Will tightened his grip and turned her towards him, his dark eyes alight with an expression she had never seen before. With his free hand he took a handful of her golden hair and wound his hand in it, pulling her close to him. Then he kissed her.

It all happened so quickly that she had little time to protest. His lips felt soft but very hot and they seared her own, while his arm held her so close that she thought her body would break.

She was incapable of resisting or controlling the urge to respond to his kisses blindly, instinctively, until she was gasping for breath. Only then did she come to her senses.

"Please stop. I—I can't."

Tightening his hand in her hair, he murmured, "You already have," and his lips sought hers once again. . . .

Other ACE Books by Justine Sommers

SO WILD, SO WONDERFUL

The Heart Must Choose

BY

Justine Sommers

ace books
A Division of Charter Communications Inc.
A GROSSET & DUNLAP COMPANY
360 Park Avenue South
New York, New York 10010

THE HEART MUST CHOOSE

Copyright © 1978 by Justine Sommers

An ACE Book

First ACE Printing: September 1978

Published simultaneously in Canada
Printed in the U.S.A.

Chapter 1

Lucinda and her brother Davy, their hands clasped tightly together, stood on the main street of Sacramento watching the confusing, noisy bustle all around them. Eleven-year-old Davy's blue eyes were open wide with astonishment, and even Lucinda was bewildered by what she saw. The street was flanked with weathered shacks that looked as if they'd been hastily erected to cater to the spontaneous needs of a burgeoning population. Banks and saloons stood side by side with gambling halls and blacksmith shops. Establishments purveying dry goods, provisions, picks and shovels and pans for gold, men's sturdy work clothes, blankets, saddles for horses and mules—all clustered together looking as if one strong gust of wind would blow the whole town into splinters.

Although the street was wide it seemed too small to contain the many creatures and vehicles trying to push their way through it, especially as it had been raining and the road was one huge mud bath. Every manner of wagon, coach, and buckboard was represented, drawn by horses or weary oxen. Men on muleback and horseback converged in the center and sloshed through the mire spattering everything within reach.

"Gee, Cindy, there must be about a million people here," Davy told his sister in wonderment.

Lucinda too was uneasy with the huge crowds. Sacramento didn't look anything like what she had expected. But then almost nothing did.

Before leaving the farm in Illinois on which she'd been

1

born, Lucinda had known of faraway places only through the few books, papers, and magazines that had come her way. Such printed matter she had used as a guide to teach a dozen children in the schoolhouse. However, when she and her brother had joined the Wright family in their covered-wagon trek all the way to California, Lucinda had realized that a book, even one with pictures, was a poor representation of reality. Rivers had turned out to be wider and deeper than she could have imagined, mountains higher and more awesome, caverns more precipitous, the desert drier, the forests denser.

All she had known about Sacramento—and such information came from newspaper accounts—was that it had boomed during the last three years since the discovery of gold at Sutter's Mill nearby in 1848. The population had grown enormously. Still, Lucinda had been sure that her brother Tom was here among the prospectors. And if not here in town, then somewhere in the hills panning for gold.

"Cindy." Davy's plaintive voice interrupted Lucinda's meditations. "I'm getting kind of hungry. What are we going to do now?"

That was a good question, and Lucinda creased her brow in an attempt to answer it to herself as well as to Davy. As her eyes scanned the spectacle she was not consoled by what she saw.

The street was teeming with men of all sorts and apparently from many different places, but the two common features among them were their ferocious appearance and raucous voices. There were almost no women, and the few Lucinda spotted seemed pretty rough-hewn themselves, and going at a fast, no-nonsense pace that made Lucinda hesitate to accost them.

In fact, Lucinda was more timid than she would have liked to admit, especially to Davy. At eighteen she was considered fully adult in his eyes, but she was most unused to great numbers of people, in particular strangers.

She had thought somehow, when assuring her mother how easy it would all be, that some kindly, friendly person would materialize to take her by the hand and lead her to her brother Tom right then and there. Now she saw that finding him was going to be much more complicated.

A group of four men swaggered up the street laughing noisily. They were carrying heavy sacks on their shoulders and walking purposefully towards the bank just behind Lucinda and Davy.

Lucinda became alarmed and tugged at her brother's hand nervously. "Perhaps we'd better go down the street a little way," she suggested.

"What for? Why don't we just ask them? Should I?"

While Lucinda thought this over, for the men looked very unkempt indeed, Davy broke away from her and stepped right up to them.

"Excuse me. I wonder if you could tell me where Mother Lode is. I reckon she's a lady who rents out rooms—"

His voice was drowned in the wild laughter of the men.

Davy looked ruefully at them, reddening a bit, for he was a sensitive boy. He didn't see what was so funny, and neither did Lucinda. She came to her brother's rescue.

Her annoyance emboldened her to say, "We're strangers here, and if we've said something amusing I wish you'd tell us what it is. We're seeking our older brother Tom, and I assure you it's no joke to us."

The laughter died on their lips. Four pairs of eyes under bushy brows regarded the slim young girl, whose face was well concealed under her bonnet, with interest.

The oldest of the four, a gray-bearded man, actually took off his broad-brimmed hat politely. "Sorry, ma'am. Guess we ought to be used to mighty peculiar questions by this time. Why, every day dozens of folks ride in here not knowing any more about this place than a chick just hatched. Tell you what," he continued, directing his remarks to his companions, "you boys go on to the bank with my goods and I'll meet you there. I'll see to this damsel in distress."

The three men, laughing merrily, threw a few teasing parting remarks at the speaker. Lucinda was relieved to see, however, that they continued on their way.

"Now, ma'am, and you too, sonny, I'll tell you straight out that asking for the Mother Lode is like asking where California is. The Mother Lode is the place the gold is, in the hills, see, and it takes in about seventy miles. The thing is you'd have to know the name of a particular mine or claim. Or at least which river, say five miles up the American River or ten miles up the Sacramento, see?"

Lucinda saw only too clearly, and her face grew even paler than it naturally was. Her head was throbbing from the unaccustomed noise and she was beginning to feel faint from lack of food, for they hadn't had a bit to eat since leaving the wagon train that morning.

"You look plumb tuckered out, ma'am. You just get into town?"

Lucinda nodded, while Davy said petulantly, "We sure did, mister, and we haven't had any lunch or anything."

"Then you just follow me, young fella, you and your sister, because I know a right nice lady lives just up the street. She has a kind of boarding house, even if she's not the Mother Lode," he teased them gently. "Don't know as you want a room but at least she'll give you some decent grub and we'll see if we can't figure out what you're gonna do next."

Davy, with the trusting innocence of a young boy, was immediately ready to follow this stranger, but Lucinda hung back in reticence, remembering how her mother had cautioned her.

"My name is Lucinda Evans and this is Davy," she said formally, using a special tone of voice that indicated she wasn't intending to take up with anybody she happened to meet.

"I'm right proud to know you, Miss Evans," the man acknowledged quite correctly. "Jeff Boles is my name. I been in Sacramento, or leastways the gold country, for nigh on a year, and Mrs. Tiller, the lady I was telling you about, will sure vouch for me. In fact, I got a wife and five kiddies back in Missouri. Reckon the oldest is just about your age."

Lucinda was reassured, and taking Davy's arm she followed Jeff Boles down the muddy street.

Mrs. Tiller turned out to be as motherly a woman as Lucinda could have wished. All smiles, Mrs. Tiller soon had Lucinda and Davy washed up and seated at a long wooden table eating hot soup, beans, and biscuits, followed by mugs of steaming coffee.

While they ate, Davy, who always had been very talkative, told Mrs. Tiller practically his whole life story, while Lucinda interjected a few pertinent remarks now and again to keep him on the right track.

The point was that their older brother Tom had gone to California in 1849. For six months he'd prospected for gold, and then wrote that he'd had some success and would be coming home. That was in the autumn of 1850. By spring of 1851, when he still hadn't returned or sent word, Lucinda and Davy had made their plans to come out here and find him. It was now summer. As far as they knew he hadn't arrived home yet, and they intended to search for him.

"Dear me, dear me." Mrs. Tiller shook her head sadly, looking at them with her quick bright eyes. She was a tiny woman, so plump she was almost as wide as she was tall. "This gold prospecting is a tricky business. My own husband's in it up to his elbows. Makes about fifteen dollars a day but that don't buy much out here with prices so high, so I run this place and I do almost as well as he does. I keep saying we should go back to Pennsylvania but he won't hear of it. Keeps expecting to strike it rich. Real rich, so we can go back home with a pile to keep us for the rest of our days. But that don't happen often."

"But Tom wrote he was coming home. We just wonder why he never got there," Lucinda said, frowning.

Mrs. Tiller took Lucinda's hand in her own. "So many things can happen, child. All this talk of gold has brought a lot of bad people to California. They let others find the gold and then they just take it, so folks have to start all over again. Or, could be your brother got the gold fever. My husband has it so I know what it's like first hand. No matter how much gold you get it's not enough. Just one more day, one more week, one more month. . . ."

"Yeah, but Tom would have written us. He knows how hard it is to work the farm without him," Davy said, between mouthfuls of food.

Lucinda was silent, and after a glance at her face, Mrs. Tiller closed her lips as well. For they both suspected that something must have happened to keep a dutiful son and brother from returning or sending word.

The rest of the afternoon went quickly. Jeff Boles returned from the bank and offered his help to Lucinda and Davy. He suggested that they remain with Mrs. Tiller and look around the town for a couple of days to see if they could get any information about Tom. They could ask at the various shops, and it was common practice to put up little notices on the sides of buildings.

"If that don't work," continued Jeff Boles, "you have to get you a couple of mules and provisions and ride up into the hills and look for him yourself. I sure hope it don't come to that. It's real tough, like trying to find a four-leaf clover in a meadow, especially for a young girl and a lad."

Lucinda had conflicting feelings about everything. She saw this trip as something of an adventure, and one she would never have had a chance to experience had Tom not been missing for so long. He was desperately needed on the farm, for he was the only full-grown man of the family.

Their father had died several years earlier. Davy was still too young to be of much use on the farm, and Lucinda's assistance was negligible, for she had been trained as a schoolteacher. Because she was small and frail-looking, as well as quick at her lessons, her father had urged her to take up teaching. She enjoyed it, but after her father's death she had implored her mother to be allowed to help on the farm. However, her mother had pointed out that Lucinda's wages were now vitally necessary. She hadn't been able to convince her mother that she would be able to cope with the heavy farm work. The only other members of the family were her two small sisters.

When Tom hadn't returned, Lucinda and her mother had spoken of the matter for weeks until finally Mrs. Evans had agreed to let her two oldest go in search for her son. The one possibility they had never even broached was that Tom Evans had met a nasty fate and would never be coming home.

Wise as she was, if Mrs. Evans had really known what lay in store for Lucinda and Davy she might have reconciled herself to her loss without risking two further sacrifices.

Lucinda shuddered to think of all the tales she could tell her mother that would make her hair turn white; tales of their journey through dangerous, wild country, and of the hardships they suffered. As a result Lucinda had begun to realize that Tom might have started for home and been harmed on his way.

Lucinda firmly tried to put these thoughts from her mind. She and Davy had survived, under the care and protection of the kind Wright family, so why not brave, strong Tom?

In any case, Lucinda believed that Tom was still in California and she had faith that all three would make the trip home together.

At the moment she was feeling vexed with herself for having been so naive as to think that the address on his last letter, the Mother Lode, was the house of a kindly, homey woman like Mrs. Tiller herself. By putting such an address on his letter Tom had unwittingly given his family the vain hope that they could find him in a partic-ular spot.

That night Davy and Lucinda retired very early, weary from their long trip and the bewilderment of a strange place. Davy went to sleep in a room with several men while Lucinda was given a cot in Mrs. Tiller's own room, since that lady's husband was away prospecting.

When Lucinda prepared for bed, she took off her dress and bonnet and then proceeded to brush her long yellow hair as she had been accustomed to do every night.

Entering the room, Mrs. Tiller made a gasping sound.

"What's the matter?" asked Lucinda, her arm poised with the brush in her hair.

"Oh, my dear, you must keep that hair hidden in your bonnet at all times!"

"But why?" asked Lucinda, puzzled.

Mrs. Tiller sat Lucinda down and gave her a frank little lecture that had the girl's pale cheeks turning bright pink with embarrassment. She had never even imagined the sorts of things Mrs. Tiller was telling her, for until she had left her farm she had hardly ever spoken to a man except for her father and brother. At a party or a dance—and those were infrequent enough—she general-ly had stuck close to her family. Of course she had ob-served some of the young men but she would never have dared to look at them directly or show them the least amount of interest.

Her mother had, of course, given her a certain amount of hesitant instruction, but it was nothing like the blunt warning now coming from Mrs. Tiller's lips. That good woman was explaining that Lucinda was in a wild country, a new country where there were hardly any rules and the few there were kept being broken by those who were far from home and behaved very differently from the way they had been taught.

"You see, child, their womenfolk aren't here to keep them civilized. That's the only word I can use. Now, if you ride off into the hills you're going to be about the prettiest sight some of those men have seen for maybe a year or more. If they get a look at that yellow hair, why it will seem like gold as much as the nuggets they find in the streams. And what's to stop them from taking hold of it?"

Her face crimson, Lucinda looked at Mrs. Tiller with her blue eyes flashing. "My brother Davy has a rifle, and, and—"

"Sure he does, and that will help. But he can't be pointing it at folks day and night. That's why I say, Lucinda, to keep yourself as plain and inconspicuous as possible, just to make sure."

Lucinda absorbed the message, and when she lay down to sleep she felt more afraid than she ever had in her life before. Even during their difficult journey she had been surrounded by the friendly Wrights, who had treated her and Davy like their own children. Besides, most of the people in the wagon train were families from nearby farms. They were all going west together because they were intrigued by the "promised land" where everything, to hear tell, was lush and green, where you could get free land from the government and grow the most beautiful crops. Whereas back home it was sometimes dry and dusty. The wind would come along and blow the seed away before it took, or the rain would soak the crops until they drowned.

The few young men in the wagon train had treated Lucinda with great respect. Perhaps one or two of them had been rather sweet on her, Lucinda allowed shyly, but they knew her purpose for going to California, which was different from theirs. Unlike them, she would be returning to Illinois. Understanding the impossibility of courting a girl on a search mission, they desisted. They had been brought up to do their duty.

Lucinda was firmly determined to do her own duty, and no gold-hunting ruffians were going to prevent her. That settled in her mind, she fell into a deep sleep.

The next morning she insisted that Davy have a proper bath, to which he acquiesced only after much grumbling, and then she had one herself. She put on a clean shift and stood in front of the small mirror in her room brushing her hair.

Shyly she took quick glances at herself. Her mother didn't hold with self-admiration, and Lucinda had not been encouraged in small vanities. Now, however, after Mrs. Tiller's warnings, Lucinda tried to see herself objectively, as Mrs. Tiller saw her.

Lucinda's face was small and perfectly oval, her skin almost transparent in its pale delicacy. Her nose was small and pert, her lips full and red. with rather a pouting expression until she smiled. Her most startling features were her large eyes, of a vivid cornflower blue, framed with thick long lashes that looked darker than their individual golden hue. Above her high forehead she wore her silky yellow hair parted in the middle, and it fell almost to her waist.

Lucinda had never considered herself to be particularly pretty. Of course, when she observed her face in repose in the mirror she was seeing only the raw material. She didn't realize how animated she grew when she was enthusiastic about something, how her eyes could shimmer with excitement or joy, or the way her shapely mouth curved into the most tantalizing smile. She little knew how enchanted another might be to watch this rather cool and self-possessed young lady suddenly begin exuding vitality and warmth.

True, she exhibited this side of herself only rarely. Up to now her life had been quiet and well ordered, devoted to duty, and with very few pleasures.

Sighing, Lucinda put on a gingham dress, pinning her

purse with all her money into the bodice, adjusted her bonnet, and went to find Mrs. Tiller.

That good lady had lost no time in making inquiries for Lucinda. Already notices containing information about Tom, provided by Davy, were posted in prominent places along the street.

The day passed pleasantly enough. Lucinda insisted on helping Mrs. Tiller with the housework. Afterwards they went shopping together. With her hair in a knot concealed under her bonnet and her eyes demurely on the ground, Lucinda excited few stares from the men milling about the streets. They were either gathering provisions and preparing to go into the hills or returning, if lucky, with sacks of gold dust and nuggets to be weighed at the bank and exchanged for money.

Davy, in his artless, friendly way, scampered all over the town, talking to everyone he met, asking about Tom, about equipment for gold prospecting, about everything under the sun, for he was a curious youngster and interested in all sorts of things.

They passed two days this way, under the welcome protection of Mrs. Tiller. Unfortunately, by the end of that time they were no wiser about the whereabouts of their brother than when they arrived.

Jeff Boles, who was also boarding with Mrs. Tiller, spoke to Lucinda on the evening of their second day. He was gathering supplies and heading into the hills and he offered to help outfit them and also to ride a bit of the way with them to start them off in the right direction.

Grateful for his kindness, Lucinda agreed. She was extremely apprehensive about venturing into the gold country, but she could see that Davy was full of eager anticipation.

"Don't worry, Cindy. We'll find Tom. And that's not all we're going to find," he predicted, his eyes shining.

He was thinking of gold, Lucinda knew, and she smiled with affection at her little brother. He resembled her only in the color of his eyes, for his hair was brown, like Tom's, and his snub nose had a sprinkling of freckles.

The only optimistic note Lucinda could cling to was that Davy had remembered the name of a river Tom had mentioned in one of his letters. At least that would narrow their search somewhat, for Jeff Boles had told them that a prospector, as a matter of superstition, usually explored a river from start to finish rather than flitting from one to another.

Lucinda, tense with nervousness, slept hardly at all that night and she rose as soon as it was light.

After breakfast Jeff Boles took them to see a mule seller. She was highly dismayed to learn that the cost of the two mules ate up almost all their money. Even Davy appeared concerned, and he kept glancing anxiously at his sister to see if they would be able to afford the purchase.

Jeff Boles, noticing Lucinda's worried expression, whispered to her, "It's a real good investment, ma'am, because providing nothing happens to these here mules you can always sell them when you come back down, and they'll fetch what you paid and maybe more depending on how big a call there is."

Davy, overhearing Jeff, immediately became elated. "Sure thing. Anyway, we're going to find Tom and when we do we'll be rich enough to buy a thousand mules."

"That's it, lad," laughed Jeff Boles, ruffling Davy's hair. "Always look on the bright side. The golden side, you might say, eh?" He and Davy laughed gleefully, and even Lucinda managed a wan smile.

In truth, she was feeling far from optimistic. In a way she was glad that she had started on her journey from the farm in such innocence. She never would have had the courage to embark on this venture if she had thought it would lead her into hazardous, unknown places with only a small boy and a rifle for protection.

When Lucinda and Davy took their leave of Mrs.

Tiller she kissed them both and wished them every success. Taking Lucinda aside, she pressed a tiny pearl-handled knife into her hand.

"Keep this on you at all times. Heaven hope you never need it but it might make you feel good just to know it's there."

Lucinda accepted the gift with trembling fingers, wrapped it well in a handkerchief, and pinned it to her petticoats.

Jeff Boles, walking his own mules, led the way out of Sacramento and towards the mountains rising in the distance. Just the sight of the majestic range awed Lucinda and Davy. They had, of course, seen mountains in their trip across the continent, but they had been raised in such flat country that they were still unused to such a spectacle.

Her brow puckered with trepidation, Lucinda kept worrying that they had left something behind. She ticked off all the items they had purchased: flour, sugar, bacon, beans, sourdough for biscuits and pancakes, coffee, cooking utensils, a waterproof tarpaulin for putting on the ground under their blankets, and even a shiny new pan for washing gold. Davy had looked at it with such longing that Lucinda hadn't had the heart to deprive him. She figured that they had already spent so much money that the little extra would make scant difference. Besides, if there really was so much gold about, Davy might just find some and make the investment worthwhile.

As they wound their way up into the hills, Jeff Boles talked over his shoulder, instructing them on the art of camping out, which was quite a bit different from doing so with the protection of a covered wagon.

"Watch out for snakes wiggling from rocks, and don't go nowheres near a grizzly bear. Don't you try to shoot it, neither," he addressed his warning to Davy. "Those things are monsters. Come at you even with a ton of buckshot in 'em. And be sure when you put out your

camp fire you stomp on it real good. There's so many
trees that one spark carried by the wind could burn
down the whole forest."

When they stopped for a meal, Jeff Boles showed
them how to light a proper fire, how to cook their food,
and how to find the best site for sleeping. "It's good to
be sort of with your back to something no varmint can
climb down from, like a big, slippery rock. So's if you
hear a nose in the night you know you only have to look
right in front to see what the danger is."

The more he spoke, the more petrified Lucinda grew.
She was quaking with uncertainty, and were it not for
the picture of Tom in her mind—and blurred at that,
after all this time—she would willingly have turned
back.

It was the thought of her older brother, her gentle,
laughing, kind, much adored brother that caused her to
bite her lips to keep them from trembling and determine
to have the courage to go through with this ordeal.

"Well, ma'am, I reckon you two are gonna be just
fine. I'm gonna leave you here because I'm taking a
quick shortcut miles upriver to look for a new place.
Back along here, where you're starting your search, the
gold's either been dug up or the vein is so rich that
there's established claims here, all registered and all.
And these folks don't take kindly to claims jumpers. Be
sure you tell them you're only looking for Tom and not
aiming to grab their claim right from under them."

The idea that a frail young girl and her little brother
could be a threat to the tough miners struck Jeff Boles as
absurd. He shook their hands, repeating that they'd be
all right.

"Who knows, we may run into each other on the trail.
Anyways, I'll sure keep a lookout for your brother. If I
have any word I'll send it back down to Mrs. Tiller."

With that he bade them goodbye. Lucinda was deso-
late at seeing him ride off into the distance. She didn't
dare show any fear in front of Davy, however, so she

briskly issued her instructions for packing up their camp and going on until it grew dark.

The sun shone down on them through the trees, and the air had a wonderful fresh fragrance. All around them birds twittered in a friendly manner. Occasionally a curious squirrel scurried up a tree trunk and observed their progress.

Once they were actually underway Lucinda's heart lightened considerably. For several hours they rode without seeing a soul. Then, just as dusk was beginning to descend, they came upon two men washing gold in a stream which branched off the main river.

"Howdy," Davy called out in his high, clear voice as they approached slowly on their mules.

The men, after a quick glance at them, continued their work.

Lucinda and Davy stopped a few feet from the prospectors. They both had long black beards and looked as if the closest they had come to water in weeks was to stand knee deep in it with gold pans in their hands.

Lucinda's heart was pounding, but she sat demurely on her animal, her head well down, only occasionally glancing at the two, while Davy did all the talking. That had been their agreed approach.

"We're looking for our brother, Tom Evans. He'd be about twenty-one. Medium tall and thin with brown curly hair and blue eyes. Came out from our farm in Illinois in '49. You see anyone like that?"

Without bothering to lift their heads, the two grunted a negative reply and went right on panning for gold.

Davy was stung, torn between hurt feelings at the men's indifference and interest in their activities.

"Davy," Lucinda called, inclining her head. She could see at a glance that they would be wasting their time. These two had no interest in them or their quest. Why, she had the feeling that even if Tom Evans had passed them by ten minutes ago they wouldn't have bothered to say so.

"Never mind, Davy," Lucinda consoled her brother when they were some distance from the taciturn prospectors. "Not everyone we meet will be so unfriendly," she finished, hoping that was true. She'd begun to realize the obsession that had taken hold of these men. Gold they were after and gold they must find. Nothing else mattered.

The next person they met was a lone prospector as little inclined to engage in conversation as the earlier two had been. After Davy had gone through his speech the man confined himself to a "Nope" and went on panning.

Just as it was growing dark and Lucinda thought they should find a place to camp they came upon half a dozen men working what appeared to be a well-established claim. Here, again, the men were bearded and very unkempt-looking but they weren't unfriendly.

"What is it you want, young feller?" one of them asked, spitting a plug of chewed tobacco into the stream.

Davy made his set speech. The men shook their heads. "Heck, you're not likely to find him around here after all that time. We been working this claim about a year. This part of the river's dug up for miles. You gotta go much further upstream."

While Davy conversed with the two or three that were talkative, Lucinda grew most uncomfortable under the gaze of the others, who were frankly staring at her.

Although it was dark and her bonnet was low over her face, Lucinda perceived that they didn't much care what she looked like. These men had probably not sighted a woman in ages. Just the fact that she wore a dress was enough to interest them.

She felt her face burning hotly under her bonnet. As she listened to the conversation she could tell that what the men were imparting to Davy was of little practical use. It was obvious that they hadn't seen Tom Evans, and that was the only information that interested Lucinda.

"Davy, we must be going," she called out to her brother in a voice that sounded more tremulous than she would have wished.

"Hang on there," one of the hitherto silent men suddenly called out.

"You the sister?" he asked gruffly.

Lucinda was silent. She wanted to turn and ride quickly away but she was afraid to be openly rude. The mule wouldn't get them very far if that big, long-legged fellow were determined to pursue them.

"It's getting late," the stranger pointed out. "Ain't you a-feared of traveling in the dark? Why not stay here with us?"

Davy looked at his sister questioningly but she shook her head firmly.

"But Cindy, it *is* getting dark and I'm kinda hungry."

Lucinda made a gesture of impatience. Davy was always hungry. "We'll go on a bit longer, thank you, sir," she said politely to the man. "Come on, Davy."

"What's your rush, ma'am? We got plenty of grub here. A nice fire to warm you." The man grinned suggestively, his eyes looking her over and the expression on his face indicating that he was pleased by what he saw. "I'll tell you what." He reached into his pocket and pulled out a large yellowish stone.

"It's gold, isn't it?" Davy cried out with excitement. "Oh, mister, please, can I see it real close?"

Laughing, the man handed it to Davy. With wonder the boy turned it over and over in his hand, while a panicky feeling stole over Lucinda.

"Give it back, Davy, we have to go now," she said, a warning in her voice.

Davy was too much intrigued by his first gold nugget to heed her admonishment. "Look at it, Cindy, it's as big as my thumb!"

"Sure it is," chimed in the owner of the nugget. "And it's all yours, lad. That is if your sister will be nice to me."

"For real, mister? What's she got to do?"

The man smiled wickedly, while his companions downstream exploded into laughter, nudging each other meaningfully.

"Davy!" Lucinda shouted at him. Her face felt scarlet, and it was only her anger and shame that gave her the courage to speak at all. "You come with me this minute, hear? Or I'm going on and leave you by yourself!"

Stunned, Davy realized finally how angry his sister was. So seldom did she speak to him this way that he grew pale and anxious. Regretfully he handed the nugget back to its owner.

"Thanks, mister, but I guess my sister is upset about something." With that, he turned his mule and smacked him on the side, for Lucinda had already begun to ride away from the camp.

"Cindy, wait up. What're you so riled up about?"

Lucinda prodded and refused to stop or utter a single word until they came upon a spot she thought would do for making camp. It was slightly off the trail against a steeply rising cliff.

Davy gathered wood for a fire while Lucinda readied the ingredients for their meal. As they ate she finally broke her silence. "The reason I was so upset back there is that those men weren't being friendly at all. I know it's hard for you to tell the difference between men like that and, say, Jeff Boles, so you'll just have to watch me and act accordingly."

"What made you so sore, though, when he asked you to be nice to him! Shucks, he would have given us a gold nugget!"

"Exactly! Do you think people who work so hard to find things like that just give them away for nothing? What he meant was, was—" she paused and her cheeks grew very pink.

Davy watched her in wonderment.

"You know how courting couples behave, Davy?"

The boy continued to regard his sister blankly.

"Remember, in the wagon train, there was a wedding between that couple—"

"Oh, yeah, I reckon. What's that got to do with being nice to that man?"

"He wanted—he meant—holding hands—" Her voice petered out into a whisper. She didn't see how she could explain it to him.

"Oh, I know!" Davy's eyes suddenly lit up with understanding. "Kissing and smooching, and like that," he added, his boy's face wrinkling with distaste.

"Yes, exactly," breathed Lucinda, relieved. "You don't want me to behave like that with a stranger, do you? That's the sort of thing a proper girl doesn't do until she's married. No matter if she's offered a gold nugget the size of a boulder, hear?"

Davy nodded, now in perfect agreement with his sister. "Shucks, I don't see why anybody wants to hold hands and such even if they're married. I hope you don't ever want to."

Lucinda smiled indulgently at him. "That's very unlikely, at least for a long time yet." She knew that some girls married very young but she didn't think she'd be one of them. At only eighteen, she thought of marriage but rarely, and then as something for the future.

Davy began to clean and oil his rifle. "Don't worry, Cindy. If anybody says that to you again I'll know what to do." In illustration, he lifted his rifle and pointed it at an invisible suitor.

Much relieved, Lucinda laughed. Then they made ready for bed, rolling up in their blankets close to the fire.

A feeling of optimism took hold of Lucinda as she lay looking up at the stars. Here, away from the bewildering crowds of Sacramento, it seemed possible to imagine locating her brother. They would slowly explore the whole river. Tom was bound to be somewhere among those bearded and wild-looking men. She would keep a careful lookout and not be deceived by immediate appearances.

Chapter 2

The following seven days passed very slowly for Lucinda. During that time sister and brother painstakingly wended their way along the banks of the river, exploring every little side stream and byway to be sure they didn't miss out on any camps. The farther they went into the gold country the more prospectors they met.

Their encounters began to be repeated with monotonous regularity. Usually it was a solitary prospector they met, perhaps two men. For the most part Lucinda and Davy were regarded with indifference at best, suspicion at worst. Few miners seemed to wish to pass the time of day chatting. Nobody admitted having seen a person remotely resembling Tom Evans. Nobody seemed to care whether he had or not. The only time the men bestirred themselves was when their interest in a female passerby diverted them temporarily from their pursuit of gold.

At such moments Lucinda would grow red with shame, while Davy would point his rifle at them, his eyes serious far beyond his years. His threatening gesture usually drew a laughing response from the men, but at least they didn't consider it worthwhile to insist. Perhaps it was just the excuse they needed, after making a token show of masculine appreciation, to bend their efforts again to the true love of their lives—gold.

At night Lucinda and Davy slept huddled in their blankets by the fire, trying to keep warm in the dark chilliness which contrasted with the sunny warmth of the days.

Lucinda found it difficult to keep up her spirits. It became only too apparent that they knew little more of Tom now than they had at the beginning, although they had narrowed the field somewhat. In other words, they knew where Tom was not. According to the few taciturn people who had bothered to speak to them at all, it was unlikely that a prospector would double back to hunt for gold where he had already been. No, the idea seemed to be to go ever onwards, operating under the theory that the farther into the hills one went the more gold there was likely to be.

Indeed, Lucinda and Davy noted the scars sometimes left in the hills by miners who had worked their claims for all they were worth. Although the signs were not so apparent in the streams, there were large, angry chunks carved out of the hills by pickaxes. Apparently as time went on the miners were coming up with more sophisticated equipment. No longer were they content only to stand in an icy stream while their feet became numb inside their boots, shaking their pans and hoping for a little gold dust to settle on the bottom. They attacked the rocks and soil of the hills with the ferocity of coal seekers, dreaming of coming upon gold deposits the size of boulders.

Aside from the ravages of the gold seekers, Lucinda found the splendor of the scenery quite breathtaking. It felt wonderful to be able to look down from a great height into a valley or canyon or a freshly bubbling stream. Back home Lucinda had never been higher than the hayloft of their barn. Here instead of the flat, tree-less land for miles around, hills looped up, down, and around, the rocky paths flanked with forests of sweet-smelling pines, or with meadows abloom with orange poppies. And oh, the magnificence of the reddish-brown trees with trucks as thick as a house and branches reaching so far into the sky that their tops were invisible.

The forests were alive with all manner of birds and small animals. Sometimes Davy succeeded in shooting a rabbit to supplement their meager diet. Mostly, though, when they stopped to rest Davy would rush to get his gold pan and try washing the dirt in the hope that his pan would yield up some gold dust. Lucinda could see that he didn't really know the proper technique. She couldn't help him there, and thus far none of the prospectors they had met had seemed approachable enough to ask.

Lucinda began to be concerned about their food supplies. They hadn't been able to take too much with them on their two mules. In fact, their friend Jeff Boles had discouraged them from overstocking. He undoubtedly hadn't expected them to persevere for any length of time.

He just didn't know the Evanses, Lucinda thought grimly. She was not about to surrender so easily. Not as long as it was humanly possible to continue the search. The thing she feared, though, was that they'd run out of food before they reached a large mining town and would have to go all the way back to Sacramento to replenish their supplies.

When they had finished their lunch Lucinda saw that their provisions would hold out for scarcely another two days, for they couldn't leave themselves with nothing to eat on the way back.

Ruefully they packed up their remaining supplies. Lucinda wished they had purchased more when they had had the chance. Of course, their money was almost gone, too.

Lucinda must have had a woebegone expression on her face, for Davy divined her worry.

"We can't quit yet," he said, looking sideways at his sister. "We got to keep going. We'll find Tom, Cindy, you'll see."

Lucinda managed a fleeting smile, thankful for her brother's optimism. She also marveled at his unerring sense of direction. No matter how the river snaked in and out, no matter how many minor detours they made,

Davy was always able to find the right track. Without him Lucinda was sure she'd have been traveling in circles.

Doggedly they went on, coming upon a camp with three fairly young men digging in the hills. When they caught sight of Lucinda and Davy they stopped their digging almost as if they were glad of an excuse.

They were on the tall side and very skinny. From the family resemblance among the clean-shaven youths Lucinda guessed that they were brothers. The oldest one, perhaps only slightly older than she, looked at her with the kind of hungry expression that Lucinda had learned to mistrust.

"Hold on there. No need to rush off," the oldest brother said boldly. "We'd be obliged for a bit of company. This here is lonely work."

Davy, by now experienced in the handling of men who made eyes at his sister, raised up his rifle.

"Hey, look at him," tittered one of the younger lads, nudging his brothers. "Bet you can't shoot that thing."

Davy smarted under the insult. "You want to try me?" he challenged.

"Never mind, Davy," Lucinda said, not finding anything menacing about these lads. "We're looking for our older brother," she continued.

The boys listened patiently. Then the oldest thought for a few minutes. "Was someone passed this way only a day or two ago. He was on his own, dressed in funny, raggedy clothes and acting mighty peculiar. Remember him, Ben?" he asked the next younger boy.

"Oh, yeah, the one who was talking to himself."

"Heck, that isn't our Tom," Davy said in disgust. "He wouldn't have been talking to himself."

"Hush, Davy," Lucinda interjected. "This fellow. How tall was he, and how old would you say?" She was taking no chances on allowing a single clue to go uninvestigated.

Just then a noise behind the boys startled Lucinda.

She was even more surprised to see a woman emerging from the woods. At least, Lucinda thought it was a woman. She was big and square, dressed in trousers and a shirt like the boys. The only feminine touch to her costume was a rather bedraggled bonnet.

"Hey, Ma, these here folks are looking for someone."

The woman drew closer, squinting through rather small, puffy eyes at the newcomers. She had no welcoming smile on her face. In fact, she was actually scowling. "Did I give you boys leave to stop your digging? Get on with it. I'll see to these here folks." She beckoned them to follow her back to a clearing where they had their camp.

"Why don't you set yourselves down and rest a spell," the women invited them.

Lucinda was only too glad to dismount. Her limbs felt stiff from the long ride. Besides, she was terribly curious about this woman, the first she had seen actually in the hills with the prospectors.

When they had taken their seats in front of her tent, the woman stared first at Davy and then at Lucinda. "Take off your bonnet off, child, and get yourself comfortable."

Lucinda politely declined. "I'm fine as I am, thank you."

The woman shrugged. "Who you looking for?"

Lucinda told her, not forgetting to mention what her oldest son had said about a strange man passing through recently.

"Yeah, come to think of it, we did see someone like that. You think he could be your Tom?"

Lucinda swallowed painfully. "Tom was—never given to odd behavior. But—but of course, out here for two years—"

"It happens," the woman said, nodding her head. "It sure happens. Folks get took awful funny if they stay up here too long by themselves. My sons' daddy. He worked these hills until he just gave out. Buried him right where he was digging. That was a year ago. Ain't had much luck since," she added suspiciously.

Lucinda doubted that this was true, but it was an impression most of the prospectors tried to convey to strangers.

"Yeah, well like I said. Maybe that there fella who passed this way was the very one you're looking for. You might just catch up to him if you go real quick. Well, it's been nice talking to you."

She rose heavily to her feet, indicating that their interview was at an end. Lucinda felt somewhat disappointed that she hadn't asked them to join her. She had no fear of the sons while the mother was around, and it would have been nice for a change to be sociable.

Obviously, however, the woman was as driven by gold fever as her husband had been, and perhaps more than her sons. She wasn't going to risk having to guard her finds from a couple of strangers.

Davy, too, looked hurt. He peered at the woman with baleful eyes just like a puppy, but she had already turned her back on them and picked up a shovel. Without looking behind her she ambled towards her sons.

"Let's go, Davy. Have to make camp by nightfall," Lucinda advised, her voice more cheerful than she felt. "After all, we want to try to overtake that man they saw."

Reluctantly, Davy mounted his mule. "Aw, I don't know. I don't think it could be Tom. He wouldn't be going around talking to himself."

Lucinda was inclined to agree with Davy but she didn't say so. Instead she tried to get her mule to go faster. Once the sun went down in these hills it darkened very quickly, and it was always better to scout out their camp before that happened.

After a while they were ready to halt but were diverted by the sounds of loud talking and laughter, as if there were a rather large party up ahead. Lucinda thought it would be better to ride ahead and look for a spot far

away from the group, whoever they were. If they stayed
put they might be surprised unpleasantly in the middle
of the night.

Sister and brother soon came upon a mine advertising
itself with a wooden sign saying "Masterson Bros. Registered Claim." It occupied a very large clearing, and
through it ran the river. There was a lot of equipment
Lucinda had never seen before. Several fires were burning at the campsite. Lucinda noticed that there were
some tents and two wooden shacks, indicating that the
miners had been here for some time.

A tantalizing smell of pancakes and beans rose from
the pans over the fire. Lucinda saw her brother's
freckled nose twitching as he sniffed longingly. To stave
off his recurrent theme of how hungry he was she told
him they'd be eating soon themselves. It was a question
of getting their business over with first so that they could
be on their way.

Lucinda's face grew very warm under her bonnet as
she saw the men nudge each other and heard them whispering about the newcomers. She could well imagine the
sight she and Davy presented—a small girl in a faded
gingham dress and bonnet sitting rather dejectedly on
her mule, followed by a thin lad bravely shouldering a
rifle.

Before Davy could speak a man detached himself
from the others and came forward, regarding them with
curiosity. He was carefully dressed, Lucinda observed
with surprise, and when he spoke she was even more
reassured.

"Good evening, ma'am. It is seldom we receive such
unusual visitors. Aren't you a long way from home?"

His voice was soft and educated, with a pleasant
drawl about it. He had removed his hat as he spoke, and
Lucinda was most encouraged by his neat appearance
and polite demeanor.

She noted that he was a very nice-looking, clean-shav-
en young man, his smooth brown hair neatly cut. Even

in the dim light she could see that his brown eyes had a clear, candid expression and that his features were finely molded and intelligent.

Although still shy, Lucinda had no fear of this polite man, and so she spoke, instead of Davy. "Yes, we are a long way from home, which is Illinois, as a matter of fact. We're trying to find our brother, Tom Evans." She continued while her listener seemed to consider every word carefully.

"I can't say offhand that I recollect anyone of that description, Miss Evans, but we've had our claim here for nearly two years. A great many men have passed this way. It takes a bit of reflection, perhaps. Smells good, doesn't it?" the man suddenly said to Davy, grinning at him.

"It sure does, mister," Davy allowed, smiling in return.

Lucinda felt embarrassed that Davy's sniffing had been so noticeable. Before she could reprimand her brother the man had spoken once more.

"James Masterson is my name," he said, addressing himself to Lucinda. "My brother and I are working this claim, in a limited partnerhsip with these other prospectors. I suggest that you dismount and come and warm yourselves by our fire. I'd be most obliged if you'd consent to share our supper with us. We can consult with the others and see if anyone recalls having seen a fellow pass this way who might be your missing brother."

Davy looked expectantly at Lucinda. It was obvious he was eager to accept James Masterson's offer. In a way, so was Lucinda, but she hesitated briefly. So far his conduct had been impeccably correct, and she was inclined to trust this well-mannered man. On the other hand, she was acutely conscious of being the only woman among more than a dozen men, most of them of the usual rough variety. Even if Mr. Masterson meant them no harm, could she trust him to keep the others in check?

"I'd be much obliged if you'd consent to join us, ma'am," James Masterson said again, his quick eyes following her own wary gaze. "These are all honest, hardworking men. They won't cause any trouble, I give you my promise."

So earnestly did he speak that Lucinda was reassured at last. "Thank you," she said simply, alighting from her mule with dignity as he gave her a helping hand.

Amid the murmur of voices, Lucinda and Davy were led to a fire and given seats on blankets, while one of the men dished up beans and flapjacks.

Davy's eyes grew wide and he fell to, much to the amusement of the men.

Lucinda, trying to sit in such a way that her well-bonneted head was back in the shadows, admonished her little brother. "Davy, don't bolt your food. Remember your manners!"

"It's all right, ma'am. We understand what hungry work this searching can be," James Masterson said soothingly. He handed a plate of food to Lucinda, who thanked him shyly and began to eat. James spoke pleasantly to sister and brother, asking questions as if he really were interested in helping them.

Lucinda glowed under the unaccustomed politeness and attention. "You see, Mr. Masterson, it's so unlike Tom to have vanished without word. He was always so considerate. Oh, I'm sure you'd remember him if you'd ever met him. He always had a kind word for everyone. He was so much fun, so jolly to be with, always saying things to make one laugh, so thoughtful of everyone's feelings—"

"Hey there, ma'am," interrupted a big fellow with a large moustache. "It sounds like you're kinda sweet on this fella. You sure he's your brother and not your sweetheart you're hunting down?"

The men guffawed loudly at that until James sharply intervened. "That will do, Jake. I know you only mean your remarks as a friendly joke, but Miss Evans is not in the mood for jokes. Her brother's disappearance is a serious matter to her."

Jake said he was sorry, which caused more merry laughs from the others. Lucinda knew her face was crimson and she was glad that it was hidden from view. She greatly warmed to James Masterson for his kindness and fervently hoped he might have something of interest to impart regarding Tom's whereabouts. She was sure that this sort of thoughtful man would have an accurate memory for passersby.

"At a camp a while back, Mr. Masterson, a woman and her three sons said a man had passed their way a day or two ago. A—a rather strange fellow, poorly dressed, who—who was talking to himself."

"That's not our Tom," insisted Davy, polishing off the remains of his meal.

"Perhaps not," Lucinda allowed, "but we mustn't ignore any leads, just—just in case circumstances have turned somebody a little strange."

"I see what you mean, Miss Evans. Come to think of it, I did notice such a person. Yesterday afternoon, I think it was. He was bearded and long-haired, so it was difficult to tell his age. He was very suspicious of us, refused to stop and talk, but he was mumbling to himself. Sometimes the loneliness of the single prospector becomes too much to bear. A person might develop one or two peculiarities, but—but it doesn't necessarily follow that a reunion with a friend or, or a sister, for example, wouldn't completely banish the strangeness of having lived without human contact for so long."

Lucinda looked at him gratefully, appreciative of his understanding. She questioned him about the stranger who had passed through until she was satisfied that James Masterson had imparted every small detail he had observed about the man.

The other prospectors, having little to contribute to

the conversation and constrained to behave themselves, began to drift away. Soon only James Masterson remained.

"Perhaps my brother saw him too. Will, come here a moment, please."

Lucinda turned her head slightly in the direction James was facing and made out a figure sitting on a box in front of one of the shacks. She couldn't see his face, only the smoke from a pipe held in his mouth.

"Not now, James," the man called out. "I'm fine as I am. I haven't anything to add to your usual acute observations. I believe you saw the stranger better than I did."

The voice was similar. Soft and apparently educated, but there was an edginess to the tone that was quite lacking when James spoke.

"I guess that's the best we can do regarding this particular fellow, Miss Evans," James said. "As for others, it's so difficult to remember. The only time someone is outstanding is if he's a foreigner."

Davy looked curiously at James Masterson. "You speak so good Cindy hasn't corrected you once, and she's a schoolteacher."

"Speak so well," Lucinda corrected her brother quickly, to cover her embarrassment.

"See?" Davy pointed out.

"Well," laughed James, "It's nice of you to say so, Davy, but my brother and I are farmers ourselves, from Virginia. We did get quite a bit of schooling, though."

Davy looked pityingly at him. "I get as little as possible. I'd much rather ride a horse or hunt or do real exciting things like prospect for gold," he finished with shining eyes.

Lucinda now understood the excellent manners of her host, for he was a gentleman farmer from Virginia, a place of legendary hospitality and learning.

After asking Lucinda's permission to smoke, James filled his pipe with tobacco and lit it, while Davy watched him with wide eyes. Lucinda knew her brother couldn't wait to grow up and do such adult things as smoke a pipe.

"Our own tobacco, this is," James said, puffing. "We'll soon be out of it but I don't rightly know if we'll be going back to Virginia. There are a lot of Mastersons back there. Our older brothers seem able to manage without us. I suppose you might say we came out here for the excitement, and to prove that we could be successful on our own. I might have stayed put, I suppose, but Will really did have itchy feet. He read every newspaper account of the gold strike and he talked of nothing else for months, until finally I agreed to come with him."

"And have you found lots of gold?" asked Davy breathlessly.

"Davy, that's not the sort of question—"

"Oh, it's quite all right, ma'am," laughed James. "To be truthful, we have found some, Davy. This is a good spot and that's why we've made our camp here."

"Gee, I sure wish I could find gold," Davy said wistfully.

"There's no reason you shouldn't. You're not too small to pan for it—"

"I got me a pan and everything," Davy broke in excitedly. "But we're always moving on and I hardly get a chance to try."

James, with his quick sensitivity to what Lucinda was feeling, hastened to assure Davy that the gold would be there for a long time to come, and that his first priority was to help his sister search for Tom.

Lucinda then requested that Davy see to the mules. She wished to have a frank word without unduly frightening Davy.

Her brother went willingly. Lucinda could see from the way his bright little eyes darted around the camp that he would soon be making friends with the other miners.

James Masterson puffed on his pipe, listening quietly as Lucinda imparted her fears that something had happened to Tom. She was grateful that he didn't try to soothe her with platitudes about not worrying or unfounded reassurances that she would locate Tom if she persevered. He merely confined himself to saying he hoped she would prove successful in her search.

"I—I wonder, Mr. Masterson, if you could tell me how far it is to the next general store."

"I'm not exactly sure, for a big mining town disbanded some months back. I think there is one up the main body of the river, but if you're thinking of buying anything it's better to do it in Sacramento if possible. The mining towns charge exorbitant prices for everything. Are you short of anything important?"

Shyly Lucinda admitted that this was so. She paused, hoping he would offer to sell her some of his own.

"I wish I could offer you something, ma'am, but unfortunately we're nearly out ourselves. In fact our cook has gone to Sacramento to replenish our own stores. He's due back in about a week, and then we'll be fine, but in the meantime—"

"Oh dear, that's quite all right," Lucinda said quickly, embarrassed at having put him on the spot. "I'm sure we'll manage very nicely with what we have. Besides, Davy shoots very well and keeps us in game. And if we find Tom before too long. . . ."

While she rambled on, talking what sounded nonsense to her own ears, James continued to look at Lucinda steadily. She was glad that the bonnet hid her face and hair. Even her form was well concealed under her shawl.

"Can you cook, Miss Evans?"

The unexpected question stunned Lucinda into stopping her flow of chatter. She grew warm under the directness of his approach. "I—I suppose so, I mean, I used to help my mother, of course."

"I have a little proposal to make, and I hope you

won't think it presumptuous of me." James went on to
say that since their cook had departed life had become
more difficult. Each man tended to prepare his own
meal, and it took too much time and effort.

"As for the results, Miss Evans, you can imagine that
not a one of us can dish up anything really edible, as
perhaps you noticed tonight."

Lucinda was too polite not to disagree, but in truth
she imagined she could do better. James assumed that
such was the case, and he proposed that she and her
brother remain in the camp with them until their cook
returned.

"This way, ma'am, if you just cook our breakfast and
supper you'll not have to dip into your own supplies.
Although we don't have enough to let you have sacks of
provisions, the small amount of food you and your
brother eat with us won't leave us short. You can spend
your days continuing your search nearby, so your time
won't be wasted. When our cook returns I'll be happy to
let you have whatever you need to get you to the end of
the river."

Lucinda sat silently for a few moments considering his
offer. She could not, after mulling the situation over in
her mind, imagine that his offer was not completely
straightforward. He was kind enough not to wish her to
be forced to return to Sacramento. At the same time,
asking her to remain as a guest would have been unac-
ceptable. By offering her a job to do, which needed
doing, he had left her in the position to accept without
feeling she was being given charity.

What were her alternatives? If they returned to Sacramento they would waste another two weeks at least. Ad-
ditionally, they would have to exhaust their money. On
the other hand, if they continued on to a mining town
she might discover that they didn't have enough money,
and then how would they get back to Sacramento? She
shuddered to imagine being at the mercy of some of the
types of people they had encountered en route. Whereas

if she accepted James Masterson's offer her meals and Davy's would be assured for the next few days, during which time they could explore the area immediately available to them. They might even find Tom close by after all. At the very worst when the cook returned they would go on, well supplied. having lost almost no time at all.

Lucinda was on the point of calling Davy over to confer with her when an impatient movement behind her showed a miner approaching and scowling at her.

"Miss Evans, this is my brother, Will Masterson."

"I—I'm pleased to make your acquaintance," Lucinda murmured.

Will Masterson nodded coldly and addressed his brother. "Of all the impractical suggestions you have ever made this sounds the most foolish. A lone girl in a mining camp is bad luck and you know it!"

Lucinda was quite taken aback at the man's rudeness and the hostility in his tone. Will Masterson had the same refined way of speaking as his brother but the anger in his voice made his words sound most disagreeable.

James rose to his feet, regarding his brother ruefully. "I hardly think that objection is exactly applicable in this case. Miss Evans is not merely a girl seeking pleasure and adventure. She is looking for her brother—"

"I know what she's looking for," Will again interrupted. "I've been listening to the conversation."

With those words he turned his glowering look upon Lucinda once more. "I beg your pardon, Miss Evans. I'm not deliberately trying to be rude, and I don't even mean this personally against you. It's simply that women and gold-prospecting don't mix, like oil and water. My brother knows it too, but he's kinder than I am so he won't say so. We don't need a cook half as much as peace of mind to get on with our work."

"I can see no way that Miss Evans would be interfering with our work," James countered, his voice calm and steady. "It would be a question of breakfast very early. Then Miss Evans and Davy would explore other camps in the vicinity, leaving us quite free to do as much work as we please. They wouldn't return until evening—"

"Damn it, James, are you being deliberately obtuse or what? You know what I mean, and so does Miss Evans!"

Stung by his venomous tongue, Lucinda grew bold enough to say, "No, Mr. Masterson, I don't know what you mean. How would I interfere with any of the miners?"

"Since you ask me to spell it out for you, your interference would come merely from your female presence. These are red-blooded men who are not naturally made to live like hermits. They forgo the company of women in order to prospect, and defer their pleasure until they reach the end of the rainbow, which is supposed to hold a pot of gold. It's easier to do so when the women exist only in their imaginations. Whereas a living, breathing female on the premises, and young at that, even if unprepossessing, is too great a temptation."

"That's quite enough, Will," said James sharply. "I think we get the idea—"

"If you get the idea, James, you'll withdraw your offer and Miss Evans will be on her way.

Lucinda felt mortified. Never had she been spoken to in such a tone, nor cast such angry looks. She hadn't even decided whether or not to accept James Masterson's offer. But now Will's harsh, ill-mannered objections made her angry and stubborn. How dared he think that she was interested enough in any of these ill-bred men to wish to disrupt anything by look or word or deed! Perhaps she was most stung by his description of her as "unprepossessing." Of course, as yet he had scarcely gotten any kind of look at her to be able to make such an assessment.

"You're on a wild goose chase, Miss Evans," Will

Masterson continued. "Thousands of men have swarmed over these hills like ants, and just about as indistinguishable from each other. A man comes out here and loses his former identity. If the gold fever doesn't get him some actual illness may."

"Stop trying to discourage her," James said, becoming exasperated. "She is having a hard enough time without your adding to her woes."

"I'm not adding to hers but merely trying to subtract from ours," retorted Will.

Lucinda sat on the ground in the shadows, her eyes darting back and forth between the brothers as they stood facing each other, her presence nearly forgotten.

There was only the most superficial resemblance between the two Mastersons. Will was only slightly taller but much more strongly built. His very broad shoulders tapered to narrow waist and hips. There was a kind of arrogant swagger that was absent from James' more slender, tentative form. Will's face, too, was much the stronger of the two. His jaw was firm and well defined, his finely shaped, expressive mouth now curled in sneering contempt. Will's nose was longer and slightly aquiline, and he had a deep cleft in his chin. His hair was black and his eyes, dark and brooding, quite disturbed Lucinda. They were the kind of eyes that could bore a hole through the object at which they were staring.

Davy appeared just then and crouched next to his sister.

"What're they fighting about?"

Lucinda had no chance to answer, for Will suddenly fixed his coal-black gaze upon her. "If you have any sense you'll turn right around and go home to Illinois. This is no place for a girl and a kid. You'll never find anyone here."

"Oh, yes we will!" contradicted Davy. "What do you know about it, anyway!"

Ordinarily Lucinda would have reprimanded her brother for being sassy to a grownup, but this time she agreed with him and stubbornly made no effort to restrain him.

Ignoring Davy's outburst, Will continued to glare at Lucinda. "All sorts of things could have happened to your brother. He could have missed his footing in the river, hit his head on a rock, and goodbye forever."

"Will," James said warningly.

"Shut up, James, and let me have my say. Your brother, Miss Evans, could have been attacked by bandits and buried in a hole in the ground, with nobody the wiser," Will continued brutally. "Now you come along two years later to follow a trail as cold as the water in this river."

Lucinda felt Davy clutch at her arm convulsively, and her anger grew at this impertinent young man who was frightening Davy, as well as her, by his horrible stories.

"The most likely explanation, Miss Evans, is that your brother went down to the saloon, so excited by his few grains of gold dust that he thought he'd double his stake by betting it at cards. Or maybe he drank it up, or spent it on some fancy woman and then was afraid to come home. So he melted quietly into the beyond, never dreaming that his sister would be foolish enough to come all the way out here to search for him."

"Our Tom wouldn't have done any such thing!" Davy shouted at Will, his small face ablaze with fury, which brought out his freckles more strongly. Davy reached for his rifle and pointed it at Will Masterson. "You take that back or I'll make you!"

Will Masterson laughed suddenly, making Davy even more angry.

"Put the rifle down, Davy," Lucinda said tightly. "You needn't agree with what the man is saying, but this sort of argument certainly can't be settled by a shooting match."

"Do I detect a note of sanity creeping into these proceedings? Is the young lady going to be sensible after all?"

Lucinda loathed Will's sarcastic words, and she set her lips grimly. Rising to her feet, she turned to look at James Masterson, trying to stand up to her full height. She was dismayed that her head barely reached up to the shoulder of either brother.

"Mr. Masterson, does your offer still hold?"

"Yes, Miss Evans, it certainly does," James Masterson said firmly.

"In that case I am pleased to accept it," Lucinda finished. She looked Will Masterson in the eye without shame or apology.

"Good. Then it's settled," James said. "Sorry, Will. I did make the offer. It wouldn't be gentlemanly to renege. It will work out, you'll see."

Will turned away in disgust, swearing horribly under his breath. Then he stomped off, leaving Lucinda triumphant but shaken. She marveled at her own daring, for she really found the younger Masterson brother most alarming.

"I wouldn't pay him much mind, Miss Evans. I'm afraid my brother is rather sour on the subject of women. You see, he had a girl in Virginia, and when we came out here she wed another."

"That's hardly surprising," Lucinda said, more sharply than she had intended.

"Can someone tell me what's going on?" Davy queried petulantly.

Lucinda explained to him the substance of James' offer and what it would mean to them. Davy was delighted and said so.

"I'd be most obliged, Miss Evans, if you and your brother would do me the honor of utilizing my little shack. I can bed down by the fire outside."

Lucinda thanked him warmly but insisted that they wouldn't dream of putting him out of his house. She assured him that she and Davy preferred the outdoors. In this Davy heartily backed her up, so James reluctantly accepted their decision.

Lucinda didn't say so, but added to her reason was the equally strong wish not to be right next door to the shack of James' brother.

Lucinda was determined to stay away from the irascible Will Masterson. And from all the others, for that matter. Will was wrong about her, and she was going to prove it.

Chapter 3

Lucinda awoke when the first rays of the sun filtered through the trees onto her face. She could hear the sounds of the men stirring, and even the crackle of a fire catching.

Davy was still fast asleep, so she left him rolled up in his blanket while she went a bit farther upstream to wash. After brushing her hair she tucked it well into her bonnet, which she pulled as low as she could.

When she approached the fire she found James Masterson there, boiling water for coffee.

"Good morning, Miss Evans," he said politely, tipping his hat. "I hope you slept well."

"Yes, thank you, Mr. Masterson, very well. My brother is still at it," she finished, smiling and busying herself with the breakfast preparations.

"I do wish you'd agree to use my cabin. I hate to think of you all curled up on the cold ground."

"No, really, it's fine. I'm quite used to it."

James Masterson observed her as she put rashers of bacon in the frying pan and began to mix a batch of sourdough for pancakes.

"Do you have everything you need?"

"Oh, yes. I see you have a bell here," she noted with amusement. "I'll ring it when breakfast is ready."

"Fine. I'll leave you to get on with it," James said, and slowly walked away. Immediately Lucinda wondered if she had behaved rudely. He had looked as if he wished to linger and talk to her.

Better not, she decided as she worked. She was more

40

self-conscious when she was watched. In addition she must be careful not to become too friendly with James lest her interest be misconstrued by the others—and especially by Will.

By the time she'd finished the first batch of pancakes, the men were milling around her, and there was no need to ring the bell.

Jake, the big man with the mustache who had teased her about her sweetheart the previous evening, was first in line.

"My, oh, my, ain't they fine. These are the best flapjacks I ever ate in my life. I'm gonna come back for seconds, you can bet on that," he bellowed, grinning at Lucinda. In his loud, deep voice he proclaimed the merits of the pancakes far and wide. Soon Lucinda was wishing that Davy were there to give her a helping hand, for her own two didn't seem to be enough.

As each man approached and handed her his tin plate, she piled it high with food and then poured coffee into his mug. Suddenly she felt a prickly sensation at the back of her neck. When she looked up at the man whose plate she was filling she saw it was Will Masterson.

"Good morning," she said in a low voice. Immediately she bit her tongue, for she hadn't meant to open any conversation with him. The greeting had popped out automatically. Apparently it wasn't in her nature to be impolite.

"Good morning," he responded glumly.

She was careful to keep her eyes down, for she was conscious every moment of being the only girl in the camp and it made her jittery. Fortunately Will did not add to her anxiety. He took his plate and cup and moved away.

Lucinda breathed with relief, although she stole a quick look at his retreating form. He was wearing a bright red flannel shirt, which only added to his forceful personality and proud walk in making him stand out among others.

"Mm, that sure smells good, Cindy," proclaimed Davy ambling towards her, rubbing his sleepy eyes with one hand and trying to tuck in his shirt with the other.

When the men had all been fed Lucinda sat down with Davy to eat, and they discussed which route to follow that day. Davy was all for riding northeast, the direction the stranger had been observed to choose, and Lucinda concurred with the plan.

James Masterson came up as they were departing. "Just wanted to wish you both every success."

"Thanks," Davy said. "Who cooks your lunch when we're gone?"

"Oh, we make do. Most of the men don't stop except for coffee, or we open a can of beans. Besides, we had that wonderful breakfast to start us off. I'll be saving my appetite for dinner."

James Masterson's eyes were twinkling, and Lucinda blushed under his compliments. She noticed that James kept looking at her from different sides, as if trying to catch a better glimpse of her features, but she recoiled from any closeness. Although she liked and trusted him up to a point, she felt it would be best to follow Mrs. Tiller's advice and keep herself as inconspicuous as possible.

And when she remembered Will Masterson's nasty comments regarding her presence at the camp, she became even more determined to prove him wrong. She would keep to herself. When she finally departed from the Masterson camp none of the men would know any more of her than they did at this moment.

Lucinda and Davy mounted their mules, waved at James, and set off on the trail.

After having ridden but a short time they came upon a two-man claim, and from then on found the riverside thick with prospectors, some of them working independently within sight of each other.

When inquiring about their brother, Lucinda and Davy were met with the usual blank expressions and negative gestures. However, when Lucinda mentioned the peculiar stranger she was gratified to learn that he had been seen to pass this way.

"Oh, Davy, we must hurry. Perhaps it would be best not to mention Tom at all but just keep asking about that stranger. That way we can go faster."

Davy agreed, although he still insisted that the stranger bore no resemblance to his brother.

Lucinda didn't say so but by this time she had begun to think that if Tom was still alive and in the gold mining country he must be much changed. No doubt they would do better to follow tangible leads and not expect a description of Tom (as they remembered him) to be of much value. She saw how easily men reverted to half-savage ways when they were away from women.

The immediate exception of the Masterson brothers came to her mind. At least in appearance Will Masterson was as civilized as James, even if he behaved more savagely himself.

Annoyed with herself for thinking of Will at all, Lucinda tried to turn her thoughts to their task at hand. The irritating feature of questioning the various prospectors along their route was the very vague sense of time they seemed to have. When asked if the stranger had passed a day ago, or one hour, or seven, they tended to shrug in disinterest.

She supposed time meant very little to them, although they were likely to remember the very hour of the day that they struck gold.

By the time Lucinda and Davy stopped for lunch the day had grown much warmer, and they both felt sticky and out of sorts.

While they ate Davy grumbled, "I sure wish you could ride out by yourself. Maybe then I could get the hang of gold panning. I'm never going to find anything if we spend all day on those silly old mules."

"That will do, Davy. There will be plenty of time for gold panning later on."

"Maybe there won't," her brother pouted. "When we find Tom you'll want to start right for home. Anyway, he'll probably have found all the gold we need and you won't want to let me try for any."

"Come on, old grumpy," Lucinda laughed at him. She finished her lunch and poked him in the ribs. "Last one to the river is a tortoise," she cried, scrambling to her feet and running down the river bank.

Davy, making a whooping nose, sped after her and of course reached the river first. They made a game of washing their plates and mugs. Lucinda was glad to see Davy have some fun, as a boy of his age should. She regretted that the nature of their venture was causing his brow to wrinkle with worries far beyond his years.

Davy took off his boots and began wading in the water. "Ouch! It sure is cold, but then those old boots are so hot," he called out.

Smiling at him indulgently, Lucinda led the mules while Davy waded in the river, commenting on the current and also the various fish that went by.

He didn't see the prospector until he was almost upon him. Davy stopped short and stared at the stranger.

Lucinda, from the path, observed him as well. She saw immediately that he answered the description of the man they had been tracking, and her heart thumped with anticipation.

As the others had said, he had such long hair and such a big beard that it was difficult to tell his age or almost anything about him.

Davy, too, was struck by the resemblance of this fellow to the one their informants had seen. He couldn't quite come out and ask the stranger if he was his own brother, so he stood there mutely, waiting for his sister to make the opening move.

While Lucinda and Davy regarded the stranger and puzzled over him, the man himself totally ignored the other two. He stood in the stream with a gold pan, muttering indistinguishable words at it.

Lucinda beckoned to her brother to climb out of the stream. "Put your boots on, Davy," she whispered.

"You don't think that's Tom," Davy said, wrinkling his nose in the greatest skepticism.

"It's too soon to tell. Now, just stay by me and let me do the talking."

Leading their mules, Lucinda and Davy slowly went up the very narrow trail near the river. The ground began to rise so that when they were parallel to the stranger in the stream they were several feet above him.

It was then that Lucinda noticed that the man's pan was empty. He kept bending low and brushing his pan over the surface of the water. When he picked it up again, however, it was dry. Still, he shook it back and forth as Lucinda had seen the miners do.

"Cindy," Davy whispered to her, "that man is loco. He's shaking an empty pan."

Davy's eyes were big in wonder, while Lucinda's heart sank. She felt of two minds. On the one hand she wished the stranger would turn out to be Tom so that at last their search would be ended. The man was alive, at least, and perhaps could be nursed back to health. On the other hand the idea that her darling brother Tom might be roaming the hills and passing his days in this fruitless, mad activity quite chilled her blood.

"It couldn't be Tom, could it, Cindy?"

"We must find out for sure," Lucinda replied.

"Tom! Tom Evans!" Lucinda cupped her hands around her mouth and shouted the name at the stranger several times.

"Tom, it's Lucinda and Davy. We came all the way from Illinois. Ma sent us, and we have kisses from Betsy and Annie."

The man continued to observe his ritual just as if he hadn't heard a word Lucinda was shouting at him.

Lucinda's voice grew tired. "You try, Davy."

"But what should I say?"

"Anything. Anything at all that will get his attention.

But don't anger him, of course," she amended hastily.

"Hey, how about showing me how to pan gold?" Davy shouted in his clear young voice. "Hey, Tom how about showing—"

"What? What?" The man suddenly stopped his motion, picked up his head, and stared in their direction. His eyes were wild and bloodshot. Even from this distance Lucinda saw that it couldn't possibly be Tom.

"Sutter. John Sutter is my name. This is my gold mine. Git away from my gold mine!"

Davy cringed. The man's voice was eerie because it had a childlike quality that was totally out of keeping with his hirsute appearance.

"Oh, Cindy," Davy breathed, his voice full of horror.

"It's not Tom," she consoled him quickly. "Don't be frightened. He doesn't mean to harm us, poor man."

"I'm sorry, Mr. Sutter," Lucinda shouted to him. "We were mistaken. We're going now."

"Git off my land! It's mine, I tell you," the man babbled over and over.

Lucinda mounted her mule, and Davy followed her example. Clicking her tongue and smacking the animal on his flank, she turned him and started back in the direction they had come.

She saw with dismay that it was much later than she had realized. They should have begun their return long before. And their trip had been in vain after all. Against her volition the hated term "wild goose chase" came to mind, the very words that Will Masterson had used the previous evening to describe their venture. Now she saw for the first time how applicable the words might turn out to be.

When the path widened she rode alongside Davy. His face was pale and his lips trembled. It was his first brush with such a strange, tortured person. "What was wrong with him?" Davy asked.

Lucinda explained that the lonely life of gold prospecting, especially when the dream of success was unrealized, might cause a person to escape into a fantasy. "He thinks he's John Sutter, the poor man," Lucinda murmured. "John Sutter's mill was the place gold was originally discovered."

"You mean—you think—that the same thing could have happened to Tom?" Davy looked at his sister in fear. " 'Cause he maybe lost his gold or something, and then he was so upset that he thought he was rich, or—or—"

"Hush, Davy," Lucinda soothed him. "I didn't really think it was Tom all along, and it's not likely that our sensible brother would be so fanciful. Anyway, Davy, we know for sure now. Isn't it better than if we hadn't caught up to the man and kept wondering?"

Davy acknowledged that it was, but Lucinda could see, with sadness, how her young brother's innocence was being assailed by knowledge that should not have burdened him at such an early age.

"Tell you what, Davy, you're so good at scouting, why don't you go ahead and see if you can whip up that mule of yours to make some speed back to camp and dinner."

The boy brightened at the prospect of his dinner, as Lucinda had hoped he would, and in the next few moments his worries about the stranger vanished in his attempts to concentrate on the trail and the speed he could make along it.

"Here! Here's the way we came, only it's wider on this side of the river so we can ride faster." Davy was excited now, and proud of his skill at "scouting."

Although Lucinda was weary and more discouraged than she would have admitted to her brother, she did her best to join him in his enthusiasm and desisted from complaining or giving in to her wish to tumble off into the grassy knoll and have a rest. They simply had to get back to camp on time, for Lucinda didn't wish to fall down on her part of the bargain. She could well imagine the grumbling of the miners when they stopped their labors and found no meal waiting for them.

For some reason she thought again of Will Masterson, of the scathing words he would say if she returned to camp late and too much exhausted to do her job.

Fortunately, thanks to Davy's expertise, they made it back in good time. The men were putting away their tools, and they greeted Lucinda's return with shouts of welcome.

"Hey, there," Jake called out. "Here's our purty little cook back. Leastways, I think she must be purty, but she covers her face like she got scars all over it," he joked.

The men laughed loudly at that, while Davy fretted at them indignantly. "She doesn't either have scars. Why, she's the prettiest girl in the whole state of Illinois!"

"Shh! Davy, you stop it now! Remember what I told you about—about courting."

"Oh, I forgot." Too late Davy clapped his hand over his mouth. His statement had already aroused the curiosity of the men close enough to have heard his impassioned defense of his sister's beauty.

"Let's get that bonnet off her then, so's we can see for ourselves," Jake bawled.

"Jake, that will do," called out a calm, sensible voice. It was James Masterson, standing in front of his cabin.

"Sure, boss," laughed Jake, pulling his mustache nervously. "We was just passing the time of day."

Lucinda felt mortified, and especially so because Will Masterson had come to the door of his own cabin and was standing there listening to the banter, his expression insolent and smug. Hadn't he said the presence of a girl would cause trouble in the camp?

Furiously, Lucinda grabbed a couple of buckets and rushed to the river to get some water. She was sure that her red face could be seen from afar, even half-hidden under her bonnet.

Forgetting her earlier weariness, Lucinda bent over her cooking with a vengeance. With her fingers flying busily she was kept from thinking. While the men ate she quickly mixed up a light batter and heated oil in a deep pan. The men found they had hot, sugary doughnuts to go with their coffee.

Murmurs of appreciation rose in the camp, and Davy, at least, was mollified at the praise his sister's culinary talents drew from the men.

"She sure can cook," Jake acknowledged to Davy. "But," he continued slyly, "that don't mean she's pur-ty."

Davy smarted under the teasing words, unable to contradict them without calling Lucinda's wrath down upon him.

After their meal some of the men gathered around another fire and brought out a deck of cards. Fascinated, Davy wandered over to the group.

"What's that?" he asked.

"Faro. It's a game we play, a gambling game. Not for you, sonny," one of the men murmured around the cigar in his mouth.

"Why not? I like games. Why can't I play?" the boy queried.

"What would you put up as stakes, sonny? You got any gold or money? You can't play without a stake, see?"

While Davy pouted, he watched the men, trying to understand the game.

Lucinda glanced towards him occasionally as she cleaned the pots. She was opposed to gambling but didn't want to call attention to herself by trying to whee- dle Davy away from the men. Neither of the Masterson brothers was playing cards, Lucinda observed. James was sitting at a table in his cabin with the door open, looking through some papers by the light of an oil lamp.

Will Masterson was nowhere to be seen. Lucinda was annoyed with herself for looking up now and again, as if expecting to find him standing by her side.

Other men not in the card game sat around their own fire talking, smoking, and figuring out their share of the

gold mined that day. One of the miners picked up a
guitar and bagan to strum it, while another took a harmonica from his pocket.

Keeping to her own fire, Lucinda brought out some
clothes that needed mending. Although she felt quite
tired it was a pleasant feeling, and made relaxing in front
of the warmth even more sweet. When she was left alone
Lucinda was able to see the prospectors as ordinary
men, some of them hardly more than boys, who, under-
neath their bluster and swagger, weren't too terribly different from the ones she had known back home.

She learned from snatches of overheard conversation
that some of these gold hunters were former farmers,
just as Tom had been. Others had been seamen who left
their boats smack in the middle of San Francisco harbor
to join in the gold craze. Nearly all of them talked about
going home when they had made enough money to live
in luxury for the rest of their lives.

While she sewed contentedly, Davy went around the
camp in his friendly, good-humored way. The men made
something of a pet of Davy, teasing him and joking with
him, and also telling him fantastic stories because he was
so gullible.

"A gold nugget for your thoughts, Miss Evans," said
James Masterson, who had come up to her fire un-
noticed.

"Oh, I was just thinking about Davy, about how this
experience, whatever its result, will broaden his outlook
in a way that would never have been possible on the
farm."

"Not only his outlook, I should think."

"Mine too, of course." Lucinda looked up at him as
he hovered nearbv. "Would you—care to sit down?" she
asked, not knowing what else to do.

"I was hoping you'd invite me, ma'am," James said
happily, positioning himself across the fire from Lucinda. He lit his pipe. "How did your day go?"

"Well, it was rather mixed. We didn't find Tom, needless to say, but we did dispose of the mysterious stranger who passed through here, poor wretched man." When she told James of their encounter he nodded his head in sober understanding. "Sad to say he's not the only one. Will and I have been here since the beginning, and we've seen quite a few good fellows go under. Their failed dreams simply become too much for them."

"Why don't they just go home?"

"Some of them do. But others are too ashamed to face mothers and wives and sweethearts."

"I see." Lucinda bit off the end of a thread and put the shirt she had mended to one side. "My brother Tom isn't that sort of person. Anyway, he wrote us that he'd 'had a mite of luck,' as he put it. I—I don't suppose if I wrote a letter it could be delivered to the mail boat at Sacramento before I return there?"

"Of course it could. Men are coming and going here every day. We have quite a turnover. In fact, one of our number is leaving in a few days. I'm sure he'd be glad to take your letter."

"Oh, good. Then I'll write one." Lucinda hesitated. "You say you've had many men working for you. Do you think it's—it's possible that Tom did come through here at one time?"

"I honestly don't know. I've been racking my brain trying to think, but I just can't come up with anything. You see, there's nothing really outstanding about your brother, except to you, of course. I mean no strange feature or noticeable quirk of personality. The way it seems to me, your brother was one nice lad among thousands. That isn't the sort of thing that stands out two years later." James looked at Lucinda with compassion, and she knew that he would have done anything that he possibly could to have helped her.

She was beginning to think that next to Tom and her father, James was the kindest man she had ever met.

Now he glanced up at the sky. "It's clouded over and it smells rather damp. There's a good chance it will rain tonight. I do wish you'd reconsider about taking my cabin."

He shot her such a friendly smile that Lucinda almost gave in, but she felt firmly that his kindness had already been very great. Her mother had brought her up not to be indebted to folks.

"Thank you, Mr. Masterson, but I'll sleep outdoors just the same. If Davy and I grow too fond of our comfort we won't be able to go on our way. You might be stuck with us for longer than you expected," she said mischievously.

He took her seriously, however. "Miss Evans, I'd be more than happy to extend our invitation. I don't want to say anything mean about our cook but he doesn't hold a candle to you."

Lucinda thought he said those words rather wistfully, and she felt herself blushing. To cover her confusion she asked him what hour it was, immediately jumping up to exclaim that it was way past Davy's bedtime.

She excused herself and went in search of Davy, finding him sitting next to some prospectors who were weighing up their gold. Davy was turning the nuggets over and over in his hand, his eyes greedy.

"Bed, Davy," Lucinda said firmly. He looked up at her gloomily, but he really was tired, and he realized it himself as he stifled a yawn.

"Before you roll up in your blanket I think you need a good wash, hands and face, and behind your ears."

The two things that Davy most hated were getting up in the morning and washing. Often Lucinda found it expedient to make a game of it, so, looking at his pouting face, she offered to race him to the river's edge.

Davy would have beaten her even if she hadn't been so tired. Finally, the wash accomplished, she wearily made her way back to camp. Davy, in the meantime, had found second wind, and he became as playful as a puppy. He threw the soap at her. Grabbing for it, she missed, and down it went in the grass. Davy began scurrying around on all fours, making canine noises.

"You'll get dirty all over again," laughed Lucinda, trying to pull him to his feet.

Switching his imitation from dog to cat, Davy began mewing and swiping at his sister with his "paw."

Somehow his hand got caught in her bonnet strings and they became undone. Her bonnet came off with a jerk and her beautiful golden hair cascaded to her waist.

Suddenly all activity ceased in the camp. There was absolute silence as the men stared at Lucinda, getting a real look at her for the first time.

In her flustered condition she appeared even more lovely than usual. Her pale face was tinged with pink at the cheeks, and her rosy lips had parted as she caught her breath with embarrassment. Her large, clear eyes looked bluer than ever, while her hair, to those gold-crazed men, seemed like nothing less than spun gold itself. With her shawl thrown off her shoulders in the confusion, the men could see that her tight-fitting dress concealed a slim and shapely form.

Desperately Lucinda tried to gather her hair into a knot once more. While she struggled the flames of the fire suddenly caught a big log and shot higher, further illuminating Lucinda's beauty.

"Bed, Davy," Lucinda hissed, furious with herself. The thing that added the most to her discomfort was the glimpse she had of a red-shirted man standing in the doorway of his cabin, his dark eyes glittering.

After what Lucinda considered the shameful exhibition she had made of herself, she decided to retire with Davy. However, she was much too distraught to sleep.

She lay awake looking up at the stars and thinking of her home, of her mother and two small sisters, of how uncomplicated her past life had been. She had gone every day to the schoolhouse, where she derived a true satisfaction in teaching the little ones their letters. Everyone she met in their small town would greet her and behave towards her with the greatest respect.

And now—and now she was in a place full of strange men, who dared to look at her as they had, who knew nothing of her background or the precepts by which she lived, who were ready to do—goodness knew what, if they got the chance.

Of course she was under the protection of James Masterson but even he—he had looked at her as steadfastly as any of the others when her hair had come undone. He, too, was without feminine companionship. While he might be a good deal more cultured and polite than the others he was also a man, and Lucinda mustn't forget it.

Ruefully she realized that she was probably safer with Will Masterson than with any other man in camp because he so disliked her.

Lucinda was abruptly awakened from a sound sleep when her brother jumped up from his blankets, shouting, "Who's there?"

Her heart pounding with fear, Lucinda raised herself on her elbow. Their fire had burned to embers, and she could see nothing in the blackness ahead of her.

"Who's there?" shouted Davy once more.

After a few moments, a figure loomed in front of them. Even in the darkness Lucinda recognized the clumsy, big form of Jake.

He moved up close to brother and sister, his suggestive look fastening on Lucinda, who was without her bonnet, of course, although her hair was contained in two plaits.

"I was just thinkin' about you here, ma'am, all by your lonesome."

"I'm with her," Davy flung at him.

"I mean without a man's lovin' arms to kinda keep the chill off of you."

Lucinda was too frightened and humiliated to speak. Also, she wasn't quite sure if this was real or if she was dreaming.

Her brother, however, was wide awake. He reached for his rifle. "Git or else."

Lucinda lay down again and pulled her blanket up over her head, to indicate how she felt about Jake's innuendoes.

"All right, all right," laughed Jake. "I didn't mean no harm." He melted into the shadows.

"Don't worry, Cindy," Davy consoled her. "He won't be back." The boy patted the rifle at his side.

Nevertheless sleep had vanished for Lucinda. She wondered how many more men of the camp would now wish to keep her from being "lonesome." Oh, if only her bonnet hadn't come off! If only they had found Tom within the first few days! The entire adventure began to take on a nightmarish quality. Lucinda wondered if perhaps she would wake up in the morning in her own bed back in Illinois, to find that Tom had returned and all was well.

The voice that addressed her out of the darkness was not at all dreamlike. "Miss Evans."

It was Will Masterson. Lucinda sat bolt upright, drawing her blanket around her shoulders. "What—what is it?" she asked in a tremulous voice.

"I will help you to move your things into my cabin."

The blood rushed into her face, and for a perilous moment she thought she would swoon. Was he—did he dare suggest—

"Heck, we like sleeping out here," Davy said. "We don't want to sleep in any old cabin."

"You may sleep where you wish, Davy, but your sister will kindly utilize my cabin. I have put my gear in James' place and we have settled the matter."

As her panic slowly subsided Lucinda managed to find her voice. "As Davy says, Mr. Masterson, we're perfectly all right out here—"

"Don't argue with me, Miss Evans. It's all decided between James and me. Perhaps you don't need uninterrupted rest, but I assure you that my men won't be worth anything if they spend the night sniffing around your camp fire. Jake was only the first, you can take my word for it," he finished grimly.

Lucinda was silent, for she had no answer, realizing that Will might be correct. Still, she felt terribly vexed at having to give into him.

"Maybe you'd better, Cindy," Davy suddenly said. Even he could see the wisdom of her being out of reach in the cabin.

Trying to retain her dignity, Lucinda murmured, "Very well, if I must." With misgivings, she unwrapped herself and rose to her feet, drawing her shawl closely about her.

Immediately Will was kneeling beside her gathering her blankets together.

"I can do that," she said sharply. Somehow the thought of his touching the place that was still warm from her body was most disquieting.

"Just for once, try doing as you are told," Will retorted, a harsh note creeping into his voice.

"Do I have to sleep inside too?" Davy asked his sister.

"The best place for you, Davy," answered Will, before Lucinda could get a word out, "is right outside in front of the door of the cabin, so anyone trying to get in will have to deal with you first."

"Gee, that's great. I'll do that. All right, Cindy?" Davy was strutting with his rifle on his shoulder. Will Masterson had taken just the right approach with her brother, Lucinda thought with reluctant admiration.

Holding her head high, she swept past Will and walked towards his cabin, trying not to show how angry she was. She hated the idea that he was getting the better of her. If only that foolish Jake had minded his own business she would not be forced to undergo such humiliating treatment at the hands of her antagonist.

For that was how she thought of Will Masterson. To him she was as annoying as a fly, and just about as important. He kept flicking at her with his sharp tongue. She was a nuisance, that was all. And now she had to be exiled to his shack, almost as if she had committed a crime and was being taken prisoner.

Lucinda was unaccustomed to being ordered about, and she didn't like it one bit. She wished they had had enough supplies for her to have been able to tell him what she thought of his insufferable insolence, but she mustn't let her anger make her incautious. The important thing was to find Tom, she kept reminding herself. Nevertheless she couldn't help wishing that she could avenge herself somehow and make Will pay for having so offended her.

Will followed her in and made up her bed on a straw pallet. She could only stand by helplessly, fretting inwardly. The embers of a fire were visible in the small fireplace, and the cabin felt warm and cozy.

Will moved quickly and deftly, and she noticed that he had strong, graceful hands, the fingers long and tapered.

A slow shiver worked its way up Lucinda's spine, and she trembled involuntarily.

Davy's head appeared at the door. "I fixed my blankets out here, so just shout if you need me, Cindy," Davy said importantly.

At last Will straightened up from his task. He stood facing Lucinda, so close that she could have reached out and touched him.

Without meaning to do so, she lifted her blue eyes to his face and saw that he was looking at her with a resentful expression in his eyes.

For a few seconds they stood thus. And then Lucinda flinched under his gaze and turned away, fussing with her shawl.

"I hope you'll be comfortable," he said evenly. "It may grow a bit cold towards morning but the sun heats this place very quickly."

"I'll be fine, thank you," Lucinda replied, mustering

every shred of control and dignity. Her tone was a dismissive one.

"Good night, then," Will murmured in a low voice. He turned and in a moment was gone, carefully shutting the door behind him.

It was difficult for Lucinda to banish his disturbing image from her mind, and even in sleep his glowing dark eyes haunted her dreams.

Chapter 4

When Lucinda opened her eyes she couldn't determine for a few frantic moments where she was. The sun streamed in through the window, and Lucinda jumped up in a panic.

Slowly it came to her that she had slept in Will Masterson's cabin. She had dreamed so extensively the previous night that she had been almost sure her remembered episode with him had been part of her dream life.

Now she knew it had really happened. As she dressed she looked around the cabin curiously. There was a wooden table and a chair, as well as some hooks on the wall where Will apparently had hung his few items of clothing.

She noticed a couple of books on the table whose titles indicated that Will was well educated indeed.

Tucking her hair into her bonnet, Lucinda opened the door and stepped outside. From the bustle all around she saw that she had overslept, and she hastened to start her breakfast preparations.

Several of the men tipped their hats and bade her good morning in so polite a way that Lucinda was struck by their change of attitude. Perhaps it hadn't been such a bad thing for them to have had a good look at her and see that she was not the sort of girl they had at first thought but one quite accustomed to courteous treatment.

While cooking breakfast she noticed that several men had already begun their day's work. Some of them were hovering downstream, around a peculiar wooden structure, but her eye immediately was caught by two figures nearby in the river. Davy was standing next to Will Masterson, who was showing him how to pan for gold. Will's voice was gentle as he spoke to Davy.

"No, not like that, Davy. Here, you wash the dirt this way, and then drain off the sludge. When you get all finished, if there's any gold dust it will have settled in the bottom of the pan. That's better, that's the idea."

Why did he not use the same tone to her, Lucinda wondered with resentment. Why was he so hostile to her? Then she remembered what James had said about Will's lost love, the girl who had married someone else. Even so, that was no reason, surely, to dislike all women.

As such thoughts flitted through her mind, her hands busily working of their own accord, Lucinda saw James approaching her. His attitude, at least, was unchanged. Still polite, still friendly, he apologized for the bad manners of Jake the previous night, reiterating that the fellow had meant no real harm.

"I'm certainly pleased, ma'am, that you agreed to sleep in the cabin. I felt simply awful thinking of you out there in all sorts of weather. I regret that this place is not equipped for young ladies."

To cover her slight feeling of embarrassment, Lucinda mentioned that she had seen an occasional woman prospecting alongside her man, and related her encounter with the woman and her three sons.

"Oh, yes, you find some women as eager to find gold as the menfolk. But—but not quite like you, Miss Evans," he continued, glancing at her shyly. "Those are a different sort, whereas you are more like the young ladies of Virginia, made for gentle pursuits, for tea parties and balls, and to grace a home with their charming presence."

"Oh, goodness, I wasn't raised quite like that," Lucinda hastened to say, flushing, to correct his impression of her. "Our farm is a poor one, indeed, and there aren't any balls to speak of, only a simple country dance now and again."

Lucinda had read newspaper accounts, illustrated with drawings, about the gracious way of life among the rich in Virginia. She could remember looking with delight at the pictures of elegant young ladies dressed in beautiful gowns of intricate design and no doubt fashioned from rich fabrics. How Lucinda had envied them their white, smooth hands holding fans coyly in front of their faces, and their eyes that beckoned flirtatiously. Had Will Masterson been jilted by such a girl?

Just the thought made Lucinda blush. She lowered her head from the constant gaze of James who, of course, had no idea what she was thinking.

"Did I say something to distress you, Miss Evans?" he asked anxiously.

She was saved from replying by Davy, who bounded up to her, shouting with excitement, "I found some gold dust! Look, Cindy, I found some!"

Sure enough there was something in the bottom of the pan Davy was holding under Lucinda's nose. She looked at it, surprised at the sight of what appeared to her ordinary-looking particles of gravel. For one agonized moment she worried that it was all a joke. Perhaps Will had played a cruel trick upon her brother for the amusement of the other men.

The next moment she felt ashamed of her thoughts, as the men exclaimed over Davy's find, and she saw that Will was smiling at Davy. So the discovery was genuine. That smile on Will's face made her heart lurch, for it quite changed his appearance. His dark eyes glowed with happiness, and his face crinkled into warmth that was far more pleasant than his usual cold scowl. Reluctantly she had to admit that Will was a handsome man. Immediately she chided herself for noticing him at all, since the smile was not meant for her.

Lucinda felt unreasonably annoyed at the way Will had taken to Davy. Davy, on his part, had responded to

Will's interest in him with all the innocent affection in his nature. Never one to bear a grudge, Davy had completely forgotten his first angry meeting.

"How much is this dust worth, Will?" Davy shouted.

"How much would you guess?" Will shot back, still smiling at the boy.

"Gee, I dunno. Ten dollars?"

"Heck, son, you got about three times that there," one of the others averred.

"Yippee!" Davy hooted, jumping up and down.

"Careful, lad, you don't want to drop it on the ground and have it blowed away again. Do you have a little pouch to put it in?" another asked.

The men crowded around, eating and drinking while they advised Davy on the best way of securing his gold.

It took every bit of Lucinda's persuasion to get Davy to saddle the mules and prepare to ride out as they had planned. Of course he was eager to go right back to his panning. It was only by promising him he could get to work whenever they stopped for a rest that Lucinda convinced Davy to get moving.

They rode out in a southerly direction, again finding numerous prospectors. Lucinda had to do most of the talking, since Davy had become a victim of the gold fever himself, and his contribution mainly took the form of carefully observing the prospectors at work.

Lucinda cautioned her brother to be more careful, pointing out that these men were very jittery about claims jumpers. "After all, Davy, if you found a good spot you wouldn't take kindly to some stranger coming along and sticking his nose right into your pan, would you?"

"No, I guess I wouldn't," the lad admitted.

"Remember, our first task is to find Tom. We mustn't lose sight of that, no matter what. You may have been lucky this morning, but even thirty dollars doesn't buy much out here when folks are so rich and prices are high in keeping with it."

Davy promised to behave more cautiously in future, and then completely forgot when they next came upon two men in the stream bending over what appeared to be a child's cradle.

Davy waited impatiently while his sister inquired about Tom. As soon as the men had shaken their heads and bent once more to their work, he jumped off his mule and waded into the river, ignoring Lucinda's attempts to call him back.

"Gee, how does it work?" he asked in an awed voice.

They took a brief look at the lad. One prospector, well over six feet in height and quite burly, showed no fear of skinny little Davy and explained the operation to him.

The miners used their picks and shovels to gather up the dirt and put it into the wooden rocker. Then one man poured water into it while the other man shook it back and forth. The water washed out the sludge, and any nuggets were caught behind the cross peices in the bottom.

Lucinda had quite a job tearing Davy away from such a fascinating spectacle.

When they stopped for lunch Davy took his plate of food into the river with his gold pan. Over and over he bent down, filled the pan, and washed it.

Nevertheless he found nothing, and his face indicated his intense disappointment. He bounded up then, proclaiming that they must move on, for obviously there was no gold to be found here.

Wearily Lucinda didn't insist on traveling too far or too quickly. She was now of the opinion that Tom wasn't anywhere in the vicinity—if he was even still in the gold country; if nothing had happened. Lucinda forced herself to banish such disagreeable possibilities from her mind.

"It's time to start back," she called out to Davy. "You can pan on the other bank of the river," she added, as further inducement.

Davy's face brightened visibly, and that was just what

he did. Although their progress was slower, Lucinda didn't think that it mattered greatly. It was as good a way to spend the time as any.

In spite of their meandering they were, Lucinda found, returning to camp quite early. The sun was still visible when Davy proclaimed that they were less than a mile from the camp.

Just then they reached a place where a small stream branched off from the main body of the river and widened into a pool.

"Look, Cindy, doesn't that look like our old swimming hole?" observed Davy.

"You're right, it does, and I could do with a swim." Lucinda felt dusty and sticky from the trail. It suddenly occurred to her that this was the best place she had yet seen for proper bath. The water in the pond was deep enough to come up to her neck, surely. And unlike the river, with its swiftly moving current, the water in the pond was almost still.

Lucinda asked Davy to ride back to camp, fetch some soap and a change of clothes for both of them, and come right back again.

He agreed sullenly, for he preferred to pan for gold back at camp.

As he rode away Lucinda alighted from her mule and tied it up behind some tall pine trees. It was shady and cool here, and absolutely deserted.

Lucinda looked down at the water longingly. On impulse she removed her bonnet, loosening her hair, her gingham dress and petticoats, and stepped carefully into the water, wearing only her shift. How cool it felt, and very clean.

She splashed about quite happily for a little while, expecting Davy to return any minute. Jutting out of the water was a flat rock which would be ideal for washing clothes. Paddling to the shore, Lucinda got her dress and bonnet and brought them to the rock. Of course she would need the soap to do a proper job of washing the garments.

Shading her eyes with her hand, she peered off in the direction of the camp. Still no Davy. Surely he should have returned to her by this time. With her dress and shift soaking wet she had no choice but to await her brother's arrival.

In a mood of gentle euphoria, Lucinda lost track of the time. She swam around the perimeter of the little pool, being careful to stay away from the center because of the deeper water.

Eventually Lucinda grew tired so she stood up for a moment, pushing her long wet hair back from her face. Where had that brother of hers got to, she wondered with impatience.

Suddenly she had the most eerie feeling that she was not alone any longer and that someone was watching her. Frightened, she crouched in the water to be sure that only her face was showing. Was it her brother, playing hide and seek with her?

"Davy," she called out tentatively.

A figure detached itself from the trees and walked slowly towards her. Her face turned crimson with distress, for it wasn't Davy at all. It was Will Masterson!

How long had he been watching her? Had he seen her swimming, had he heard the absurd gurgles of contentment that she had uttered, thinking she was totally alone? And even worse, had he—had he seen her stand up in the water wearing nothing but her wet shift?

She would willingly have died right then and there.

"Your brother sent me on an errand, Miss Evans," Will Masterson said in a conversational tone, while he stared at her with a glint of amusement in his dark eyes.

"Where is Davy?" she asked sharply, though her voice shook.

"When I left him he was panning for gold. But he didn't forget you. Here's the soap." Will extended his hand, while what she could only describe as a smirk appeared on his handsome face.

"When I get my hands on that boy I'll beat him within an inch of his life," Lucinda mumbled to herself.

"I have your clean clothes here as well," Will called out to her.

"Just—just leave them there on the shore, please," she said to him, her words barely audible. She was mortified to imagine him handling her garments, the dress, the petticoats, the shift—Oh, how stupid and helpless she felt, kneeling in the water while her wet hair swirled around her as if she were a mermaid.

"I can put the clothes down, but don't you want the soap? Ma'am?"

He stood close enough to the water's edge for her to observe that his mouth was twitching in an effort not to laugh, and she could well imagine how ridiculous she seemed.

"Yes, I want the soap!" she blazed at him. "Just throw it in, please."

"Throw it in?" he asked, his voice mocking. "Why then it will sink to the bottom, Miss Evans, and you'll have to dive down for it. You can dive, I presume?"

She could do no such thing, and he surely knew it. Oh, she was so furious she felt like a small girl ready to stamp her foot! Never in her life had she been in such a predicament, and in front of her sworn enemy, too. If it had been James rather than Will she could much better have handled her embarrassment. At least James would not have added to her discomfiture. He would have done his utmost to ease the tension.

"If you were a gentleman you'd put the soap on that rock, turn around, and just walk away from here," she called out hotly.

"Would I, indeed! Just because you say so? If you were a lady you would speak in a gentle voice and not issue instructions like a schoolmarm instructing her pupils. That tone may work with Davy but I consider it damned impertinent when directed at me!" He was angry now, and his dark eyes flashed at her.

She was about to demand that he not swear in her presence, but he would no doubt take that as more schoolmarm instruction. The presumption of the man left her spluttering with helpless rage.

Taking a deep breath she tried to gain control of herself. "Would you please be so kind as to put the soap on that rock next to the clothes?" she choked out, trying to keep the sarcasm out of her tone.

"Certainly, since you ask me politely!" Still smoldering, Will stormed over to the rock and banged the soap down, the next minute having to lunge for it as it started to slip into the water.

"Thank you. I can manage now, if you will kindly leave me."

While she was speaking Lucinda had been backing off, because it had occurred to her that the water might have been clear enough for him to have seen her shift while she remained so close to shore. She stepped back too far, however, and suddenly found herself in deep water.

Taken completely by surprise, Lucinda began to thrash her arms in a panic. Never before had she been in water over her head, and she didn't have any idea of what to do. She felt herself sink down and swallow water, while she wildly flailed her arms in an effort to come to the surface.

The next moment a terrific splash next to her informed her that Will was in the pond with her. Her panic grew, and she couldn't stop swallowing water.

"Blast it, woman, stop that thrashing. I'm not going to hurt you. Here, you simpleton, I've got a blanket."

She felt something heavy and wet thrown over her while a strong arm grabbed her around the shoulders and pulled her to the shore.

It was all over in a matter of seconds. Will lifted her up in the blanket and placed her on the ground. Then he climbed out himself, panting and cursing under his breath.

"You little fool, you nearly drowned the two of us!"

Gasping and coughing, Lucinda tried to curl her legs up into the blanket as well as her arms, but it was much too short for that. It concealed only her torso.

"I—I wasn't drowning," she gasped. "I just lost my footing for a moment. All you had to do was turn your back—"

"Never mind that now. The sun has gone down and it's chilly. Better dry yourself off and get dressed," Will said, making it sound like a command.

At least he did have the grace to turn around and walk into the woods a little way.

Her teeth beginning to chatter, Lucinda clumsily unwound herself from the sodden blanket and dried herself with a towel. Of course she was too jittery to do a proper job, and she kept her eyes glued fearfully to Will's back to be sure he didn't whirl around in the middle of everything. With trembling fingers she hurriedly pulled on her clean shift, petticoats, and dress. She was still quite wet but at least her limbs were covered.

During those few awful moments in the water Lucinda had died a thousand deaths and she could almost wish that Will had let her drown. At least she would have been spared the humiliation of ever having to look at him or speak to him again.

Picking up her hairbrush she drew it through her tangled hair ruthlessly, thinking of how she would absolutely tar Davy for having reneged on his promise and causing her to be put in such a humiliating position.

"All right now, Miss Evans?" called Will, turning around and walking towards her.

"Stay back!" she shouted in alarm.

He stopped and looked at her sullenly. "What's wrong now! You do have your clothes on, so what gentlemanly principle am I violating? Surely it's not against the law for me to see you brush your hair. Or do you have special rules all your own!"

His voice was scathing, and she felt embarrassed all over again. How could she tell him that he had a way of looking at her that made her feel naked even when she was fully clothed?

Will's trousers were still wet, and he had removed his shirt. With his damp, tousled black curls he looked like a gypsy standing there in bare feet holding his boots and shirt.

Quite against her volition she stared at his broad shoulders and strong chest, tanned by the sun, at his muscular arms that only recently had carried her from the water and deposited her rudely on the bank.

The thought once more sent a flush right through her.

"I see you observe me carefully, Miss Evans. I suppose that is out of concern for my welfare, to be sure I did not do myself an injury when I jumped in to save you. That careful scrutiny, no doubt, is your own peculiar way of saying thank you." His voice mocked her.

"You, you—how insufferable! I wasn't anywhere near to drowning. I—I just lost my footing briefly. I would have been all right again in a moment, if you hadn't jumped in almost on top of me and started to maul me," she cried, her blue eyes flashing darkly with anger at him.

"You were, I assure you, very much in danger of drowning because you were in a panic. It is possible to drown in two inches of water, Miss Evans, if one loses one's head. As for mauling you, I should think you'd have the common sense to realize that one can't pull a drowning, wildly struggling person from the water without putting hands on her. At least I was considerate enough of your modesty, such as it is, to have taken a blanket with me."

"My modesty! How about your own? I suppose you think you ought to have a medal!" Furious and completely beside herself, Lucinda clapped her sodden bonnet upon her wet hair, picked up a handful of dripping clothes, and marched towards her mule.

She mounted, holding the wet bundle in her lap, and smacked the animal smartly on the side. "Get up!"

The mule started forward, shaking itself with annoyance at all the water dripping down its neck.

"Watch out you don't drown your mule as well," Will called out after her, and then she heard him laughing.

Lucinda had never been so enraged, and she cast about for some way to have her revenge. She would beat Davy with a stick and throw his gold pan into the river. She would go directly to James and tell him what a brute his brother was. She would pack up everything as soon as she got back to camp and ride right out from there without so much as saying farewell!

During the half hour it took to return, her anger abated somewhat. It was dark now and she realized that, in spite of her dire threats, she would have no time to do a thing except start supper. However ill disposed she might feel at the moment towards Will Masterson, the others did not deserve to miss their meal.

When she arrived at camp she found herself the center of all eyes, and she well understood that she looked quite a sight in her damp garments with water still dripping from her bundle of clothes.

At least Will wasn't there to mock her. It was James who came up to her in some perplexity and concern to ask what had happened.

She decided the best thing would be to say little so she confined herself to explaining that she'd washed some clothes and gotten wetter than she had intended.

As for Davy, he was bending over the fire he had lit and was gathering the food and utensils for supper. "Gosh, you sure are late, Cindy. I thought you'd never get here. Didn't you get the soap and things all right?"

Fortunately he omitted to mention Will's name. Lucinda nodded briefly and tried not to look angry at her brother, but it wasn't easy.

It wasn't until she had finished serving all the men

that Will made his appearance at the fire. He had changed his trousers and shirt, and she was thankful that at least he had spared her the embarrassment of prancing over to be fed looking as wet as she was, thus occasioning most unwelcome comments from the others.

Nevertheless she kept her eyes down as she dished out his food, and he didn't break the silence. When his plate was full he withdrew from the fire.

Lucinda's temper had not cooled. When the pots and pans were dried and put away, she beckoned to Davy to follow her to the cabin, where she could speak to him in privacy.

"Now, Davy, perhaps you would care to explain yourself."

The boy hung his head. "I got interested in the gold, I guess. Jake was showing me what they call a long tom. I sort of thought, being it has the same name and all of our Tom, that it might bring me good luck," he finished softly.

Lucinda just couldn't find it in her heart to berate him, for he seemed so contrite. He was still a child, after all.

"And did you find any gold dust?"

He shook his head. "Not this time."

"Didn't it occur to you that I was waiting for you?"

"Yes, and I'm—I'm sorry, Cindy. I said how I had to go back and take the things and, and Will was standing right there so he offered to take them for me."

Lucinda's cheeks burned. "Are you sure he made the suggestion first? You didn't ask him to do it?"

"No, ma'am, I wouldn't have asked him. He offered, I swear, Cindy."

"Don't swear." She paused, not sure of how much of the proceedings she should impart to her little brother. He might, when they finally returned home, say something impetuous that would cause her mother grief in retrospect.

"You see, Davy, I had quite some uneasy moments. When Mr. Masterson came along I was in the water in only my chemise. And—and I didn't get to wash my clothes properly. . . ."

She had said enough for Davy to imagine that the scene had been unpleasant, especially since he could see that his sister's face was scarlet as she told him her story.

He apologized again and offered to have a proper bath on the following day. Lucinda sighed and forgave him with a hug.

After Davy had gone Lucinda lit the lamp and sat on the chair brushing her hair until it was dry and glistening. She had no wish to wander outside this evening and was content to remain in the cabin and immerse herself in one of the books Will had left out.

The more she thought about her encounter with Will, the more ashamed she grew over her behavior. It was true, of course, that he shouldn't have offered to bring her things in Davy's stead but ought to have encouraged the boy to obey his sister. And having found her thus in the pool, Will should have left the things and taken himself off. Nevertheless, when she floundered in the water he had jumped in after her. The thought made her blush anew. Still, things could have been worse. What if there had been no blanket?

She tried to turn her attention to her book once more but it was no use. Her thoughts had agitated her. In addition she now felt tired, and the flickering oil lamp hurt her eyes.

What she needed was a quick breath of air. At the same time she would suggest that Davy prepare for bed.

When Lucinda emerged from the hut she found only a scattering of miners playing cards outside. From a light burning in the Masterson cabin she assumed that the brothers were keeping to themselves this evening.

She walked all over camp without finding Davy. Finally she struck out on the path hoping to catch sight of him in the woods.

The night was very fine, and the cool air felt good

against her cheeks. A soft breeze gently wafted through her hair, for she had neglected to pin it into a knot. In fact, she had left her bonnet inside the cabin. That hadn't been very prudent of her, she now realized, but she had expected to be out only for a moment to fetch Davy.

She stopped short, for she suddenly came face to face with Will Masterson.

"If you're looking for your brother, you'll find him north of camp with some of the men. They're setting traps to catch game, and he wanted to be in on it."

"Thank you for telling me," she said, wondering why her voice sounded so weak and shaky, and why she was trembling slightly. Surely she had nothing to fear from Will now.

"All dried off, Miss Evans?" he asked, and once again she heard the mocking note creep into his voice.

"Yes, I am. I—I apologize for my rudeness back at the pool. I realize now that—you thought you were—saving me from drowning, although I don't—actually think I was. However, I have—I have chosen to—to accept your interpretation of the affair, and I thank you."

The words came out in short breathless gasps, as if it cost her quite an effort to say them, and indeed it did. She hated to be beholden to a man who so clearly thought of her with contempt.

"Ah, how very generous of you, ma'am, to accept my own explanation of what happened instead of granting me the benefit of your superior understanding. I must be growing in your estimation. It's quite a thing to celebrate, when a teacher admits she may not know best after all."

His voice fairly dripped with sarcasm, and Lucinda was stung into fury once more. "Can't you ever just accept any statement at face value? Do you always have to assume that an apology, as in this case, was intended as an insult? You really are too much to bear, Mr. Masterson."

"I might say exactly the same of you, Miss Evans."

He took a step closer to her, his eyes hooded in anger. "I'm not accustomed to being given clearance as to my motives or, as a matter of fact, to being chastised by members of the female sex. Our Southern women, Miss Evans, have the sense and the courtesy to allow the men to take responsibility for their own actions. I'm not your mule, to be prodded this way and that."

"I don't see why not," Lucinda countered hotly. "You're every bit as stubborn. Oh, I've no doubt I don't remind you of your grand ladies back home. But then, they have servants to do for them, haven't they, and gracious mansions to live in. They aren't constantly surrounded by a bunch of ruffians who—who stand by the water's edge, as you did, enjoying their discomfort."

"Of all the ungrateful—I simply brought the things you wanted. I assure you I wasn't lurking behind a bush spying on you. I was about to leave you alone when you began to thrash around like a kitten that has somehow gotten itself into deep water, and I then—"

"I wouldn't have thrashed around, as you so elegantly put it, if you hadn't been looking at me so—so—"

"Go on, Miss Evans. How did I look at you?"

Lucinda was silent. She had been about to say something presumptuous, and she had caught herself just in time.

Will divined her thoughts nevertheless. "You may be the only female present in this camp, Miss Evans, but that doesn't mean that you are totally irresistible to every man here. The fact that someone looks at you may merely mean that he is admiring the species and not necessarily the particular example."

Lucinda whirled and began to run back along the path. She couldn't have explained why her eyelids stung with tears, why her chest was heaving in great distress, and why she wished with all her might that she had never set eyes on Will Masterson.

When she reached the clearing she halted and stood for a moment patting her hair and trying to collect herself. The men were back, Davy with them.

Although Lucinda felt shaken by the encounter with Will she was determined not to show it. "Bedtime," she said sternly to her brother.

A noise behind them startled Lucinda. She spun around to see Will.

"I found this on the path. It is yours, I presume, Miss Evans."

She saw that he was holding out to her a tiny gold locket on a chain which had been her grandmother's. Automatically her hand went up to her throat and found it bare. "But—but the chain must have broken."

"No, merely came undone." Instead of handing over the locket Will stepped quickly behind her and fastened it around her neck, his fingers gently moving her hair so that it didn't become entangled in the chain.

The touch of his burning fingers on her skin made Lucinda quiver suddenly, and the strangest tingling sensation went down her arms to her very fingertips.

It was all over in a moment.

She thanked Will in a whisper; he inclined his head in recognition, and walked swiftly away.

When Lucinda lay in bed that night she wished with all her might that the cook would return on the following day. She had had enough of the Masterson camp, and especially of Will Masterson. She sensed a great danger in remaining here, even though she couldn't exactly define it. She knew only that she must flee. Will aroused in her stronger emotions than she had ever believed possible, and she didn't like it one bit.

Chapter 5

Lucinda dawdled after breakfast the following morning, her eyes alert for the return of the cook. When there continued to be no sign of anyone, she reluctantly faced the fact they they had better ride out as usual and hope for the cook's return by evening.

The camp was quiet because the men, along with Davy, had gone to investigate the animal traps. Will Masterson was with them. Lucinda was angry with herself for noticing but found that she kept looking around for him. It wasn't that she wished to see him. On the contrary: she merely wished to ascertain his movements so that he wouldn't come up out of the blue and surprise her. For whenever that happened her heart would begin to pound and she would feel the palms of her hands grow moist. It was fear, she decided. Hadn't the same symptoms occurred when the wagon train had faced danger? That was it. Will Masterson constituted some sort of danger, and she would do well to avoid him as much as possible.

At the moment it was James who approached her, a sheaf of papers under his arm. "Are you riding out today, ma'am?"

"Yes, I am. As soon as Davy returns."

"In the meantime, I wonder if you would mind assisting me," James asked diffidently, his soft brown eyes appealing to her.

"Of course, Mr. Masterson. I'll be happy to help in any way that I can, though I don't see what I could do that you couldn't."

James laughed. "It's figures, ma'am. I'm not much good with them. I used to be the despair of my mathematics teacher. Now I struggle and struggle to make sense of these, having to determine the hours worked and the value of the gold mined, and so forth."

"I'm only a country schoolmistress, Mr. Masterson, and I can't do much more than simple arithmetic—"

"But that's splendid. That's all I need, only my arithmetic is so poor. Every time I add up or multiply or divide I get a different answer—with the same numbers."

He moved his table and chair out into the sun in front of the cabin. Lucinda sat down and he leaned over her, watching her as she worked and listening carefully to her explanations.

"It seems so simple when you do it, Miss Evans. I can run a tobacco plantation and I know a good deal about agriculture and animals, and now a fair amount about gold mining. It's just those darn numbers that defeat me."

"I can do the figures, but most of the other things you mention would be a total mystery to me, so you still are way ahead, Mr. Masterson," Lucinda said, smiling up at him in an effort to soothe his masculine pride.

A murmur of voices indicated that the men were back. Lucinda noticed that Will was right up front and that he was glaring at her and at his brother. Apparently he had seen her smile at James. Why should that distress him?

"Any luck, Will?" James asked.

"No. Couple of tiny rabbits. Not enough to make a meal so we released them."

While he spoke, Will flicked his dark eyes insolently over Lucinda's face. She was wearing her bonnet rather far back on her head and hadn't bothered to tuck in her hair. Under his rancorous gaze she grew warm and uncomfortable.

"Let's go, Davy. We're late starting today," Lucinda said briskly to cover her confusion.

As they walked towards the mules she had the disturbing feeling that Will was looking after her.

They rode due north that day, meeting with the usual indifference and blank responses from the prospectors they encountered. Davy spent much of the time panning for gold but came away empty-handed, which put him in a glum mood.

Lucinda, too, was feeling out of sorts. She determined that all this searching in the vicinity was a waste of time. Tom must surely be farther up in the hills. "Let's hope the cook returns today," she remarked to Davy.

He looked at her curiously. "You in a hurry to leave camp?"

"Well, of course I am. I think Tom must be miles away. This part of the Mother Lode is either worked out or well established, as the Masterson claim is, and Tom isn't there, is he?"

"I thought you liked the camp. At least you sure seem to like Mr. Masterson."

"I do not!" Lucinda contradicted sharply. "I loathe him. Why, he's the most conceited, arrogant, ill-tempered—" She stopped and reddened, because her brother was staring at her strangely.

"James Masterson?" he asked her incredulously.

"Oh. Oh, no. I thought you meant—oh. I—I like James Masterson, of course. He's been extremely kind to us. But we mustn't lose sight of our purpose for being here. Come on, Davy, let's see if we can go a bit faster."

Lucinda was vexed at having misunderstood Davy's words. Of course he had meant James Masterson. Why anybody could see that she hadn't the slightest liking for his brother!

The day proved fruitless and on the way back Davy pouted and grumbled. He felt restless with failure, Lucinda could see, and although she was equally discouraged she cast about for a way to cheer him up.

"Look, Davy, there's a rabbit. It might be you could shoot something and take it back to camp. I think the men are missing meat, and they're so busy prospecting they haven't time to hunt. I understand the cook generally does that."

Davy brightened and reached for his rifle. "Where's he got to, that rabbit?"

Lucinda fixed her blue eyes on the spot she'd first seen it. There was a slight movement in the brush. "There," she whispered, pointing.

Davy raised his rifle, took careful aim, and shot. He jumped off his mule and ran to the spot. "I got it, I got it," he told Lucinda excitedly.

Greatly encouraged, Davy kept his eyes open as they continued on their way. Amazingly, he bagged two more rabbits before they rode triumphantly into camp.

"Look! Look what I have!" Davy began shouting as soon as they hit the clearing.

A number of the men were clustered in the river, and they seemed so preoccupied that they didn't even look up. Suddenly Davy's attention was diverted by the crowd in the river and he rushed down to see what was happening.

The miners had erected a wooden sluice that spanned the river, into which they shoveled dirt and gravel. Then they washed it with water. The sluice was ridged, like the rockers, and any gold nuggets collected behind the cross pieces. Now they had fashioned two large wooden water wheels to feed the sluice from upriver and speed up operations.

When Davy came up to the miners they were removing a few heavy pieces of gold ore.

There were great shouts of joy from the men, and even Davy began jumping up and down in excitement although none of the gold belonged to him.

Lucinda smiled as she bent over her preparations. They had returned early so there would be plenty of time for the rabbit stew to cook.

In fact it was only when the tantalizing aroma of the big kettle began to waft into the air that the miners left the sluice and clustered around the fire to determine the source of that wonderful smell.

"It's rabbit stew!" Davy informed them importantly.

"Rabbit?" Will questioned him. "Where did that come from?"

"I shot us three rabbits!" Davy yelled proudly.

"Hooray," shouted the men. They lifted Davy onto their shoulders, treating him like a hero. Davy's face was wreathed in delighted smiles, and his enormous happiness moved Lucinda. This was the first time in Davy's young life that he had done something truly worthy of being appreciated by grown men, and he was basking in his quite deserved glory. How proud their father would have been of Davy. And Tom, too, Lucinda thought, with a catch in her throat. Their father was gone, but surely Tom was somewhere to be found.

It would be just too cruel if, if—No, she told herself sternly. She mustn't think unhappy thoughts at a time like this.

"Something the matter, Miss Evans?" came Will Masterson's voice directly behind her.

She whirled to face him, her face warm from the fire and her confusion at having been surprised when she least expected it.

"I—no, nothing."

"You can be proud of your little brother. He's going to grow into a fine man," Will said admiringly. For once his tone was sincere, and Lucinda warmed to him for his praise of Davy.

She managed a slight smile. "Yes, I'm sure he will. I was just thinking how awfully proud of him Tom would be. Davy was only a small child when Tom left, and—" Her throat closed up and she couldn't go on. She was too close to tears, so she bent over her stew pot and stirred it vigorously, although it didn't need it.

"Smells mighty good, Miss Evans. Don't oversalt it with your tears," cautioned Will as he moved away.

Lucinda's hand holding the spoon began to shake.

Why did Will always have to spoil everything by injecting a sour note into the proceedings? Just when she began to think perhaps he wasn't so bad after all, he immediately caused her to reverse her opinion. It was almost as if he wished her to think badly of him.

The meal was a great success. Man after man took the trouble to compliment Lucinda personally on the excellent stew, pronouncing it the best they had ever eaten.

"Shucks, that's not all she can do," Davy boasted on her behalf. "If we had a stove here why she'd bake us the best bread and biscuits and cakes you ever ate in your life."

Lucinda went crimson under the compliments and the stares they produced.

"Hush, Davy," she whispered frantically to her brother.

"She'll make a right good little wife, won't she?" Jake said, nudging James Masterson in the arm and winking broadly.

Flustered at Jake's words, Lucinda peeked under her bonnet at James and was surprised to see a slow flush suffuse his features. Without daring to look at her, James immediately changed the subject.

After dinner the men sat contentedly around the fire. The unaccustomed hearty meal had put them in a good mood, and they laughed and joked while they cared for the equipment and their boots, scraping off the caked mud and oiling them.

Lucinda sat off to one side, close enough to the fire to be able to see the letter she was writing but not too near the men. Even so, Jake called out something about writing to her sweetheart.

It was the first time Lucinda had communicated with her mother since they had taken to the trail. Without giving too many details, Lucinda tried to convey that she and Davy were fine and had high hopes of locating their brother. What else could she write to her mother to keep her from worrying?

"Let's have a song," someone said.

"What about 'Clementine,' James," the guitarist requested. "Bet Davy doesn't know that one."

James agreed to sing the verses if the others would join in the chorus. He had a pleasant, clear baritone, and Lucinda kept looking at him, smiling, as he sang verse after verse about the Forty-niner and his daughter, Clementine. When James came to the part proclaiming that Clementine wore shoes size number nine, "herring boxes without soxes," Davy rocked back and forth with laughter.

After that song, James added some logs to the fire, looking shyly at Lucinda. "I hope we're not making too much of a racket and disturbing you, ma'am," he said softly.

"On the contrary. I love listening to you, and you have such a fine voice, Mr. Masterson. I think the songs are simply wonderful."

James' eye was drawn to Lucinda's nimble fingers, busily darning Davy's jacket.

"He manages to get a hole in it daily," she said, laughing. As she glanced again at James she couldn't fathom the strange expression on his face. There was a longing there. Of course, she thought, he must miss his mother and sisters.

"There is only this button left to sew on, Mr. Masterson. If you have any mending that needs doing I'll be most happy to attend to it for you."

James started from his trance. "Oh, I—I didn't mean to give the impression that I was hoping you'd make such an offer."

"But I don't mind at all," she cried. "It's the least I can do, after all your kindness."

"Miss Evans, you don't owe us a thing. Why, that meal you cooked this evening would compensate for a thousand kindnesses. It's certainly the finest rabbit stew I ever tasted."

"Well, thank you." Lucinda laughed self-consciously

to be compared with what surely were good cooks on the tobacco plantation. "I can't say my mending is anything special, but truly, Mr. Masterson, if you need a button on anything or a hole darned—"

"Well, come to think of it, ma'am, if you could just put a button on my best jacket I'd be mighty grateful. We're having a little celebration tomorrow evening for Ed, there. He's going home after being with us almost a year. We thought we'd say goodbye as best we can."

James brought her his jacket, which Lucinda took in hand. "Do you have any idea of when the cook will be returning?"

"I can't say for certain, Miss Evans. You never know what's going to come up on the trail to delay you. It may be that when the cook reached Sacramento he found they were out of some of the things we need so he was forced to hang around for a couple of days waiting for supplies. But he's a reliable man and he'll be back surely within the next few days."

James looked a little hurt. Lucinda didn't wish him to get the idea that she was anxious to leave because of anything he had done.

"It's just that I feel we're not making much progress here." She went on to tell him her theory that Tom had ventured much farther upriver.

While they talked she could hear the miners making music in the background. Her attention was suddenly caught by a ballad being sung in a husky, arresting voice.

Turning her head, Lucinda was astonished to see that Will Masterson was strumming the guitar and singing:

On top of old Smoky, all covered with snow,
I lost my true lover, from a-courting too slow.
Now a-courting's a pleasure, and parting's a
    grief,
But a false-hearted lover is worse than a thief.

The song was hauntingly beautiful, and Will sang it with such mournful, restrained passion that Lucinda was quite moved by it. His husky voice sent a tremor up her back.

Silently she wielded her needle, trying not to stare too much at Will lest James catch her doing so. Will must have loved that girl very dearly to sing about her thus so long afterwards.

Why, then, hadn't he married her? Why had he come here instead and left her behind to wed another?

Lucinda desperately wanted to question James about his brother but she somehow didn't dare. She was afraid she would turn all colors and reveal what strong emotions Will aroused in her, for which she could offer no explanation.

The poignancy with which Will had sung that song was disturbingly touching to Lucinda. She had glimpsed another side of Will. He could be kind to Davy and romantic with a guitar in his hands. Only to Lucinda was he wretched. Right from the start he had been antagonistic to her. After all, she hadn't done him any harm, had she? It seemed strange that a man who could sing so movingly of one girl, who had betrayed him, could behave so rudely to another who had never done a thing against him.

When the song ended, Lucinda stole a look at Will, to see that he had fixed his brooding eyes upon her. She lowered her glance immediately, but not in time to avoid pricking her finger.

"Here, you've hurt yourself," James observed anxiously. "Let me bind your finger in this handkerchief."

"It's nothing," Lucinda assured him lightly.

"I'm sorry to intrude on this tender little domestic scene, but you were going to have a look at the water wheel, James," Will said sulkily to his brother. He had glided towards them so silently that Lucinda hadn't noticed Will until he spoke. He now stood a few feet from the fire scowling most unpleasantly.

"Sorry, Will. I'm coming right now," James said apologetically, rising and following his brother.

Lucinda watched James' white handkerchief turn red in the tiny spot where the needle had stuck her, a puzzled frown puckering her brow. What was Will upset about now? He was so peculiarly unpredictable. One minute he had been singing so nicely, and the next he was in a temper.

"Davy," Lucinda called out. "Get ready for bed, please."

Looking at him happily, Lucinda rose and kissed his cheek. "I'm really proud of you, Davy. But don't let all this fuss over you go to your head, hear? There's many a river to cross before you come up to Pa or Tom."

Her mention of Tom's name made both of them regard each other sadly.

"Say Cindy, I got me an idea. Why don't we leave tomorrow, even if the cook hasn't come back? Shucks, I can shoot enough rabbits to keep us eating, and that way we can get farther into the hills."

Davy had a point. "We did promise to stay until the cook returned. It would seem rather ungrateful of us to go off just like that, before he gets back, because you've turned out to have some skill with a rifle."

She suddenly felt vexed with herself. Why was she making excuses to Davy? Hadn't she been thinking of nothing but putting this camp behind her, and with it the disturbing encounters with Will Masterson?

Davy, however, chose to go along with her reservations. "I guess you're right. Anyway, I was forgetting about finding more gold, and that Will is going to teach me to play the guitar."

"You have to make up your mind about what you want, Davy. You can't dance at everybody's wedding," Lucinda said absently, quoting one of her mother's favorite expressions.

"Huh? Who said anything about a wedding? Say, Cindy, you're not fixing to get wed, are you?"

"No, of course not! What put that idea into your head?"

"Uh, I dunno. The men were teasing James about you earlier on."

Lucinda was silent, but she flushed slightly, distressed to find that her heart had begun to beat quickly, although it was not for James Masterson. She suddenly became aware that Davy was holding his head on one side, his wide, innocent blue eyes regarding her with puzzlement.

"Just put it out of your mind, Davy Evans! There isn't going to be any marrying around here," she said firmly.

"Not ever? Aren't you ever—"

"That's enough, Davy! Ever, never—those words have no significance out here in the wilderness with a bunch of men who are wedded to the Mother Lode. Gold is what they have on their minds, not marrying. That's for people back home, farmers and the like, sensible folks. Go to sleep now."

She walked purposefully away from her brother feeling irritable and not exactly sure why.

It was a very cool, slightly damp night, and the wind was blowing sharply. Lucinda wrapped her shawl more closely around her. She didn't intend to walk very far from the camp. In truth, she knew she ought to turn back then and there and retreat to her cabin, for it was growing late. If only she weren't feeling so restless.

"Miss Evans," called out a voice, which she believed belonged to James Masterson. "Wait up a moment."

He came up behind her, carrying a mule saddle. "Are you headed anywhere in particular or just stretching your legs?" he asked her pleasantly, as he strolled alongside.

"Oh, just walking for its own sake, I guess. After being on that mule most of the day it feels good to move about on my own."

"Am I intruding on your thoughts by walking along with you?"

"No, not at all, Mr. Masterson."

They walked in silence for a few moments. "I wish

you'd call me James. Otherwise I feel like an old gray-beard, though I realize I'm years older than you."

"Oh, you couldn't be, Mr.—James. I'm past eighteen myself, whereas you couldn't be much older than about, say, twenty-three?"

"That's my brother's age, Miss Evans. I'm nearly twenty-six myself."

"Gracious, that's no age at all. If I'm to call you James I do believe you ought to call me Lucinda." As soon as she'd said it she wondered if it was wise. Although James was trustworthy she certainly wouldn't care to have all the men in camp taking such a liberty. "You know, James, in many ways you remind me of my own brother Tom."

"Do I, indeed!" James looked sideways at her, and the expression on his face was not a pleased one.

"Oh, I meant it as a compliment, truly I did. Tom is one of the finest men in the world, and when we find him I'm going to bring him to meet you so that you can see for yourself."

James laughed then, his good humor restored. "I believe every word you say, Lucinda. My, that's a lovely name, and it does suit you."

Lucinda was beginning to feel uncomfortable, for somehow James was treating her differently from the way he usually did. He spoke once more, interrupting her thoughts.

"I'd like to clarify something, if I may. When you first came here asking about provisions I made a little deal with you: your food and board in exchange for cooking. However, I'd hate for you to think, Lucinda, that the moment cook rides into camp you have to be moving on. No, indeed. I'm obliged to you for much more than the cooking."

"I—I don't quite know what you mean," she murmured.

"Well, you've had such a good influence on the whole camp. There's nothing quite like having a woman around the place to gentle a bunch of ruffians. Not that there's any real wickedness in them. It's only that they've been away from the fairer sex far too long. Makes them forget their manners. But since you've been with us the things their mothers taught them seem to have come right back into their memories."

Lucinda warmed under the compliment. She felt flattered at the way he referred to her as a woman. She had always thought of herself as a girl, but a great deal had happened to her since leaving home. So perhaps she had become a woman recently without realizing it.

James, glancing at her from time to time, spoke again. "What I'm trying to say, ma'am, in my awkward way, is that you're welcome to stay as long as you wish."

"I'm touched by your kind offer, James, but I just can't give up looking for Tom."

"No, of course not. I didn't mean that you should. Only that you might have wearied from your travels and wish to rest a spell with us before moving on. Might be your brother, if he's up in the hills, will be coming on down at some point, and that would save you the trip."

"Yes, but what if he's ill or hurt or something? He—he may not be himself. And he wouldn't know what to do, whereas if Davy and I actually found him. . . ." Her words tapered off weakly. No matter what explanation she tried to find to justify Tom's disappearance she always was faced with the probability that something was not right with her older brother.

"Yes, I see what you mean," nodded James. Stopping at his mules, he said, "Just let me tell you once again that you're always welcome here, you and Davy. No matter what happens. Shall we shake hands on it?"

James held out his hand and Lucinda, feeling shy, put her own in his.

"That's settled then. I'll be messing with this saddle for a bit. Are you walking on or going back to camp?"

"I think I'll just go a little farther, thank you."

The night was very thin, an

"Be careful. It's always best to be watchful at night, Lucinda."

With that, James tipped his hat and turned once more to the mules.

Lucinda continued along the path for a little way, her thoughts whirling as a result of the rather strange conversation. She wondered why James had extended such an open-ended invitation to her, especially as Will so strongly disapproved of her presence in the camp. She had to grant that after the first day or two the men had behaved themselves very nicely. Lucinda had assumed it was because James had cautioned them on their manners. Now he indicated that this politeness resulted from her gentle feminine influence.

Lucinda came to a little clump of evergreens near a high, jagged rock. It was much darker here, for the stars and moon were obscured from view.

There appeared to be a cave beyond the rock, and Lucinda paused uncertainly, remembering James' warning about being watchful. Deciding to venture no farther, Lucinda stepped back into the clearing so that she could see the stars once more. The wind blew more briskly now, and she shivered slightly, breathing in the fresh, pine-laden air.

A deep sigh escaped her, for what reason she didn't know. Perhaps she longed once more for the uncomplicated pattern of life at the farm. There she had but to let one day follow another. Since she had left home every day brought new conflicts and uncertainties, and with them new decisions. She wasn't really very wise, she felt, and it disturbed her to think that Davy's safety, as well as her own, depended solely upon her. Would she choose the proper road for both of them?

Sighing over her fate, however, wasn't going to solve any immediate problems. It would be far more practical to return to camp and go to bed so that she could rise early, fresh for the new day's adventures.

Lucinda began to retrace her steps along the path, carefully avoiding jutting stones. It really was quite dark now, and when the moon retreated behind a cloud she began to be alarmed that she would not be able to find her way back to camp. It was a mistake to have walked so far. She ought to have stuck close to James.

As her fear increased she quickened her pace. Soon she had reached the spot where she had left James. The mules were still tethered but James was no longer there. At least she was on the right track.

Just as she began to relax she saw something huge in the path in front of her. At first Lucinda thought she had veered off the path and was heading for a thick-trunked tree. But when the object stirred, she realized it was alive.

Her heart hammering painfully against her ribs, Lucinda wondered what it could be, so huge and furry that it seemed a creature out of a nightmare.

Behind it in the distance she could at last see the orange glow of the camp fire. Could she possibly skirt around the creature and escape?

When it got up on its hind legs she saw that it was an enormous bear! Terrified, Lucinda stopped short and screamed. Then she began to stumble backwards in horror as the bear slowly lumbered towards her.

"Stop moving! Stand perfectly still!" a voice rang out.

Lucinda halted in blind obedience to the command. The next moment Will Masterson had sped past the slowly moving bear, picked Lucinda up in his arms, and carried her to safety.

When he set her on her feet she was shivering violently, a delayed reaction to the most terrifying thing that had ever happened to her. Or nearly happened.

Her legs wouldn't hold her, and she began to sink to the ground, kept from falling only by Will's strong arm supporting her.

"Easy, easy, now. You're all right. He never touched you. Just relax for a moment. Lean on me, that's it. I won't let you fall." With those words he put his arms around her trembling body and drew her close to his chest.

Oh, how warm it felt, and safe, to be held thus. Gently he pushed her bonnet off the back of her head and stroked her hair.

Her heart was pounding so loudly she was sure he could feel it, and the thought of how close she was standing to him began to distress her.

"I'm—I'm all right now," she choked out in a whisper, putting her palms flat against his chest in an effort to steady herself and withdraw from his embrace.

She felt his body stiffen. He stepped back so abruptly that she tottered.

"Now I suppose you'll deliver a lecture on my rudeness for handling you so roughly. Doubtless you weren't in any danger, and I only imagined that shrieking noise was coming from your lips. Perhaps there wasn't any bear at all, and I staged the whole thing just to get my hands on you!"

Lucinda looked at Will in the light of the moon, her face white and her lips bloodless. She bit them tensely. "I don't know why you're so angry. I know very well that I screamed. I was terrified. I admit it. Why don't you give me a chance to speak for myself without putting words in my mouth?"

"Since you mistook my motive last time I had no reason to expect better understanding of this situation."

"I understand it perfectly. You saved me and I thank you," she whispered.

"You're welcome," he muttered, his anger abated. "And while we're on the subject, whatever possessed you to walk so far from camp in the dark? You can't simply go strolling around here as if you were back on the farm with your milk cows."

"I—I was trying to be careful."

"Careful? Do you realize that grizzly was eight feet tall and weighed about a thousand pounds? Ordinarily they don't bother people but your scream startled him. One swipe at you with his paw and you'd have been done for."

"I'm—I'm sorry, I didn't realize." Lucinda sobbed suddenly, as the realization of what would have happened if Will hadn't been there terrified her anew.

"So now it's to be tears! Well, don't bother trotting out your whole bag of tricks for me. Save them for someone more receptive. I'm immune, I assure you. Come on, young lady, I'll see you back to camp."

"I can go by myself, thank you," Lucinda said, sniffing and trying to regain her dignity.

"Can you, indeed! How do you know that bear isn't wandering around somewhere? Or his relatives? If you think one grizzly is a frightening sight, how would you like to meet up with three or four?"

Cowed, Lucinda let Will take her arm. Through her shawl and dress she could feel the heat of his hand. Lucinda quivered involuntarily and caught her breath.

Will tightened his grip and turned her towards him, his dark eyes alight with an expression she had never seen before. With his free hand he took a handful of her golden hair and wound his hand in it, pulling her close to him. Then he kissed her.

It all happened so quickly that she had little time to protest. His lips felt soft but very hot, and they seared her own, while his arm held her so close that she thought her body would break.

She was incapable of resisting or controlling the urge to respond to his kisses blindly, instinctively, until she was gasping for breath. Only then did she come to her senses.

"Please stop. I—I can't."

Tightening his hand in her hair, he murmured, "You already have," and his lips sought hers once again.

This time she whipped her head back out of reach. "I mustn't!" she exclaimed.

"Why not? Don't tell me it's the first time. You, a girl

with only a boy for a chaperone, going from camp to camp—"

"How dare you!" she shouted hotly, struggling out of his grasp. "I've—I've never done anything of the kind! My mother always said a decent girl doesn't kiss a man until she's betrothed!"

Will thrust her ruthlessly from him, dropping his arms to his sides. He glared at her sullenly. "There's not much likelihood of that around here. It's not the same as back home. Different rules."

"Maybe for you but not for me!" She rubbed her bruised lips, slightly swollen from the way he had ravished them.

"Don't look at me so accusingly, Miss Evans. The time to say no to a kiss is before, not after."

"How could I? I didn't know what you intended," she cried, her temper rising.

Will snorted. "You expected a proposal of marriage, did you? In this place? You'll wait a long time for that around here. I'm a wanderer like my brother. That's why we left our plantation and came to California. No women is ever going to tie *me* down. Certainly not for the price of a mere kiss!"

Lucinda was stung. No wonder the girl in Virginia had married another. "In that case you'd better leave the kissing to somebody else!"

"I see. To my brother, perhaps. Do you think he means any more by his behavior than I do by mine?"

"I don't know what *you* mean, since he has never taken the liberty of kissing me. I can tell you that there is absolutely no similarity between the two of you, except for your last name! James was telling me only this evening how my presence in the camp was having a gentling effect on the men. Little did he know he couldn't possibly have included you!"

Will looked incredulously at her and suddenly threw back his head and laughed.

"What's so funny? You stop that! Don't you dare to

laugh at James! He's a true gentleman still, whereas you
left whatever manners you ever had back home in Virginia!"

Will stopped laughing and advanced on her menac-
ingly.

"Don't you touch me!" she cried in alarm.

"I'll do exactly as I please, as I always have. Don't
you tell me what to do, you little ninny! So you think
you're still the schoolmarm, shaking your finger warningly at a bunch of schoolboys. You don't have the sense
of a tadpole. Don't you know what my brother has done
to keep the men from swarming all over you?"

Lucinda grew pale. "What—what do you mean?"

"I mean, Miss Know-it-all, that James told the others
that you were his woman! That was the only way he
could keep them from breaking down your door night
after night! If he hadn't said that they would have paid
gold for you, fought over you, killed each other for you,
because you're the only woman for miles around. Your
'gentle presence' wouldn't have stopped them from
dividing you up like so many nuggets. Why there
wouldn't have been enough left of you to ship home in
a box!"

Chapter 6

Lucinda couldn't remember returning to the cabin. It was only when she was curled up in her blanket that the awful numbness left her, only to be replaced with nightmarish thoughts based on what Will had so brutally revealed. James had lied to her. Oh, they were a fine pair, the Masterson brothers!

As she lay sleepless she went over and over the humiliating meeting with Will. Yes, he had saved her from a grizzly bear, but at what cost. He had violated her person and her trust in James and, oh, the cruel things he had said to her! He had insinuated that she had been—offering her companionship and kisses to men in mining camps, that her anguished tears had been a trick she was using to gain his sympathy, that she encouraged him to kiss her. Perhaps worst of all, he had implied that she had no particular charms with which to entice men, that it was merely because she was the only woman in the area that she excited any interest at all.

Lucinda was vexed at her own naivete, for she had, indeed, imagined that perhaps her presence at the camp had been beneficial to the miners. She saw the whole plot now. The Mastersons had moved her into her own cabin so that—so that she would have privacy when—when James came to call upon her, presumably in the middle of the night!

Her breast heaved with anguish. In some ways she was more angry with James than with Will, for she had known what a disagreeable person Will was from the start. Although James had pretended to be her friend he had subjected her to such a shameful deception. She could never look any of them in the face again. Tomorrow she was simply going to have to leave, cook's return or not. That was settled.

She finally began to feel sleepy, but then the memory of Will's kiss stole over her unwillingly. During his embrace she had felt the way she had always imagined she would when she had fallen in love with her future husband. Was it possible that she would react this way no matter who kissed her? No matter how badly she thought of the person?

She tossed in her bed restlessly, wishing vehemently to forget that any of it had ever happened. Nevertheless she couldn't stop remembering the way Will had entwined his fingers in her hair and drawn her to him in a crushing embrace; of the way his burning lips had demanded her own, the weakness and the breathless excitement she had felt.

Every time she dozed off she seemed to be experiencing the kisses anew, and she would awaken with a start, her body trembling, a fluttering in the pit of her stomach.

It was the most troubled night she had ever spent. When she awoke, as weary as if she had never slept at all, she immediately went to wake Davy.

"Get packed, Davy, we're going after breakfast."

"Which way will we try today?" he asked sleepily.

"I mean we're going on. Leaving the camp."

"But the cook hasn't returned yet. You said yesterday—"

"I know. Never mind what I said. Everything's changed."

"But why?"

"Because. Don't ask so many questions. Just do what I say, hear?"

"But I don't want to leave, Cindy. What about the gold, and the party tonight for Ed and everything?"

"Please don't argue with me, Davy. I'm upset enough

as it is." As she spoke the words she saw James coming towards her.

"Good morning, Lucinda. Is something wrong? You seem distraught."

"I'd like a word with you alone, please, Mr. Masterson," she said, addressing him formally.

"Why certainly." Frowning, he let Lucinda lead the way.

She walked briskly towards the meadow behind the camp, her face grimly set. The few miners awake looked at the couple curiously, making her blush with humiliation.

When they were out of sight of the camp, Lucinda stopped and turned to face James Masterson. She paused, hardly knowing how to begin. Her face turned cherry red at the thought of having to speak to him of such a delicate matter.

"Lucinda, does this have anything to do with my brother? When he returned to the cabin last night he was in a terrible temper. He refused to tell me what the trouble was, and it didn't occur to me until just now that perhaps you had an altercation with him. He is difficult, I know, but I'm sure whatever it is can be settled amicably—"

"I'm not sure my quarrel isn't with you, Mr. Masterson," she said coldly.

"With me? But—but what have I done?"

"You haven't been honest with me."

He looked at her for a moment, his eyebrows arched in puzzlement. "I haven't?"

Lucinda lowered his eyes. "You told me it was my 'gentle presence' that was making the men so respectful. According to your brother, it's the fact that you told them—that you told them—" Her voice tapered off. The words were choking her.

"I see." His brow cleared and he looked a bit like Davy after she had reprimanded him. "Do forgive me, please. I didn't mean to compromise you, ma'am. Ac-

tually, this all happened the second night. Please don't
look at me so harshly, Lucinda. You see, after the men
had gotten a real look at you I was so afraid there would
be trouble that I said the first expedient thing that occurred to me. Obviously, if you were spoken for by Will
or by me nobody else would entertain any hope of, of—
Well, anyway it *is* true, I assure you, that you have had
a decidedly good effect on the manners of the men by
your sweet and feminine example. I do believe with all
my heart that they respect you greatly for yourself. As
for the other, well, I've sort of made it clear that we're
betrothed. When I realized the kind of girl you were—so
that they wouldn't have the wrong idea."

Although his face was now almost as red as her own,
James spoke with such sincerity that Lucinda was somewhat placated. In all fairness she couldn't have offered
an alternative to James' way of dealing with the situation. And if they were supposed to be betrothed, it
wasn't as bad as if—as if—To a certain extent she imagined she ought to be grateful that it was James and not
Will to whom she was supposed to belong.

"Lucinda?" James looked at her wistfully. "Do say
you forgive me. I apologize most humbly for any distress I have caused you."

As she hesitated, Ed, the man who was leaving, came
by swinging his shovel. "Morning, ma'am," he called
out jovially. "I'm sure going to miss your cooking."

Lucinda suddenly felt ashamed of her sulkiness. The
men were waiting for their breakfast, and instead of preparing it for them she was reproaching her best friend in
the camp.

She glanced up at James now, as he waited patiently
for her response to his apology. "I see you meant only to
keep order in the camp and that it wasn't to be taken—
personally. Although I can't honestly say I like the idea
of the men thinking that—that—Anyway, I suppose it
was the best you could do on the spur of the moment. I
—I'd better fix breakfast."

She turned and hurried away. In the clearing she found the men milling around looking rather lost and hungry. A clamor went up as they saw her head towards the fire and the cooking pots.

Davy was nowhere in sight, but Lucinda worked quickly to make up for lost time. Her brother finally came running when he had smelled the frying bacon.

"I found some more gold dust, Cindy! Look here!" Excitedly he showed her his pouch.

"That's wonderful. Have something to eat."

"Uh, are we really going today?" Davy asked tentatively, a pout forming around his mouth.

"No, Davy. I guess we'll hang around for a bit longer," she answered gently. "I'm sorry I was so grumpy this morning."

"That's all right," Davy said generously. "I'm sure glad we're staying."

Lucinda occupied her time doing odd chores and Davy went hunting, having been cautioned by his sister not to venture very far.

True to his word, he wasn't gone unduly long, and when he came rushing enthusiastically up to Lucinda he was carrying a rabbit.

"I couldn't find but one," he admitted, "but isn't that better than none?" he asked, with hopeful optimism.

"Yes, of course." Lucinda patted his head affectionately. "There's not enough to make a stew but it will enhance the beans, anyway."

One of his passions indulged, Davy next ran to the river with his gold pan. Several times he called out that he had succeeded.

Lucinda began to see that this was a very rich gold vein, since the men seemed to be successful with their nuggets and didn't begrudge Davy his quantities of dust.

By sundown Davy had completely filled his pouch. "Now we don't have to worry about running out of money," he confided to his sister proudly. "Will says it's worth a least a hundred dollars!"

"That's wonderful, Davy. You've certainly been lucky today. Now, how about cleaning up a bit for the party tonight?"

They rode their mules to the pond, and this time Lucinda took a careful survey before slipping out of her dress and venturing into the water. Enlisting Davy to keep a lookout for any intruders turned out to be unnecessary, for no red spot of color showed through the trees during her swim.

Lucinda thought it might be nice to dress up a bit in honor of the festivities, so she chose a calico dress in a pattern of blue and white flowers, the blue emphasizing her eyes, which now looked wide and clear, in contrast to their puffy appearance that morning.

Instead of pinning her hair into a knot, Lucinda parted it in the center as usual and let it fall softly over her shoulders. As she adjusted her matching bonnet, Davy teased her. "Gee, Cindy, you're about the prettiest girl in camp."

He bounded out of the cabin to start the fire for supper, leaving Lucinda to star at herself critically in the tiny cracked mirror. Her pale skin had the fine transparency of porcelain, and there was just a tinge of pink at her cheeks, a slight flush of anticipation.

When she stepped outside the miners ceased their loud conversation, and she grew self-conscious under their quiet stares. She quickly involved herself in the preparation of the meal, making it as festive as she could. The miners were pleasantly surprised to find bits of barbecued rabbit in their beans instead of pork. Lucinda noticed that the men had spruced themselves up a bit. There were wearing their clean shirts and trousers, and had scraped the mud off their boots.

Both Will and James were attired in white shirts, black string ties, and black jackets of good quality, which they obviously had brought with them from Virginia.

Although Lucinda exchanged quick glances with Will

from time to time, she noticed that he kept as far away from her as he could. James, too, preserved a respectful distance from Lucinda. She wondered if the brothers had discussed her that day.

When Lucinda began to fry doughnuts to go with the coffee, the men's delight knew no bounds. Ed, the guest of honor, kept maintaining that he wouldn't be able to leave after all.

"Shucks, whoever said that their ma was the best cook in the world never tasted these here doughnuts."

"Try drizzling some honey over them," Will suggested.

Flustered, Lucinda looked up to see his dark-coated figure standing close to the fire. He was holding out a tin of honey.

Shyly she took it. Their fingertips momentarily touched, making Lucinda jump. If Will noticed he gave no indication. He merely stood at her side watching her dip her ladle into the sticky honey and make a circular pattern on the doughnuts.

"Aren't you curious as to where it comes from? Or do you think it was sent by the gods for the occasion?"

As usual, his tone was faintly mocking. Lucinda had planned to ignore Will, but now she decided that it wouldn't be in keeping with the festive atmosphere to bear a grudge. So, keeping her voice as casual as possible, she asked about the origin of the honey.

"There are some very productive honeycombs in that cave nearby, where you made your first acquaintance with that grizzly. Bears love honey, and—"

"Me, too!" exclaimed Davy, his mouth full. "But when you gather the honey, don't the bees sting you?"

"They might want to, but I fool them," Will answered, smiling at the boy. He went on to give Davy a lesson in honey gathering.

It was apparent to Lucinda that Will really liked Davy, and it made his dislike of her that much harder to bear.

As she finished frying the last of the doughnuts she found James at her side, insisting on helping her clean up. "It would be a pity, Lucinda, to soil that beautiful dress," he murmured.

Lucinda thanked him. She was glad someone, at least, had noticed her frock. Some people never seemed to pay attention to what a person was wearing. Why, it might just as well be a potato sack, she thought petulantly, her eye seeking Will's figure, although she had no conscious desire to look at him at all.

Supper over, the guitar and harmonica made an appearance, and also a stronger beverage than coffee. Jake had gotten hold of the whisky jug, and he was dispensing quite generously.

The miners surrounded him, clamoring for their share.

At that point Will stepped in. "No more than half a cupful per man. Just enough to make him happy, not enough to cause him to fall on his face. Remember, we have a long day's work tomorrow. Gold, gentlemen, gold," he finished, shrewdly appealing to a greater weakness than their one for whisky.

"Hey, ma'am, you ain't took a drop yet," Jake called out to Lucinda, wielding his jug carelessly. "We're gonna drink a toast to Ed there. Ain't you gonna join us?"

"I don't drink whisky," Lucinda said, a bit primly.

"'Course you don't, ma'am. But on such a special occasion. Tell you what. You just hold out your cup and I swear I'll stop pouring the minute you say so."

"I think you'd better let me do that," Will said, taking the jug from Jake's unwilling fingers. "Miss Evans, allow me."

Without waiting for her reaction he took her cup firmly, poured in a couple of drops, turning away so that the others couldn't see, and immediately added some water.

He gave Lucinda her cup. Only she had been close enough to see that it contained practically all water.

For a moment their eyes met. "Thank you," she whispered, grateful for Will's intervention. If she had accepted Jake's measurement she wouldn't have dared to touch a drop. This way she would be able to drink a toast with the others.

"And now," James' voice rang out, "I should like to propose a toast to Ed, who was our first partner, and now is leaving us as rich as Croesus."

The men cheered and drank, while Ed remarked, "I don't know who that fellow Croesus was, but he couldn't have got his gold any happier than I got mine here with the Mastersons."

Although there was only a drop of whiskey in her cup, Lucinda felt it go to her head immediately, and she could tell that her face was flushed.

"Who's Croesus?" Davy asked at her elbow.

"He was an ancient Greek who was supposed to be the richest man in the world," Lucinda answered her brother.

"But Ed just said—"

"Never mind, Davy," Will's voice interrupted. He was standing close enough to sister and brother to have heard their exchange. "Ed doesn't know everything the way your sister does."

"Oh, maybe, but she only knows things out of books," Davy said with scorn, although he couldn't begin to match the mockery of Will Masterson.

"Come, Davy, let's join in the singing," Lucinda said sharply to her brother, turning away and walking resolutely towards the fire.

The men grew very jolly over their whisky. The harmonica player and guitarist struck up a lively tune.

"How about a dance?" one of the men asked another jokingly, bowing from the waist.

"Ah sure don't mind if ah do," the other replied, in the spirit of fun.

Then, tying a neckerchief around his head, the second man pretended to be a woman, as his partner twirled him around in a dance.

"Hey, lookee here, we got us a real live female," Jake called out, catching sight of Lucinda. "Ain't you gonna dance, ma'am?"

The men added to Jake's request in unison, as Lucinda stood still with her eyes down, feeling very shy indeed.

Happily James advanced upon her then and formally asked her for the first dance. She felt she couldn't refuse, so she tentatively put her hand in his and let him lead her in a lively waltz.

The ice now broken, the rest of the men clapped and cheered, while a couple of them continued to play-act, taking the role of female partners in the dance.

"Shucks," Jake called out to James, "you ain't a-gonna hog her all to yourself, are you? That ain't fair!"

"No, I guess it isn't," James then whispered to Lucinda. "Would you mind very much? It's so rare the men have a chance to enjoy themselves. I'll see to it that they behave, ma'am."

What else could Lucinda do but agree? She held herself rather stiffly it is true, when Jake took her small hands in his big bear's paws and lumbered around in a circle. He really was very bearlike, and he made Lucinda laugh. She felt hot and flushed, but she was rather enjoying herself as well.

"How about you, Davy?" one of the men called out. "Don't you want to dance with your sister?"

"Shucks no!" Davy protested fiercely. "I like the music right enough but I think all this jumping around is just plain silly."

At that a huge roar went up from the men. "You just wait a couple of years, boy," they predicted, winking at him. "Once you start you won't hardly ever want to stop. Ain't that right, ma'am?"

"Gracious," breathed Lucinda, halting suddenly and leaning against a tree. "I must rest a moment to catch my breath."

While several of the men complained that they hadn't

yet had a turn, James calmly assured them that their chance would come. They mustn't expect a member of the gentler sex to have quite as much energy as they had.

Lucinda was thankful for James' presence. She could see that without James' sober control the men could easily get out of hand. It was too bad, Lucinda thought, as she leaned her back against the tree trunk and watched the men cavorting, that there weren't any other women. A few wives or sisters would have been so welcome.

Lucinda was forced by politeness to do a turn with each of the men. Most of them really couldn't dance at all. What they wished—and Lucinda blushed deeply to think so—was to hold her hand to theirs, to put an arm around her very slender waist, and thus to remember what their lives had been like before they had been infected with the gold fever.

Some of the men, in fact, were little more than lads. Lucinda could see that they danced with her only to save themselves from being taunted unmercifully by the others.

Finally, to her infinite relief, all turns had been taken. She had danced with every last miner—except for Will Masterson. He had made no move towards her, nor had he been participating in the general merriment. Instead, he sat a little off from the others leaning against a tree, his knees up in front of him, quietly smoking.

Lucinda convinced herself that she was glad he hadn't asked her for a dance. He would probably have stomped on both her feet just from spite.

Tossing her head scornfully, she wondered why she was wasting a minute of her time even thinking about Will.

Just then James approached her and asked her for another dance. Lucinda threw him an enchanting smile and held out her hands in welcome. He took them humbly and began to turn her around in a polka.

All the while Lucinda smiled at James she couldn't help hoping that Will was watching her and seeing that she was having a perfectly good time, even though he despised her.

She begged to be allowed to rest for a while, collapsing in a heap near the fire and requesting some singing. As the hour grew late and some of the frenetic energy died away, the music became softer and more romantic.

James sang three songs in a row, looking at Lucinda in a way that caused her to lower her eyes diffidently. The ballads were meant to be sung by a man to the girl he loved. Lucinda felt she should not have been the recipient of such tender verses even if she was the only girl in the camp. Then she remembered that James may have been trying to live up to the false picture of the two as betrothed that he had presented to the men. He didn't really mean the words at all.

When the songs ended, Lucinda added her murmurs of praise. Although the fire was dying, nobody bothered to add logs, for the men were now beginning to yawn. It had been a very long day.

"Before you put that away," James said to the harmonica player, "perhaps Lucinda will do me the honor of one last dance."

Although she felt weary herself, Lucinda got to her feet in resignation. They were playing a part, and she supposed she owed it to James to fulfill her own role.

The musicians played a slow waltz. Lucinda and James hadn't been dancing for more than a few moments before a voice said behind them, "Come, come, my dear brother, you are monopolizing the only lady this evening. Although I can't claim to be as light on my feet as you, surely I am entitled to one dance?" Will's voice held just a tinge of mockery.

"Of course, Will. I'm glad the charms of our fair Lucinda have finally enticed you away from your pipe. My brother, Lucinda, never joins in the revelry. Tonight, however, he will make an exception."

With that, James handed Lucinda over to Will.

As soon as Will's hand enfolded her own and his other arm went about her waist, Lucinda grew most uncomfortable. Her warm hand turned cold as Will held it, and her breath started coming in short gasps. Automatically her backbone stiffened while her legs felt as if they were made of wood.

Was it because she really did not wish to dance with Will? Was it his mocking tone that caused her such discomfort? Or was there something in his very touch that had such a strange effect on her pulse and heartbeat?

Whatever the source of her awkwardness, Will did not seem to be in the least affected. He held her firmly, authoritatively, and negotiated the steps in a surprisingly graceful manner. Lucinda was momentarily stung with envy at his coolness. Why in the world was she falling all over her own feet?

As if to further humiliate her, Will said in her ear, "I see that you have done the best of your dancing earlier on, Miss Evans. The others had the benefit of your daintiest toes, while I seem to have won only the heels."

Fretting with indignation, Lucinda opened her lips to reply. She feared her voice would fail her, even if she could summon up the words. If the others hadn't been watching she would have stopped dancing then and there. However, she hesitated to make a further spectacle of herself by storming away from Will.

Lifting her head proudly, she straightened her back and let herself be whirled as before, without stumbling or hesitation.

Lucinda also found her tongue. "You can't expect a mere farm girl to make a gracious Southern ballroom out of a pebble-strewn clearing in a mining camp," she said fiercely. "No doubt the ladies of Virginia can float as lightly as a cream puff in their delicate gold slippers, whereas I, may I humbly point out, am shod almost as roughly as a workhorse!"

"Indeed, Miss Evans, I merely made a joke. Perhaps if you took yourself a little less seriously you would not always rush in doggedly to avenge your offended dignity, especially where no offense was intended. Besides, you have rediscovered your toes, to my infinite gratitude."

He was offensive beyond belief! In her indignation Lucinda squeezed his hand with anger and frustration. Will, however, smiled and returned the pressure, as if she had meant it as an affectionate gesture.

"A little faster," Will directed the musicians, who obligingly increased the tempo of the dance. Round and round they whirled, until the trees began to spin and Lucinda grew terribly dizzy.

"Please—I must stop. My head is going around!"

"As you wish." Will gradually slowed down until they came to a complete halt. When he dropped his arms, she nearly staggered, for she had not yet adjusted her balance.

To her utter astonishment, Lucinda saw that all the men had vanished, with the exception of the two musicians. Even James was nowhere to be seen. Had she and Will been dancing so long? Lucinda had not been conscious of the passing of time.

"It is late, Miss Evans. I shall bid you goodnight," said Will, his tone almost reproachful, as if Lucinda had been keeping him dancing against his volition!

"Yes, it is late indeed!" she fumed. "And where is Davy?"

Will did not reply. He had already turned and walked towards his cabin. The insufferable rudeness of the man!

Lucinda glanced towards her cabin, wondering if Davy was already asleep, but she couldn't see him. A sudden panic seized her. What if he had wandered off during the dancing, out of boredom, and some harm had befallen him?

She ran blindly towards the woods. "Davy. Davy," she called. The only sound that answered her call was the hooting of an owl.

Turning, she ran back to the clearing. The fire was out now, and the men retired for the night. Lucinda hesitated. Should she awaken someone and ask for help to find Davy?

She couldn't bring herself to disturb anyone. Hastening towards her cabin, she peered into the darkness in front of it to see if by some miracle Davy had gone to sleep for once in his life without her prodding. But she could see nothing in front of her cabin.

She started into the woods in the opposite direction, softly calling her brother's name. Venturing as far as she dared, and looking around her every second, Lucinda became terrified. Every tree trunk seemed to her to be a grizzly bear lurking in wait for her.

It was no use. She'd never find Davy here. If he hadn't answered her call he was probably out of earshot, for his hearing was acute and he was a light sleeper.

She veered this way and that, in alarm, and suddenly bumped violently into something in the pitch darkness.

She opened her mouth to scream when a hand went gently over it. "For pity's sake, Miss Evans, if you're going to let loose that blood-curdling shriek of which you are capable the entire camp will be aroused, and all for nothing."

Quivering with fear, Lucinda looked up at the dim outline of Will Masterson. "What—what are you doing here?"

"Following you, of course. In spite of all my previous warnings you dashed into the forest without a care for what might have lain in your path. If you behave in so reckless a fashion you won't last long in this country.

"If I don't find Davy nothing matters," Lucinda exclaimed, torn between her fear for Davy and annoyance at Will.

"What makes you think Davy is out here?"

"Well, he must be. I've looked for him everywhere—"

"In your cabin?"

"Why no. He never sleeps there. He stays outside. Why would he—"

"Nevertheless, Miss Evans, tonight I saw him taking

his blanket roll inside. Perhaps he didn't wish to be disturbed by the music, or maybe the spectacle of his sister gamboling around like an artless lamb among the wolves was a distressing sight."

Lucinda stood facing him, her blue eyes flashing, while she drew in her breath sharply.

"Aha! The lightning has struck. Can the thunder be far behind?"

"Will you stop speaking to me in that tone!"

"Yes, indeed, here is the clap of thunder. Usually followed by a shower of rain. Is that the tone to which you object, Miss Evans?" he asked, employing it to the fullest.

"You know very well that it is! What have I ever done to make you treat me with such disdain?"

He snorted. "Too many things, perhaps, to be able to tell you before red streaks slash the sky in the east, heralding the arrival of dawn. However, I shall try."

"I don't wish to continue this conversation. Get out of my way, please, Mr. Masterson."

"Don't schoolmarm me, Miss Evans, unless you wish me to stand here all night. You just asked me a question and I am bound to answer it. First, you insisted on staying here against my wishes and inclinations, after hypnotizing my brother half out of his wits. You then made yourself neatly indispensable in the matter of the cooking. Further, and perhaps most grievously, you turned this camp from a masculine stronghold dedicated to the mining of gold into a ladies' boudoir, where big brave men with the strength to wrestle with a mountain lion single-handed have been reduced to stammering, shuffling schoolboys! No drinking, no swearing, no relaxing! Tonight was perhaps your crowning triumph, as they lined up like obedient children to have their turn at dancing with you."

"And so did you!" Lucinda blazed at him.

"Not a bit, Miss Evans. I merely took the responsibility off my brother's shoulders. He was tired and wished to retire early. You will notice that he did so as soon as I had taken you off his hands."

"I didn't ask to be taken off anybody's hands! If you must know, I didn't wish to dance with any one of you! I don't like dancing, I don't like the sweaty palms and the big feet treading on my own—"

"I? Tread on *your* feet, Miss Evans?"

"If I trod on yours it was only because I felt forced to dance with somebody I loathe! Now get out of my path!"

Will was silent, and Lucinda knew that the last thing she had said finally had struck home.

For once he had no retort. With a grim face he merely stepped aside and let her pass. She strode purposefully along the path, her cheeks still burning at his words. Everything he had said cut her to the heart. His infuriating jest about lightning, thunder, and rain—well, she might have produced the first two but she'd sooner drop on the spot than ever cry in front of him again.

She despised his implications that she had made any effort at all to limit the relaxation of the miners. She had not, short of their trampling over her sensibilities. In any event, they didn't seem to mind. Will Masterson was the only one complaining.

Perhaps the cruelest sting was Will's denying that he had wished to dance with her but was merely relieving his brother of an unwelcome chore.

Stepping ahead briskly in her fury, she suddenly turned her ankle badly. She grimaced as she was forced to stop. Kneeling down she touched the injured spot and was dismayed to feel that it was very tender. When she tried to put any weight on it she felt a stab of pain through her entire foot.

"What is it now?" asked Will in a gruff voice, coming up behind her.

She refused to answer him. Gritting her teeth she limped forward for a few steps, but the pain was too much to bear.

"I see you've hurt yourself. Your anger has led you to twist your own foot as ruthlessly as you would no doubt like to wring someone's neck. In the end, of course, it is you who are hurt. Come now, Miss Evans, lean on me."

"I'd rather die!" she exclaimed fervently.

"No doubt you fume at having to accept help from someone you loathe. The alternative, however, is to damage that foot beyond healing for weeks."

His words disturbed her, for she knew that they were true. She had twisted her ankle very badly. Swallowing her rancor, she said, "I'm afraid I can't walk at all, even if I lean on you."

"In that case you'll permit me to carry you to your cabin. If you struggle when I lift you I'll be forced to throw you over my shoulder like a sack of beans."

He would do it, too, she knew. "Very well," she choked out.

Lifting her in his arms as if she were entirely weightless, Will picked his way carefully through the trees and bushes until they had reached the clearing.

She sat up as straight as possible, cursing her misfortune to have done herself such an injury that she had been forced to accept his help, for it definitely gave him the upper hand.

Her bonnet strings had loosened, causing her hat to slip off her head down to her back, where it bobbed with the rhythm of his gait. She hugged herself with her arms to avoid putting them on him. Even so, she found her closeness to him most disturbing. Her heart was making dull thumping sounds within her breast, and she felt as breathless as if their positions had been reversed.

He, on the other hand, was totally cool and impersonal, treating her as if she were an inanimate burden.

"I believe I can walk now, if you would please put me down," she requested.

"You can't walk any more tonight. Your ankle is doubtless already swollen and you'll only make it worse.

We are almost at your cabin. Surely you can bear it for a few minutes more," he finished wryly.

Just as they were approaching the cabin he tripped momentarily. Involuntarily her arms reach out for his shoulders to prevent herself from falling.

He, too, clutched at her so as not to drop her while he sought to regain his balance. For one shivering moment she felt his hot breath on her neck. He quickly recovered himself and with one hand opened the door of her cabin. Then he set her down in the chair and vanished without a word.

Lucinda could hear the measured breathing of a sleeper. Sure enough, there was Davy curled up in his blanket on the floor.

Chapter 7

Lucinda's ankle was tender and swollen the next morning. She winced with pain as she hobbled around the cabin trying to dress.

"What's wrong?" asked Davy, yawning.

She told him, and began to question him about the previous evening. "I looked everywhere for you. I was worried sick. Why didn't you tell me you were going to sleep in here?"

"I thought you'd find me when you came inside. Anyway, I didn't get a chance to talk to you. You were always dancing with somebody." Davy's sour expression indicated how little he thought of that activity.

"Davy, if you ever do anything like that again I'll tan your hide. I want to know where you are at all times. If necessary, write me a note, if you haven't forgotten how," she said testily.

"Yes'm," he agreed grumpily. "You can't walk, can you? What are we going to do today?" He looked at her with some anxiety.

"Don't worry, I'll manage." But would she? She was barely able to dress herself.

When she stepped outside she found Will waiting for her. Involuntarily her face registered the pain as her foot touched the ground. She was immediately angry with herself, for she could do without his mockery this morning.

He offered none, however. "I have brought a bandage for the foot."

Before she could decline his help James appeared,

looking at Lucinda with concern. "I hear you've twisted your ankle. Will is a sort of impromptu doctor. He'll soon fix it for you. And I've made you a crutch, until the foot is better." He held out a roughly fashioned crutch and demonstrated how to use it.

"My brother is an impromptu carpenter, Miss Evans," Will commented, smiling at James.

That smile set Lucinda's heart pounding, even though it was directed at someone else. It was the sort of smile that caused Will to appear more handsome than he had any right to be, and it made Lucinda's heart ache with an undefined longing.

The Masterson brothers were in good form this morning, and Lucinda was ashamed to spoil it. They were trying to help her, so she supposed she might as well accept it graciously.

In any case, they took her willingness for granted. Will knelt by her foot, his fingers working nimbly to bind the piece of cloth tightly around the swollen part, while Lucinda clenched her teeth to avoid crying out in pain.

The bandage in place, Will and James lifted her to her feet, or rather her good foot, and taught her how to utilize the crutch to the best advantage. But she was clumsy with it.

"One isn't enough," James decided. "I'll make you another. Then you'll be able to keep your foot off the ground altogether."

He withdrew to the woods, leaving Lucinda standing on one leg, one arm hanging onto the crutch, the other onto Will's shoulder.

"I—I have to fix breakfast," Lucinda said. "Could you please help me to get to the fire?"

Without a word he swung his arm around her waist and lifted her. In a few strides he carried her to the fire and set her on the ground, asking only if she would be able to manage.

Lucinda assured him that she would. And she would

manage much better, she thought, if he would take his disturbing eyes off her and move away. She found that under his gaze her fingers were clumsy, and she couldn't seem to recollect whether she generally fried the bacon first or did the pancakes. Or did she set the water to boil for coffee?

She became terribly vexed at her childish incompetence. Why should Will's presence make her so nervous? She already knew that he had a poor opinion of her, so she had nothing to lose by being herself. Why, then, did she feel stiff and awkward? Why did her pulse throb in her temple?

It was necessary finally for Lucinda to thank him politely and tell him that she would manage all right, so he needn't keep himself from his work. She would ring the bell when breakfast was ready.

He knew very well that his presence made her uncomfortable, and she wondered why he lingered. She had been outspoken in her wish that he leave her. For a few moments she busied herself with the pots, trying to concentrate on the task at hand. Still Will remained staring at her.

When she glanced up swiftly she saw a despondent look in his dark eyes. She felt a catch in her throat. The previous evening she had told him that she loathed him. Was he waiting for her to indicate that she had spoken in anger?

It wasn't quite true that she loathed him, of course, although he did make her awfully angry at times. When he was kind and helpful, as this morning, she found him quite acceptable. Since he obviously was waiting for something, she thanked him for having bound up her foot and expressed confidence that it would recover as a result of his ministrations.

She heard him sigh, but before he could speak James was back with a second crutch.

Over breakfast the men commiserated with Lucinda, although they also teased her about having danced the night away, assuming that was how she had hurt her ankle. Lucinda didn't contradict them. Will, his equanimity restored, disappeared immediately after the meal, while James insisted on lingering and teaching her to use the crutches.

There was no question of riding out in search of Tom today. Lucinda would simply have to rest her ankle. She hated to be idle and was totally unused to it, so she requested that any mending the miners might have should be brought to her. That was something she could do sitting down and it would help her to pass the time.

Under a tree she sat, the leaves shading her from the burning sun, and wielded her needle. Davy was happily panning in the river near the shore, while most of the others clustered around the water wheels and the sluice.

Looking up now and again, Lucinda caught a glimpse of Will's red shirt and James' blue one. After a while the red shirt was missing. Straining her eyes, Lucinda saw Will in the river working bare-chested. She felt somewhat guilty for watching him without his knowledge, but it was a compelling sight.

His broad shoulders and back were deeply bronzed from persistent exposure to the sun. He worked swiftly and gracefully, his movements sure. Although his face and hair were concealed under his broad-brimmed hat, his features now seemed as familiar to her as her own. When she remembered that he had carried her in his arms her fingers shook and grew clumsy. Once again she felt the heady sensation of having been clasped to that manly chest by those powerful arms, and kissed by those burning lips that could also curl in mockery or smile so infectiously.

Lucinda blushed fiercely under her bonnet as she wondered whether similar thoughts had passed through Will's mind when he had glimpsed her through the trees bathing in the pond. Then the very idea that he had seen her as she was not meant to be seen by any man until she was wed gripped her with shame and the fervent wish that it could all be undone. Perhaps if she had met Will Masterson under other circumstances, perhaps at a ball in Virginia, instead of as an interloper in a male stronghold. . . .

While she worked, Lucinda's imagination was given free rein. It had always been a vivid one, perhaps to make up for her rather ordinary, mundane existence. She now saw herself bedecked in silks and taffetas, her jeweled fingers fluttering a fan in front of her bosom, her eyes lowered demurely, her long lashes brushing her cheeks. She imagined herself at a fancy ball, being surrounded and admired by all the young men. They beseeched her for a dance, while in the doorway, standing tall and proud, was Will Masterson. Slowly he came towards her, parted the circle of admirers, took her hand and touched it with his lips. "May I have the pleasure of this dance, Miss Evans?"

As she blushingly acquiesced, curtsying prettily, he took her by the hand and encircled her waist with his arm. Then he twirled her around the floor while the other dancers stepped to the side to give them room and to admire them. "Isn't she lovely!" they exclaimed. "Don't they make a handsome couple." Faster and faster Will whirled her, out through the French doors and into the garden, where the air was redolent with honeysuckle and magnolia. He danced her to a little bower. Then he took her gently in his arms and kissed her, tremulously at first, then with growing passion. He crushed her to him, his lips becoming ever more insistent on hers, while she felt herself falling into a swoon. "You are the most beautiful girl in the world," he murmured, his lips against her ear.

"Are you asleep, Miss Evans?" The real voice of the real Will Masterson caused Lucinda to start violently. Her eyes had, indeed, been tightly shut. Had she been dreaming, or only daydreaming?

The color flooded into her face as she sought to banish the shameful tableau and conceal her feelings from the man who was regarding her so coolly. Tenderness and passion indeed! Lucinda felt furious with herself for permitting such fancies to take hold of her.

"I—I must have dozed off just for a second," she whispered. "Is there something you wish?"

He held out his red shirt. "I understand that you're the camp seamstress this morning, and I wondered if I could trouble you to replace these buttons."

When she took the garment and saw that two buttons had popped off at the chest, she couldn't help thinking that the shirt was too tight in that spot. The buttons would be bound to go when he took a deep breath and expanded his chest. Even more disturbing was the sight of that chest only a few inches from her eyes.

Under Will's scrutiny Lucinda found it impossible to thread the needle, and she tried again and again. Oh, why did he stand there looking at her like that!

"It—it may be a few moments. If you can come back in a little while," she murmured, forcing her eyes to remain on her work.

He turned then and withdrew. She sighed with relief, looking up to watch his retreating back.

"Stop it, stop looking at him, thinking about him," Lucinda lectured herself severely. All right, he was a handsome man, what of it? She had met many others, or at least seen them from afar. James was just as handsome, she told herself fiercely. Only his face was more kind and soft, his look less intense, his mouth less predatory.

She finished sewing on Will's buttons. Bending her head, she savagely bit off the thread. With her face close to the shirt, she suddenly felt the warmth of it, and the fragrant smell of the recent wearer. Hardly able to help herself, Lucinda buried her head in the red flannel folds for a moment, the aroma of sun and river and soap mingling with a tantalizing masculine odor. It reminded her so strongly of Will during their embrace that she could almost feel his kisses all over again.

Distressed, she lifted her scarlet face, which she was sure matched the color of the shirt exactly, and placed the garment beside her. She was only thankful that nobody was close enough to have seen her make such a fool of herself over a piece of material.

Lucinda was becoming more and more aware of the great danger of remaining here. She knew Will didn't care for her. His words were as cruel as his kisses were compelling, but she had to admit to herself that she was attracted by him.

It was James who now was coming towards her carrying two buckets of water. He knelt to kindle a fire, and she realized that the sun was directly overhead. It was time for lunch, and James apparently was going to see to the meal.

"Oh, please, let me do it, since I've little else to occupy me. Do you think the cook will be returning soon?" she asked.

As James opened a tin of beans he gave his opinion that the cook would appear any day. He had asked the departing Ed to make inquiries and speed the cook on his way, for they were certainly growing very low. The sacks of flour, coffee, and sugar were nearly empty.

"In any case, Lucinda, you don't want to be traveling with a sore foot."

"I'd mostly be on the mule so it doesn't really matter. Besides, I have your ingenious walking aids," she finished, smiling up at him.

Just then Will appeared and intercepted the smile. His own face seemed frozen with malice. Without a word he picked up his mended shirt and walked away, trying to put his arms into the sleeves so ferociously that there seemed a danger he would rip the sleeves from the body of the shirt.

James saw Lucinda gazing after his brother. "I'm always having to apologize for Will's indifferent manners. He doesn't mean to be this way, I know. I believe his resentment against women started when he was disappointed in love by Louise."

While waiting for James to continue, Lucinda stirred the beans in the kettle. "What—what happened?" she dared to ask at last.

"It's rather a confusion in my own mind, Lucinda," James explained. "Will has always been reticent about his feelings, so I can speak only from observation. Will had courted Louise, and everybody had thought there was an understanding between them, though no formal announcement of an engagement had been made. And then suddenly he began reading every newspaper account he could get his hands on of the gold strike in California. He had become obsessed with finding gold. He grew restless, bemoaning his dull life, empty of adventure." James went on to describe how Will had chafed at having to defer to his older brothers and had wished for a chance to strike out on his own. As the two youngest, James and Will had never really had the opportunity to prove themselves. So off they had gone, with the blessing of their family, for there were too many fingers in the pie, or to be more precise, in the tobacco fields. Although it was a big plantation encompassing cotton and food crops, the older Mastersons had everything well in hand.

"No, Lucinda, we haven't been missed. And in turn, I think, haven't missed the rather bland plantation life. Will, I know, is much happier out here. He has a particular knack for finding rich gold beds and we've done extremely well."

"And—and Louise?" Lucinda pressed gently, to get back to the original discussion.

"Ah, yes. After we'd been here almost a year Will had a letter from home saying that she had wed another. He was in a temper for months afterwards."

"I—I have received the impression that he doesn't wish the company of women, doesn't wish to be tied down in any way."

"Yes. That is his dilemma. I told him repeatedly that

he could hardly blame Louise for disloyalty when he had departed and showed no inclination to return."

"Was she—was she very beautiful?" Lucinda asked wistfully.

"Oh, yes, yes indeed. She was the loveliest belle of all." James sighed, as if he, too, had been smitten by her.

"Was she dark?" Lucinda questioned, ashamed of her curiosity.

"She was fair, with reddish hair, sort of the color of newly burnished copper. She had green eyes and a smiling mouth. And, oh, very charming ways, Lucinda. She knew how to flirt. She turned the head of every eligible young man for miles around. When she laughed it sounded like the ping of silver against crystal. She was truly the essence of Virginia womanhood," sighed James.

Lucinda questioned him no more. She stirred the kettle of beans so vigorously that a couple jumped out and fell sizzling into the fire. A feeling of gloom settled over her as heavy as a raincloud about to disgorge the heavens. No wonder Will treated her with such disdain! He had loved the fairest belle of all, a red-haired, green-eyed coquette who had enchanted every man she met. No wonder a simple farm girl like Lucinda seemed very unworthy in his eyes. Very crude and inelegant, in her homespun garments, with her direct gaze and candid ways, her acid tongue and ungovernable temper.

Oh, she could well see that she would suffer in comparison to such a paragon of feminine excellence. Even James had gotten a faraway look of wistful longing as he described the beauteous Louise.

Lucinda could hardly imagine such a vision of loveliness camping out in these rugged hills with a flock of untutored, loud-swearing miners. She wondered what that gracious young lady would have done if her own older brother had disappeared in the gold hills of California. Would she have ridden out in a prairie schooner, enduring unspeakable hardships, in order to find him?

Of course she wouldn't, Lucinda thought savagely, answering her own question. Louise wouldn't have had to conduct such a search herself. Why, she would have had droves of suitors offering to seek her brother in all the corners of the earth. James' description of Louise reminded Lucinda of a fairy tale. In those, the lovely princess always had knights in armor setting off against impossible odds to slay fire-eating dragons.

No, indeed, Lucinda thought sorrowfully as she dished up beans and bacon, she was not the stuff of which fantastic stories were made. She was not the sort of heroine who inspired men to do brave deeds in order to win her regard. She was simply Lucinda Evans, farm girl from Illinois, who, if she wanted something done, had to do it herself!

Only last evening she had preened herself in front of the mirror, taking foolish pleasure in her modest frock, her plain, functional bonnet. She had basked in the glow of the dance last evening, shyly pleased at the attention she had received.

Suddenly she imagined what the scene would have been like if the beautiful Louise had suddenly appeared. The men would have been rendered speechless with admiration. They wouldn't have dared to ask Louise to clump around a dirt clearing with them in the travesty of a dance.

And Will would not have asked Louise for a dance as a duty, to keep her from being an annoyance to his weary brother, oh no! Will would have been proud to take her in his arms, he would have burst with joy to have had every man in camp envying him his prize.

Will's scornful words of the past, invoking gentle Southern womanhood in contrast to Lucinda's "schoolmarm" behavior, now took on an added significance. He had lost the prize he most coveted; it was undoubtedly an affront to have to suffer the barbarity of Lucinda's crude remarks.

Lucinda made Davy carry her plate to a far corner

away from the others, while she hobbled behind on the crutches. As they ate, she questioned Davy about the gold panning, about the sluice and the water wheel—anything, in fact, that she could think of to encourage him to speak, for she felt unable to contribute a word to any conversation. She was irritable, dejected, and completely disgusted with herself and her pathetic airs, her foolish daydreams and pretensions.

Davy kept glancing sideways at his sister. He had sometimes seen her angry for good cause, but never had she appeared to him so unreasonably fretful.

"My foot is bothering me," Lucinda explained petulantly, but that was only half the truth and nobody knew it better than she. How her mother would have lectured her if she had known the way Lucinda had been daydreaming lately and investing herself with the virtues of a heroine. Well, there would be no more daydreams. She would remember who and what she was, and adhere to her humble position in life. Right now she must take care of her foot so that she would be well enough to travel in a day or two. And then, cook or no cook, she and Davy would be on their way, even if they had to subsist like the squirrels on nuts and berries.

Lucinda felt too heavy-hearted to enjoy her task. Finally she hobbled to her blanket and lay down for a rest. If only the day would pass quickly. She was impatient to be gone, to turn all her attention to the task of locating Tom. Then she would willingly leave California and the gold hunters and return to the humble farm where she belonged.

When she awoke it was late afternoon. She felt stiff and restless. Her nap, accompanied she supposed by unwelcome dreams, although she could not remember them, had left her as moody and dejected as before.

The men were drifting back to camp and Lucinda noticed James walking in her direction. Looking up, Lucinda saw dark gray clouds bunching overhead. James followed her eyes and sniffed tentatively. It was probably going to rain.

"We'd better build our fire under the lean-to, Lucinda, so if it does come pouring down at least our dinner won't be diluted." His ready smile faded as he looked at her drawn and gloomy face. "Is it your foot? Not any better?" he asked anxiously.

Lucinda shook her head. "I'm afraid not. It might even be a little worse," she confessed, wincing slightly as she rotated her ankle gently.

"Will," James called to his brother. "Do we have any of that salve left for muscle aches and so forth? Lucinda's foot is paining her."

In spite of her feeble protests the brothers insisted upon bringing out a chair for her. James undid the bandage while Will rummaged in their cabin for the salve.

When Will returned to look at her ankle he shook his head and made a clicking sound with his teeth. And well he might have done, for it was red and swollen.

"It needs a soaking in hot water," he pronounced, and went off to make some ready.

Lucinda felt foolish sitting with her bare foot extended, while some of the miners gathered around giving advice and likening her injury to those they or their acquaintances had sustained. Everyone had different remedies to offer. One said she must exercise her foot and "work the kink out of it," another, that she would be laid up for a week. A third predicted dire consequences if she dared to soak her foot in hot water, proclaiming that only icy water would bring down the swelling.

When Will returned with the boiling water, however, the crowd of amateur medical experts melted away. Now it was Will's turn to kneel at her feet, examining the tender spot again. He poured the steaming water into a basin, suggesting that she put her whole foot in it as soon as the water had cooled slightly. "It should be as hot as you can bear it."

Lucinda, gazing at his dark, glossy curls as his head bent over her foot, found her eyes swimming with tears. Will looked up at that moment, his expression showing surprise at her glassy regard.

"I'll try not to hurt you," he reassured her in a low voice, gently lowering her foot into the hot water.

It was not the pain that was causing the tears. Lucinda could have given no good reason for her despair. She knew only that she felt wretched.

While she soaked her foot, she kept glancing around for her brother. Will remained with her, lighting his pipe.

"Have you seen Davy recently, Mr. Masterson?"

"No, not that I can remember. Why? Is he missing again?" He said the work "again" in his customary iron- ic tone. He was, of course, referring to her panic over Davy the night before.

Keeping her voice calm with a great effort, Lucinda replied that Davy had apparently ridden back to camp with a rabbit. However, nobody had noticed him since. "And he's not in the cabin," she finished quickly.

Looking down at Will quickly she saw a fleeting smile pass over his face, but she didn't have the spirit to smile back at him. She determined that for the short time she was to remain in the camp she would alter her behavior utterly in front of Will Masterson. She would, above all, keep her temper. She would be sweet and reasonable, no matter how nastily or provocatively he behaved towards her. Lucinda would show him that she, too, could be a simpering female. Honey wouldn't be any sweeter than Lucinda.

When her foot had been soaking for some minutes and the water was cool, Will removed the basin. Then he applied some ointment gently to her sore ankle.

"I'm afraid it smells rather pungent," he remarked, wrinkling his nose as the strong odor of camphor emanated from the linament.

What did it matter? Lucinda imagined that Will would never have applied such foul-smelling stuff to the delicate ankle of his Louise. For her he would undoubt - edly have journeyed to Arabia to find some exquisite perfume to sweeten the ointment. But this would do for Lucinda, used as she was to cows and pigs, she thought self-deprecatingly.

"Cheer up, Miss Evans," Will suddenly said to her. "All wounds heal with time."

Did they, indeed? Had the ones inflicted upon him by the jilting Louise healed? She thought not. Of course, it was a physical wound to which he was referring.

Rising painfully, Lucinda grabbed her crutches and went at a snail's pace to the lean-to, where one of the men had kindled a fire. The wind was blowing strongly now, and the temperature had dropped dramatically within the last hour. Gunmetal gray clouds now completely covered the sky.

Still there was no sign of Davy. Angrily Lucinda compressed her lips. Was he being deliberately defiant? Hadn't she told him only that very morning not to leave camp without notifying her of his destination? Well, this time she wasn't going to worry. She would cook dinner and then eat her own. If he missed his meal, so much the worse for him. Perhaps it would teach him a lesson and he'd be more considerate in the future.

It was one thing to behave as she had intended, another to feel comfortable about doing so. For in truth, she began to be greatly concerned when it grew dark and Davy still had not put in an appearance.

James noted his absence. Because Will was listening, Lucinda shrugged and said lightly that she supposed he was somewhere around and would come home when he was hungry enough. She wasn't going to give Will the satisfaction of showing him how worried she was.

The first drops of rain began to fall, and within a few minutes it was raining steadily.

Now Lucinda grew terribly anxious, for it was altogether dark and she didn't like to think of Davy out alone in all this wetness. Besides, he must be good and hungry by now. Where could he have wandered off to, without his mule, knowing that she would be concerned?

Could something have happened to him? Even if he had been panning for gold or shooting rabbits, it was now too dark to do a thing. Oh, why hadn't he returned?

For the next half hour Lucinda tried to console herself with every sort of explanation, but it was no good. She had a terrible feeling that something had happened. Making her way slowly on her crutches, Lucinda glanced at Davy's belongings and looked in the cabin. His gold pan was there; only his rifle was missing.

Finally she could delay no longer. Putting a shawl over her head to help keep out the rain, Lucinda painfully maneuvered until she came to the Masterson cabin. She knocked on the door.

James opened it, but before he could invite her in she had blurted out her worry about Davy in a couple of breathless sentences.

If she had feared that he would pooh-pooh her concern she was mistaken. James worked his mouth in concentration. "Just let me get a lamp and I'll go and have a look. Meantime, come inside before you get soaked."

Ignoring her protests at not wishing to disturb them, he lifted her over the threshold into the cabin. It was identical to the other one, except that it was full of clothes and pipes and other masculine objects. At least it was dry and warm, and Lucinda realized that she had been quite chilled by the rain.

Will lay on a cot reading a book. Without glancing up, he merely grunted as James relayed his intention to have a look around the camp for Davy.

"Most likely he's in the middle of the card game or listening to somebody's tall stories," Will finally remarked, turning a page.

Lucinda was incensed. Will had pretended to like Davy, but now that the boy was missing he was making light of it. However, she wouldn't speak. She had vowed not to show him her tempestuous side again. It cost her quite an effort, however, to remain silent.

James fussed over her, insisting that she sit on the

chair and let her wet shawl dry in front of the fire. He promised to return quickly.

Lucinda was acutely uncomfortable, left alone in the tiny cabin with Will. If her foot had not been a problem she would not have remained there for one moment. However, the thought of getting a crutch under each arm and clumping her way to the door under Will's withering scrutiny deterred her. At least he didn't speak now but seemed absorbed in his book.

Glancing at the title, Lucinda saw it was a book about alchemy.

Will looked up then and met her eye. "Do you enjoy reading, Miss Evans?"

"Yes, I do," she said, a defiant note creeping into her voice, as if he wouldn't believe that such a creature as she would be capable of deriving pleasure from the printed word.

"Do you know the meaning of alchemy?"

"The turning of base metals into gold?" she suggested tentatively.

"That's correct." Will grinned sardonically at her. "It was left in camp by a gold seeker who was passing through. In a more skeptical moment he had purchased the book before setting out from Boston, reasoning that if he failed to find gold perhaps he could produce some from whatever the land had to offer."

"And, and did he find gold?"

Will shrugged. "He didn't say, but I can only assume so since he left the book behind. Do you believe that base metal can be turned into gold?" There was mockery in the question, and Lucinda flushed uncomfortably, for she took it personally. She was the base metal, of course, and someone like Louise the desired product.

"No, I don't," she answered firmly, "any more than I believe that you can make a sow's ear into a silk purse."

"No, indeed. Sometimes, though, one forgets that one already has a silk purse," he remarked cryptically.

Lucinda, cudgeling her brain, could only think it was meant as a rueful reference to the fact that he had had Louise, a silk purse indeed, but hadn't valued her at the time.

James stuck his head into the door. "Not a sign of Davy, and nobody has seen him since he returned with the rabbit. I'll send some of the men in different directions to look for him. Want to lend a hand, Will?"

It sounded like a request more than a question. James withdrew, while Lucinda felt a panic rising. If he was sending a search party then even he thought Davy's disappearance might be serious.

Will hadn't moved a muscle. Lucinda rose awkwardly to her feet, positioning the crutches.

"It would be best if you remained here," Will said then, snapping shut his book and rising languidly. "There's no use your going out in your present hobbled state."

"Well I can't just stay here and do nothing," Lucinda cried. "I delivered a lecture to Davy on this very subject this morning, and he promised to mind me in future. And now he's disobeyed—"

"You seem to be unfortunate in both of your brothers," Will commented, reaching for his jacket.

Lucinda fumed at his innuendo, and an acid retort came to her lips but she swallowed it down. No matter how diabolical his words she had vowed to let nothing call forth a response in kind. She had to resign herself that Will was indifferent to her feelings at best, and deliberately brutal at worst.

Lucinda must have looked totally crestfallen, for Will suddenly relented. "Don't worry, Lucinda. We'll find Davy." With those words he darted out of the cabin.

Lucinda stood poised on her crutches, her good leg feeling as if it would buckle beneath her. He had called her Lucinda for the first time. Why a tremor should have seized her she couldn't have explained. Confused, she stumbled out of the cabin, and only when she stepped into the wet night did she remember that she had left her shawl inside.

Never had she met anyone as unpredictable as Will Masterson. He was apt to change his mood from second to second. Just when she had made up her mind that he was totally hateful, he would say or do something that made her feel warm towards him. Conversely, she might be relenting in her feelings towards him, thinking that he had come to accept her at last, when he would spit out some hurtful remark, wounding her all over again.

The camp looked deserted. She could hear shouts from the tent, as the card players continued with their game. Perhaps the rest of the men were in search of Davy.

Lucinda noticed then that her brother's bed roll was out in the rain. She went towards it, and after some false tries managed to hook it around the bottom of the crutch in such a way that as she hopped the bed roll came with her. When she reached her cabin she knelt and grabbed hold of the bed roll while she tried to open the door with her other hand. She felt like an acrobat accomplishing this feat.

At last she was inside. After lighting the fire she decided to unroll Davy's blankets so that they would have a chance to dry out. As she did so a tiny piece of paper fluttered out.

Stooping in excitement, she picked it up. "Dear Cindy. I'm going to the cave for some honey, just so's you know where I am. Love, Davy."

Lucinda's throat contracted. He had left word after all. True, he hadn't picked the most sensible spot for his note but at least he had remembered.

The cave! It was not so far away, but her heart fluttered in her breast to think of Davy rooting around the honeycombs. He might have fallen from a rock, or been stung by a swarm of angry bees. In any event, that was hours ago. Why hadn't he come back?

She determined to head for the cave and hoped she'd

meet somebody on the way. The men were searching aimlessly, wasting time, while she now knew exactly where her brother was.

Lucinda was impatient with her injury. Were it not for that, she would have flown to the cave and known the truth within half an hour. As it was, she was proceeding at a tortoise's pace, and in pain, too. If only Davy was all right! If only nothing had harmed him! Perhaps he had eaten some honey, which had dulled his appetite. Perhaps he had lain down to sleep and was sleeping still? That was the most acceptable explanation for Davy's disappearance. She hoped and prayed it was the true one.

As she made her way into the forest the rain began to come down in blinding sheets. In a matter of seconds she was soaked through, her hair dripping, for she had no shawl and had left her bonnet behind as well.

With both hands on her crutches, she couldn't even wipe the sodden strands of hair from her eyes, and she stumbled forward, her progress agonizingly slow.

Then she heard voices. "Here!" she cried out, "Over here, oh, please! I found a note from Davy. I know where he is."

The next moment she heard swift footsteps. The bush parted and there stood Will, glaring at her with exasperation.

"What the devil are you doing out here? Didn't I tell you we'd find him? It's so treacherous and slippery you could have added a broken neck to that sprained ankle."

"But I know where he is," she shouted at Will, forgetting her vow to behave in a genteel ladylike manner. "He's in the cave! He went looking for honey. And the bees—oh, dear, please hurry!"

"We found him. First place I looked was the cave. I thought that's where he might have gone. Davy is quite all right. James has taken him home." With those words, Will put his arm around Lucinda's shoulder.

"But, but why didn't Davy come home himself? Is he hurt at all?"

"No. He said he had been about to start home in good time, but just then a big grizzly came into the cave. Davy remembered he wasn't to shoot at it. Neither could he get past it, for the entrance isn't very large. And there were the bees to think of. So Davy did the most sensible thing. He climbed up onto a rock as far from the bear and the bees as he could get. He thought someone would think of looking for him there. Then he fell asleep and didn't awaken until we arrived. The bear had gone by then."

"Thank heavens," Lucinda murmured.

"Davy has some sense. More than some other people I could name," Will finished sulkily.

Lucinda was so relieved to know that Davy was all right that she collapsed against Will's shoulder, all her strength dissipated. Both crutches fell away from her and she simply went limp. She forgot the rain and the wind whipping around her head. Davy was safe, and for that she was thankful.

Will lifted her and carried her all the way to her cabin. There was a light burning and a great commotion coming from inside, as James and another man tried to separate Davy from his tin of sticky honey.

Instead of putting Lucinda down in front of the door, Will carried her around to the back of the cabin, where it was dark and deserted. Lucinda was puzzled, but with her hair dripping in front of her face she could scarcely see.

Will gently set her on her feet. Before she could thank him, she felt his hands on her shoulders. Then he moved one hand to her face and pushed the strands of wet hair from it. His own hair was dripping with rain as well, but her gaze was immediately riveted on his dark, glowing eyes. He was looking at her the way he had the time he kissed her.

Before she could think he had grabbed her and kissed her again, one arm holding her to him, while the other hand caressed her wet hair.

"Lucinda, Lucinda, Lucinda," he murmured between kisses.

She forgot her sore ankle, the wetness, and all her resolve. She even forgot Davy. Her arms wound tightly around his neck in a trance and her soft mouth received his hard one willingly. She knew she should push him from her indignantly, should protest at such treatment, but she simply couldn't bring herself to do anything but respond ardently.

It was the sound of the opening of the door to the cabin, and the loud voices within, that brought them to their senses.

Will lifted her in his arms and swept her around to the front, as if they were just arriving at the cabin.

The next few minutes were devoted to the reunion between Lucinda and Davy, the withdrawal of the men, the haste to get out of their wet things.

It was a long while later, when Lucinda was lying wrapped up in her blankets, that she reviewed her encounter with Will. The last look she had had of him had shown her an expression of antagonism on his face, as if she had deliberately enticed him and he was trying to resist. But she had done nothing at all! Surely it was the other way around!

Chapter 8

By the following day Lucinda's ankle was amazingly improved. She took off the bandage herself and found that the redness and swelling were gone. Her foot was still slightly tender but at least she could walk unaided, provided she didn't put her full weight on the injured foot.

As she made breakfast she rejoiced that the day was beautiful and sunny. The only traces of the previous night's downpour were some raindrops glistening on the leaves of the trees.

Lucinda had pinned her hair into a knot and pushed it into her bonnet. When the men inquired about her foot she told them briefly that she was better, but she spoke in a reticent manner and didn't encourage conversation.

Meanwhile, she kept peeking beneath her bonnet in search of a red shirt. When she glimpsed it finally and saw that Will was coming over to get his breakfast, she was careful to keep her head well down and not to look at him at all.

"Foot better?" he asked in a casual tone.

She nodded.

"Better not use it much. One twist and it could be worse once more."

Lucinda nodded again, still not looking at him.

Will respected her mood and made no further attempt at conversation before walking away.

Lucinda was feeling very much ashamed of her behavior the evening before. Regardless of the liberties Will wished to take, she needn't have accepted as she so apparently had done. No doubt any young girl in camp would have been subjected to the same treatment. She was nothing special to Will. If only she could remember that at the crucial moment, instead of losing her head completely.

One way to avoid the problem was to avoid Will Masterson. Today Lucinda was determined to ride out in search of Tom. Even if she hadn't much hope that they could venture far enough, at least she would be out of Will's path. If only she could control herself for another couple of days.

"Lucinda," James called out, coming up to her anxiously. "Ought you to be on your feet this way?"

She explained that she was much better and that she and Davy would be venturing forth as usual today. James cautioned her against overdoing it, but she pointed out quite reasonably that as she would be riding the mule for most of the time, there was little danger of aggravating her sore foot.

It felt good to get away from the camp. In fact, as soon as they were out of sight of a certain red flannel shirt, Lucinda's spirits soared. She breathed in the air, fresh and crisp after the rain. Everything seemed clean and renewed, the colors more vivid after a day of leaden dullness. Even the birds were making every effort to sing their sweetest.

"Oh, Davy, isn't it simply beautiful!" exclaimed Lucinda, smiling happily.

"Yeah." Davy looked at his sister curiously. She was an enigma to him. He certainly couldn't fathom why she should be so full of smiles now when he had heard her moaning and even sobbing half the night. Girls were certainly strange, he thought.

Almost as soon as they began to follow the stream they came upon prospector after prospector. Instead of stopping and asking, Lucinda decided they should ride ahead and look for Tom themselves. She pointed out to

Davy that nobody was interested or appeared to have a reliable memory anyway, so they might as well save themselves trouble and embarrassment.

When they stopped to eat lunch, Davy waded into the stream with his pan. Within half an hour he had discovered a very small quantity of gold dust.

"Gee, Cindy, I wish I could stay here. I'm sure if I kept panning—"

"Not now, Davy. You'll remember where it is. You can come back another time. Today I'm determined to make some speed.

"Davy, I want you to keep your eyes open for rabbits. If you find anything we'll keep it for ourselves. We can dry out the meat so that if the cook delays much longer we'll be able to go on knowing that we'll have something in our bag to eat."

They reached the end of the stream by mid-afternoon and then rode on as they had planned, doubling back along another route. They hadn't gone very far when they saw up ahead a large collection of tents and shacks.

"What is it, Cindy, a town or something?"

"Probably a mining town," Lucinda said, brightening. "Perhaps we'll be able to get some supplies ourselves. James said the prices are very high, but still, maybe we can buy just a little to keep us going."

Davy's face fell. "I left my gold pouch back at camp. I didn't think it would be safe to take it with me."

Lucinda agreed that was probably wise, since he was so often careless with his possessions. In any case, she still had her purse of money tightly pinned in her bosom.

When they rode into the mining town they were astounded at the numbers of men and the amount of activity going on. The first thing that puzzled Lucinda and Davy was that so many people were milling about a few shacks in the middle of the afternoon instead of working the stream or digging in the bedrock.

As they rode through the muddy main street Lucinda was reminded of Sacramento in miniature. Here, however, the men looked even more disreputable. There were a number of foreigners, she could tell, both from their strange clothes and unfamiliar tongues. As Lucinda and Davy rode past the saloon they heard a great din from within. Just outside several men lounged, drinking from bottles and calling out in an inebriated manner.

A sign proclaiming that they were riding through "Dead Man's Gulch" did not reassure Lucinda in the least.

There were even women, but Lucinda tried not to stare, for they were dressed very elaborately and had painted their cheeks and lips. Davy had none of Lucinda's reticence. His mouth frankly hung open, and he twisted his head to look after them as they slowly passed by.

"Davy," Lucinda hissed at him, "don't stare so. We're looking for a general store, remember."

Davy's clear young voice sounded out of place amid the whisky-sodden rumbles of the miners and the shrill laughter of the women. He asked a group at random if there was a store that sold supplies.

The chatter lessened for a moment, and then several people began to shoot questions. Where did they come from, where were they going, did they want a drink, and how about a game of cards? The men stared at Lucinda openly, smirking and nudging each other, in spite of the fact that she wore her bonnet well down over her face and her hair was completely hidden.

Davy become flustered by all the questions, and Lucinda, much as she had been trying to remain in the background, was forced to enter the conversation. "We should like to purchase some flour, coffee, bacon, beans, and sugar," she announced in her loftiest schoolmarm tone. Instead of silencing the rude and cavalier remarks, it made the group jeer the louder. It was plain to Lucinda that all of them had been drinking, including the women.

"Supplies you want, eh? Well, ma'am, if you can pay

a dollar for a pound of potatoes and fifty cents an egg, we can help you out. Or, if you'd like a chicken to put in your pot, ma'am, that'll set you back four dollars."

The group roared with laughter at the astonishment on Davy's face.

Lucinda didn't alter her grim expression. After determining that there were no staple provisions for sale, she yanked the reins so that they might be on their way.

"Hey, wait a minute. What's the all-fired rush? Stay a while. We'd sure like some company, wouldn't we, boys?" Shouts of laughter greeted that remark, and to Lucinda's horror, the group, comprising about two dozen men and women, came out into the middle of the road and blocked the path of the mules.

Davy picked up his rifle. "You let us pass, or else!"

The sight of the small, slight boy and his menacing words caused them to rock with laughter. One of the taller men suddenly reached up and pulled the rifle right out of Davy's hands.

"You give that back! That's mine!" he said, his lip trembling, looking fearfully at his sister.

Before Lucinda could react two of the women, dressed in faded satin gowns, had approached her from both sides. One was young and might have been pretty if her face hadn't been distorted under all the paint. The other woman was middle-aged and nearly toothless. Her inappropriate gown, elaborate hat, and artificially red cheeks made her look grotesque.

Both of them reached out to touch the hem of Lucinda's plain calico dress.

"You come inside with us, dearie," the young one suggested, "and we'll give you a real nice dress to wear. And you can make more money just staying in the tent than spending all day digging up nuggets."

At this the older woman howled with laughter, her gaping smile quite revolting Lucinda.

"No, thank you," she said, icily polite. "If you will kindly return my brother's rifle we will be on our way."

One of the women put her hands on her hips and danced into the street, repeating Lucinda's words in a mocking way, thus causing further merriment on the part of the audience.

"Let's get them down off of their mules," one man suggested, and a loud clamor of agreement went up from the others.

Lucinda was terribly frightened. She grew pale and her heart hammered fearfully but she knew she mustn't show her feelings. Although she had never met such people before, she realized that a great deal of the trouble was the fact that they'd all been drinking.

Davy began to shout at them then, demanding his rifle and threatening that he knew how to use it. Far from frightening the crowd, his brave protests only increased their amusement.

"Hey, let me through here," a man's voice called out. A stocky figure pushed through the rowdies, and Lucinda and Davy were suddenly face to face with Jeff Boles, their friend from Sacramento.

"Why these here are my own kids," Jeff shouted at the others. "Lucinda and Davy, come looking for their Pa."

Even Davy could see the wisdom of not contradicting Mr. Boles, especially since his announcement had an immediate effect on the crowd. Davy's rifle was handed back and the group melted away, still merry but no longer menacing.

Within a short while Lucinda and Davy were drinking coffee with Jeff Boles outside his tent a little way out of the main part of town.

"I don't know what we would have done if you hadn't happened along at that moment," Lucinda was saying, a worrying frown returning to her face.

"I don't think anything much would have happened. Leastways not in the daytime. At night those fellers can be dangerous. After a whole day of guzzling the whisky they turn real mean and ugly."

The three went on to exchange news of each other's activities during the period since they had last been together in Sacramento.

Jeff Boles felt that Lucinda and Davy had been lucky to have been befriended by the gentlemanly Masterson brothers. Lucinda could not help but recall, with a reddening face, the ungentlemanly behavior of one of them, but of course she didn't voice her thoughts.

"As a matter of fact," Jeff Boles continued, "I was thinking of you two just the other day, 'cause I spoke to a man who had met a farmer from Illinois, and—"

"Tom! It must have been Tom!" Davy interrupted excitedly.

"Hush now, Davy, and let Mr. Boles finish his story. Tom isn't the only farmer to have left Illinois for California." Even as she spoke sensibly, to keep herself from becoming wildly hopeful, Lucinda's pounding heart told her she was almost as excited as Davy.

"Like you said, I don't know as it's your Tom. Man I spoke to only said that the feller was sort of young and was going on up the main body of the river to pick up his sack of gold and take it back down to the bank in Sacramento. Seems he was doing an awful lot of bragging about it. Not wise in these here parts, where there's some as would rather steal it than dig it up for themselves."

Lucinda's euphoria lessened. If it was one thing her brother had never been it was boastful and she said as much, in a low voice. Of course, he might have changed.

Once again thanking Jeff Boles for everything, Lucinda and Davy finally went on their way. Jeff rode with them until they were out of sight of the mining camp, to be sure they would not be molested once more.

As soon as they set out Lucinda realized that they had remained much longer with Jeff Boles than they ought to have done, for it was already nearly dusk and they were still quite a long way from camp.

Although they rode as swiftly as they could, the way

back was much longer because the path following the
stream snaked in and out. They were afraid to risk a
short cut, being unfamiliar with the area. Their map was
not detailed enough to be useful in this respect.

"Look there, Cindy. I see a rabbit," Davy called happily to his sister.

Jumping off his mule, Davy began to stalk it.

"Careful, Davy," Lucinda cautioned him. "It's quite
dark over there in the trees. I don't think you'll be able
to see properly. Let it go. We'll do better to ride back to
camp straightaway."

Davy, however, had scurried so quickly after his prey
that Lucinda's words were lost in the air.

"Davy, come back!" she shouted after him. Her
brother made no answer, but after a few minutes a shot
rang out, and then another. Then there was silence.

Lucinda waited and waited, as dusk deepened into
darkness. She couldn't imagine what Davy was doing.

After shouting after him for several moments without
result, Lucinda was forced to get down from her mule
and go in search of her brother. Her sore foot slowed her
movements and it took her some time to get to the beginning of the woods. Every few moments Lucinda
stopped and shouted her brother's name. She began to
grow alarmed when she received no answer.

Farther and farther she walked. Finally her shouts
were rewarded.

"Down here," Davy's voice called weakly out of the
darkness. "I fell in a hole. Be careful, Cindy."

Slowly she advanced in the direction of the sound,
and then she saw in front of her a small ravine. At the
bottom of it was Davy! Lucinda's heart turned over as
the name "Dead Man's Gulch" jumped into her head.

Kneeling at the edge, Lucinda called down to Davy to
see if he was hurt. He assured her he was fine, but he
simply couldn't climb out. What had happened was that
he had shot at the rabbit, and so intent had he been on
tracking it that he hadn't seen the ravine until it was too

late. He had tumbled in and there he was. He had been calling to Cindy, unheard, ever since.

She knew it was no good crawling down after him, for then they'd both be stuck. Lucinda wasn't good at climbing. She hadn't had any practice in the flat fields at home and she suspected that Davy wasn't much better.

First, she called him to come as close as he could to her. She reached down with the longest branch she could find, but it still fell several yards short of reaching Davy. And, according to him, the sides were sheer vertical rock.

If only she had a rope. Well, she didn't and one wasn't going to materialize out of the air. She would have to think of something else.

"How big is this gulch, Davy? Can you see?" she shouted down to him.

"I don't know. I can't tell. It's too dark."

Indeed, the clouds hid the moon, and there were very few stars.

"Davy, stay as close to the sides as possible and just start to move slowly to your right. I'll follow you up here. Maybe it will be less difficult to climb out at another spot."

They did as she had suggested, slowly groping their way in the dark. Lucinda feared that they might come upon a bear or a snake, or worst of all, a mountain lion. On and on they went, and they both realized that it was a much wider ravine than either of them had first supposed. Worse, it grew steeper instead of more shallow.

Just as Lucinda was about to direct her brother to backtrack and try the other way, he called out in jubilation, "It's better here, Cindy. I think I can climb a little."

He could, and soon Lucinda saw that he had managed to get halfway up, although he had nothing to hang onto for the rest of the way.

Once again Lucinda sought the longest branch she could find. Instead of picking one up from the ground, which might be dead and dry and snap under Davy's weight, she decided to cut a fresh one from a tree. But how? Davy's knife was back at camp.

Then she remembered the little pearl-handled knife Mrs. Tiller had given her for protection. She had continued to wear it pinned to her shift. Now, with trembling fingers, she undid it. It looked terribly small to do the job of cutting through a branch, but she found to her eager delight that it was razor sharp.

Choosing a slender but very strong-looking supple branch, she spent some minutes cutting it through.

As she went towards Davy she prayed that it was long enough and that it would hold his weight. The length turned out to be fine, and she made him test it several times before permitting him to start his climb.

Lying on her stomach, her feet clasped around the root of a tree, Lucinda extended the branch, fearful that Davy's weight would be too much and both he and she would tumble into the gulch.

Fortunately Davy proved very agile. As she hung on for dear life, gritting her teeth, for her ankle was painful held in this position, Davy slowly climbed his way up.

They hugged each other with relief and then made their way back to the mules. Lucinda's foot was throbbing now, but she paid it scarce mind. What worried her was that they would be returning hours late to the camp. She would have missed cooking the men's dinner. More than that, the Masterson brothers would probably be concerned about them. At least James would. Knowing how unpredictable Will's moods were, Lucinda could scarcely project how he would react at a given moment.

The sky was like a checkerboard of clouds, and the moon kept appearing, only to disappear in the next moment. It made the going rather slow. By the time they reached the main body of the river, it was near ten o'clock.

As they rode, she suddenly saw looming up in front of

them a figure on a mule. Lucinda reined in her animal, and Davy did the same. He took the rifle from his saddle and pointed it at the unknown stranger.

"Well it's about time," the man said angrily. "Where in blazes have you been?" There was no mistaking the irate tone of Will Masterson.

"Oh, howdy, Will," Davy greeted him brightly, putting down his rifle. "You coming to look for us?"

"So it seems. Once again I've been pressed into service."

Brother and sister started forward again and rode up to Will. Lucinda's heart was pounding in the same irregular way as when she had faced the various perils of the trail. She wondered if he knew that she considered him as menacing as Dead Man's Gulch.

"Aw, don't be sore, Will. I'll tell you what happened. We were—"

"Just a moment, Davy. Let me signal James. He took the other route." Will lifted his rifle and shot into the air twice.

"All right. Let's go. James is on horseback. He'll catch up to us."

Then Davy launched into his tale with gusto. He was an excellent story teller, Lucinda thought proudly. And a very complete one, for he didn't leave out any of the details. She rode silently behind Davy and Will, flushing with distress when Davy reached the part of the story about their encounter with the inebriated men of Dead Man's Gulch and their painted female companions. In fact, Lucinda had the distinct impression that Davy was dwelling overlong on the details of that incident, hoping for further enlightenment on Will's part. She could tell that Davy was consumed with curiosity about the women.

When Will offered no insights, Davy couldn't resist asking, "Why do they dress up like that, Will, and put that stuff on their faces?"

Will remained silent for a moment. Just as Lucinda was on the point of admonishing Davy not to ask questions, Will spoke.

"They do it to display their wares. The same way, for instance, if you were selling saddles you might polish them so that they would show to their best advantage."

"But what are they selling?" Davy asked, puzzled.

"That will do, Davy," Lucinda called out firmly. "Some things are hard to understand now. You'll have to wait until you grow up." Her tone indicated that Will had said too much, and she hoped he would take the hint.

Instead, he half turned on his mule to look at her. "Don't you think that the boy is better off knowing certain realities of life than being raised like a butterfly in a cocoon?"

"Not in this instance," Lucinda objected. "This particular reality of life, as you call it, doesn't exist on the farm in Illinois. That is where Davy will be when he comes to the age to be interested in that kind of purchase."

It was only Lucinda's annoyance that had made her speak so boldly of such a forbidden topic. For she knew very well that Will had been hinting that those brazen painted women were at least honest, implying that she herself was not!

They heard horses' hooves behind them, and the next moment they were joined by James. He greeted them with great relief and concern over their whereabouts. When Davy showed every sign of repeating the long tale to James, Lucinda suggested that he continue to ride ahead with Will and she would fill James in on the important details.

Seeing James restored Lucinda to good humor. It was easy to talk to him, to describe the day's events in such a way that they evoked his sympathetic comments. One of the things she liked about James was that he responded appropriately to her remarks. So if, for example, she

told him of the ruffians in the mining town of Dead
Man's Gulch he exclaimed that it had been an unfortunate experience, and rejoiced with her that Jeff
Boles had intervened. When she came to the part about
Davy's tumble into the ravine James seemed to hold his
breath as she related how she had helped to rescue her
brother.

She was careful, however, to minimize the danger, unlike Davy who had told the story to Will as if he were
inventing a tale of horror with which to frighten small
children.

"And how is your foot after all that?" inquired James
solicitously.

Lucinda assured him that it wasn't too bad, though it
was throbbing at that moment. She felt warm towards
James for having remembered. He was concerned about
her and Davy, whereas Will seemed disgruntled at having been enlisted to look for them in the first place.

Whenever she compared the two brothers as to politeness, kindness, modesty or sensitivity, James always
came out far and away the more considerate of the two.
Why, then, did thoughts of Will occupy so many of
Lucinda's waking hours? Was wickedness just more interesting than goodness of heart? Or did it simply irk her
that James thought so highly of her and treated her with
so much respect whereas his brother mocked her and
took unpardonable liberties?

Perhaps it was that Will was such a formidable presence, compared with his gentle, almost self-effacing
brother. Even the way they sat on their animals was in-
dicative. James, although nearly the same height as Will,
rode hunched over, his shoulders sagging slightly, his
head jutting forward as if in tacit agreement that the
rider deferred to the animal. Will sat up straight and
proud, carrying himself like a king in the saddle and
proclaiming to all the world that he was the master here
and the beast had no choice but to obey. In fact, Will
behaved the same way with people.

Lucinda was unaccustomed to domineering men. Her father had been a rather happy sort of man. In spite of his hard life on the farm he had always had a jolly word for everyone, was always ready with a joke on his lips. She remembered Tom the same way. Neither of them had forced her to do anything. They were firm, but Lucinda had always felt that what they advised was for the best. James was like her father and Tom. Will, on the other hand, seemed simply to want to show her who was boss. At times she felt that he actually enjoyed making her squirm.

Yet, even as she had these thoughts they were tempered by the kind way Will treated Davy. Once again her mind went in circles, and she came back to her original assessment that Will was a perfectly fine and decent man—to other men. His treatment at the hands of Louise, however, had caused him to be suspicious of all members of the female sex. Lucinda obviously wasn't going to be the one to change him for the better.

Riding along thinking about the Masterson brothers, and listening to James chatting amiably of this and that, Lucinda was suddenly startled when her mule stumbled and stopped short. He then let out a loud braying sound.

"What's the matter with him?" Lucinda asked James.

"I'll have a look," he volunteered, clambering down from his horse. He examined the mule closely.

"Careful he doesn't kick you in the head, brother," Will called out from some distance away, where he and Davy had stopped to wait for the other two.

"He's got something in his foot, I think. It's too dark to see properly. I think you'd better get down, Lucinda, and let him make his way alone without a weight on his back, even such a light one as yours. I'll see to him back in the clearing. Meanwhile, jump up here in front of me. We can gallop back. You must be weary after your ordeal."

James bent and lifted Lucinda up on the saddle in front of him. It felt very strange to Lucinda to be sitting so close to a man on a horse. James held her around with one arm, maneuvering the reins with the other.

To cover her embarrassment, Lucinda turned her attention to the horse. "He's nice," she said, patting the horse's neck affectionately. "Did you buy him in California?"

"No, I rode him all the way from Virginia. Will had a horse as well but he went lame and we had to shoot him."

"Oh, dear, you won't have to shoot my mule, will you?" asked Lucinda in alarm. "He cost so much to buy, and I was planning to sell him again once we returned to Sacramento."

"Let's hope it's nothing serious. I won't be able to tell you definitely, Lucinda, until I've had a look at him." James smiled down at her. "Will's the doc with people, but I'm better looking after the animals."

Lucinda thought that it should have been the other way around but she refrained from saying so.

When they reached camp Lucinda went directly to her cabin to wash and to comb her hair. By the time she emerged into the clearing Davy was sitting in the center of a group of the men talking to his heart's content and, if she heard correctly, adding a few embellishments to the truth. He was getting into the bad habit of telling exaggerated stories just like the miners.

After she and Davy had had a bite to eat Lucinda went in search of James and her mule. She found Will holding the lamp while James examined the animal's hoof gingerly.

"Ah! Here's the trouble," James exclaimed, bending his head lower. "Nail came loose from the shoe and injured the left forefoot. I'll just put some salve on it. He should be all right."

Lucinda and Will watched silently as James worked. When he finished he told Will he wouldn't need the lamp any more. Turning to Lucinda, James offered to help her back to her cabin, for he could see that she was again favoring her sore foot. "If you lean on me it will make it easier for you to walk."

Lucinda did as she was bid, although she felt unreasonably nervous with James' arm around her waist because Will was following their progress with his resentful glance.

"I suppose you must be very weary after your harrowing day and wish to retire immediately," James said a little regretfully.

Lucinda had the feeling that he wished to speak to her but was trying to ascertain her mood.

She assured him that she was perfectly all right.

"In that case, ma'am, would you mind if I brought your chair outside and we had a little talk?"

Lucinda readily agreed. Within a few moments she was sitting comfortably in the chair, her sore foot on a wooden box that James had thoughtfully provided for the purpose, while he reclined on the ground by her side.

Patiently Lucinda sat in silence, waiting for James to speak. She was surprised that he said nothing, almost as if he was too shy to begin. That wasn't like James. Did he have some criticism to make that he was reluctant to make for fear of hurting her feelings?

"Is—is something the matter?" she asked him at length.

"What?" James jumped, startled. His mind evidently had been far away. She repeated her question.

"No, nothing at all is the matter, Lucinda. I—I was just going to say that, well, when you and Davy are ready to leave the camp and continue the search for Tom I would be mighty proud to accompany you. Now, before you raise any objections, I wish you'd listen to my point of view." He went on to explain that a great many dangers lurked in the hills for a young lady and a boy, some of which they had experienced that very day. It was inadvisable for her to go even farther into the hills. The greater the distance from civilization the greater the hazards.

Lucinda let him speak. Although he was trying not to frighten her unduly, and he had a way of putting his case and touching on the most horrifying contingencies with great delicacy of manner, Lucinda became thoroughly alarmed.

"But your mining activities, and—"

James met all her objections patiently, pointing out that the operation was running smoothly and Will could adequately supervise it. It wouldn't take more than a week to explore the river to the end. If, by that time, they had not succeeded in locating her brother, it would be clear that he had either transferred his activities to another river or a different explanation must be contemplated.

"Have you—have you discussed this with your brother?" Lucinda asked James cautiously.

James was honest enough to admit that he had not. "But don't think that makes any difference. My brother and I have an understanding in this partnership, that each of us can go our own way whenever we wish. Even if Will had any objections to my accompanying you it would make no difference."

It would make a difference to her, however. Although in some respects Lucinda was tempted to accept James' offer, she felt in her heart that it would be unfair of her to do so. Surely James was simply unable, like the Virginia gentleman he was, to permit a lady to travel unescorted, even if he had to drop his own activities in the process.

"It's extremely kind of you, James, and I am most grateful for your offer, but I simply couldn't accept. You have already done more than you should—"

"No, I have not. Besides—" James stopped then and his face took on a sheepish look.

Lucinda had the impression that James had not yet revealed everything he had intended to say.

She took a deep breath. "James, I wish you would speak absolutely plainly to me. We are friends, are we not?"

She thought his face deepened in color at her words.

"Yes, of course we're friends," he murmured, but still he hesitated.

"Whatever it is, James, I promise I won't be angry if only you'll tell me."

"Well, then, Lucinda," James began, clearing his throat nervously. "I—"

He stopped, flustered, as he saw Will approaching with long angry strides. "So sorry to break into this cozy little huddle but I could do with some help unloading the supplies and storing them in the shed."

"Supplies?" James repeated, dazed by the interruption.

"That's what I said. The cook has returned at last," reported Will, taking his brother's rather unwilling arm and helping him to his feet.

Casting a look of apology in Lucinda's direction, James let himself be led away.

The last sight Lucinda had of the brothers was the resentful scowl that Will shot at her before they retreated from view.

Chapter 9

When Lucinda went to bed she found she couldn't sleep. The cook's return had evoked feelings that tore her several ways at once. She wanted to be free to continue to search for Tom. She wanted to be free of the Masterson brothers, for that matter, because the kindness of one was beginning to distress her almost as much as the disdain of the other. However, after having been under the protection of James and Will she also feared to be on her own once more with Davy. Whatever had happened on their day trips, she had been secure in the knowledge that there was her little cabin to which she could retire with safety and warmth.

Now James' offer to accompany them on their travels lent a new dimension to her worries and confusion. Having James with them might be easier as far as the various dangers were concerned, but she would feel conscience-stricken at having kept him from his work. She might be costing him more than a hundred dollars per day. It was out of the question.

And yet, and yet—things had changed since she had come to the Masterson camp. When she and Davy had first embarked on their search they had been like two babes in the wood. She knew now what difficulties they might experience, as they had in Dead Man's Gulch, and no Jeff Boles would come forward to protect them. Then what? Hadn't she seen with her own eyes that not all the men along the gold trail were solely occupied in prospecting? Wherever there were quick riches to be had, entrepreneurs stepped in to sell whisky and tempt the men further with gambling and—and women.

Lucinda was haunted by the dissolute painted faces of
the women she had seen. Had any of them, perhaps,
once been simple self-respecting girls like Lucinda who
had been enticed, or even forced, to go astray?

Sighing profoundly, Lucinda realized that she had
grown very wise over the last few months. She wondered
fleetingly if she would ever again be the carefree girl who
embarked on this journey, if she would be able to return
to her simple life once more. It was one thing to read
about exciting happenings in books, quite another to
have experienced them yourself.

No matter how she tried to fool herself, her recent life
had been exciting. Every new day had brought with it the
possibility of fresh adventures and a new and cherished
freedom. No doubt about it, she had been her own mis-
tress recently. Even—even in the matter of accepting or
rejecting the embraces of Will Masterson. At home there
would have been no question of such a choice. She
would always have been chaperoned. A well-brought-up
girl did not dally with a man unless they had reached an
understanding.

The very thought of it caused the blood to rush madly
through her veins. Lucinda supposed she had to admit
to herself that she was fascinated by Will. If the situation
had been different, if he had been a farmer she had met
back home, and if he had wished to court her, she
wouldn't have discouraged him.

But those were an awful lot of ifs, indeed! It was all
very well to be so candid with herself, since she knew
that Will hadn't the slightest intention of doing any such
thing. She remembered his curling lip when he had said,
"No woman is ever going to tie *me* down. Not for the
price of a mere kiss!" Yes, those were his very words and
she had no reason to believe that he had changed his
mind, even if he was willing to kiss her.

Lucinda was glad that nobody could see her now. Her
face grew pink when she began to wonder if Will ever

rode up to Dead Man's Gulch, or some place like it, and availed himself of the "wares" on display by some of the women of the town. For if he liked kissing so much, and he wasn't the marrying kind. . . . Lucinda could well imagine Will imperiously plunking down his gold and taking what he wanted brutally and without a thought for the other person's feelings. Did that sort of woman have her sort of feelings? Or did the whisky she imagined they all partook of deaden such finer sensibilities?

The knowledge that men like Will might have taken their pleasures with painted women didn't exactly come as a surprise. Her mother had told her everything she needed to know before setting out on this trip. What came as a shock to Lucinda was that she should have been in any way attracted by such a person as Will against every bit of sense and reason that she could muster. How disappointed her mother would be in her if she knew that her daughter was so weak in character as to permit the embraces of a man who was only playing with her, and didn't even pretend to be doing otherwise.

Lucinda thought the night would never end. Every time she fell asleep an array of faces whirled in her mind's eye: her father, her mother, Tom, Davy, James, and Will. Especially Will. He seemed to have many faces at once: smiling, mocking, cruel, brooding, passionate, angry, proud.

She was glad when it was morning and she had an excuse to leave her bed and go into the chilly air to prepare the men's breakfast.

She'd forgotten that the cook was back. When Lucinda came to the fire she found a rather small, wizened-looking man with a white fringe around a bald pate busily flipping pancakes in the skillet.

He called out a cheery greeting to her, adding that he understood he would be forever plagued with comparisons between his grub and her own superb concoctions.

He was full of uncomplaining smiles as he said this,

and Lucinda found that she rather liked him. She offered to fry the bacon while he finished the pancakes, and he readily accepted her help. When the men ambled to the fire to fill their plates they found two people serving the meal.

"Hey there, Cookie, ain't you heard that too many cooks spoil the soup? Maybe you better let the little lady see to the whole durn meal," Jake called out good-naturedly.

Lucinda protested, of course, adding that she and Davy would be on their way right after breakfast.

"I fear not, Lucinda," said James, approaching in time to hear her words. "I've just been having a look at your mule. You'd better give him another day to recover, or he could go lame permanently."

Lucinda was forced to agree to postpone their departure, although she greeted that piece of news with complicated emotions. She was sorry that they couldn't set off immediately and at the same time glad she would have one more day without the dreaded perils of the trail.

Davy gave vent to his joy by a loud "whoopee," as he ran for his gold pan and plunged into the river helter-skelter.

Lucinda smiled with indulgence, and her heart went out to her little brother. This might be the last day he could pan for gold without restrictions.

Lucinda told the cook that she would wash the dishes, and she carried them to a shallow part of the river. As she knelt with the pans, she had a glimpse of her reflection. She was wearing her bonnet, but her golden hair hung loose.

It was amusing to see the reflection of her face in the water, especially as an occasional school of tiny brightly colored guppies swam by and appeared to be brushing over her features. Fascinated, Lucinda put the pans aside and concentrated on the little fish. They were adorable things, and she wondered why they swam so closely together. Putting her hand in the water, Lucinda felt a slight tickling sensation as the fish fluttered their little fins against her fingers and then detoured around them.

Laughing delightedly, she made funny faces into the water at them. Suddenly, she saw reflected in the water a bright red shirt, and then the dark head of Will Masterson.

"I should think you'd rather use a glass to admire yourself than this muddy river," Will remarked derisively.

Lucinda spun around in such haste that the pile of pans clattered into the water and began to float downstream. Jumping up, Lucinda plunged in after them, heedless of her dress and pantalets, which were immediately soaked up to her knees.

"Hold on there. I'll get them. No point in compounding vanity and clumsiness with recklessness," he finished, striding in his high boots after the errant cooking utensils.

"I may be clumsy but I am not vain!" Lucinda shouted at him, beside herself with rage. "I wasn't admiring myself at all, I was looking at the little fish. Why you must always jump to conclusions—"

" 'Thank you for retrieving the pans, Will,' " he said mockingly to her.

Lucinda stood up straight and put her hands on her hips, her lips quite white and trembling. "Nobody that I have ever met in my entire life has made me as angry as you!"

"Careful not to strike too dramatic a pose on one foot or you may lose your balance and go floating down the river." He was laughing at her!

She knew she looked ridiculous but she simply couldn't help herself. He was always surprising her in compromising positions. "I'd rather float out to sea than stand here putting up with your rudeness!"

She tried to swerve but only succeeded in causing a twinge to the bad ankle.

In a moment Will was at her side, his face showing his concern. "Be careful! I was only jesting. Must you take everything I say so literally?"

Lucinda didn't answer, for he had taken her around the waist and was supporting her while she tried to regain her footing and step out of the water.

"Tsk, tsk," he clicked his tongue at her. "You alternate, Lucinda, between behaving like a brave woman and a sulky child. Sit here, now, and let's get those shoes and stockings off before the mud dries and cakes."

"I can do it myself," she told him fiercely, but he paid no attention. She was too overwrought to argue with him, so she let him remove her shoes.

"I will do the stockings myself, if you will be so kind as to turn your back," she requested sullenly.

When he looked into her eyes she felt a stabbing at her heart as if he had thrust a knife there. She lowered her gaze immediately, for she knew her face was growing red and she hoped he would turn away before seeing it.

He did turn his back, and she hurriedly pulled off her wet stockings.

"All right? May I look now, or are you planning to have a swim?"

Lucinda opened her mouth to protest, the last moment realizing that this was yet another jest. She had always been accustomed to chat lightly with people and didn't consider herself overly serious. Why then was it only with Will that she was so touchy, that her sense of humor deserted her?

"Turn around if you must," she said, regarding her muddy toes ruefully.

"Here, let me have a look at that ankle," Will commanded. His tone left her no choice but to obey.

He touched the spot gently with his fingers, looking up at her to see if there was any pain.

I

"It's all right, really it is."

"In that case we'll just concentrate on cleaning off the mud. Put your foot in the water."

She did so, and he rubbed off the mud of first one foot and then the other. Taking a handkerchief from his pocket he proceeded to dry her feet.

To her mortification, Lucinda began to laugh helplessly. "I'm sorry," she exploded, "but it tickles!"

Her laugh was infectious, and Will was soon laughing with her. He raised himself from her feet, and their eyes met and locked.

She saw again that look she had learned to dread, the look that made her breath come in excited gasps. She forced herself to turn her head and squirm away from him because she had that scared feeling that he had been about to kiss her again.

"I'd best be getting back to camp," she announced breathlessly.

"What's your hurry? The cook has returned. As far as I can see you haven't a thing to do for the rest of the day. So you might as well let your things dry in the sun and talk to me."

It was the first time Will had ever made what might be construed as a friendly overture to her.

With her heart pounding madly, she knew she should refuse. She should immediately walk back to the clearing. Instead she heard herself saying, "Very well. What shall we talk about?"

He shrugged and pulled his pipe and tobacco pouch from his pocket. "What do you talk about with the men back home?"

Her color deepened. "I don't talk to men at all. Not —not by myself. I mean—"

"I understand what you mean. Never mind. I've been wanting to speak to you about Davy. I know you're determined to comb the gold fields until you locate your missing brother, but I wonder if you realize that Davy is developing a bad case of gold fever."

"He—he is?" she whispered, her blue eyes suddenly solemn.

"He's only a boy, of course, but he has the idea that finding gold is easier than it actually is. It's partly our fault, for we encouraged him. We understood from Davy that you had spent almost all of your money and, well, we have plenty of nuggets here to be able to spare a little dust for Davy. But you see, Lucinda, he may have gotten the idea that he has only to wield that pan of his in any part of the river and it will come up pay dirt."

"I see. Thank you for your concern, Mr. Masterson. I'll try to explain to him. And very soon Tom will be able to help me. I know that you really don't expect us to find Tom but I am confident that we shall."

Will ran his fingers through his black curls. "I guess you're right about my pessimism. I've seen too many men come and go to hold out much hope of miracles. But find him or not, there's no reason you have to go on calling me Mr. Masterson, Lucinda, when you call my brother James." His voice had grown husky, and he looked at her with such burning eyes that she recoiled from their intensity.

"Won't you call me Will?" he repeated huskily.

"Very well, Will." She tried to keep the quaver out of her voice but didn't quite succeed.

She found his nearness most disconcerting. She suddenly had the absurd thought that a bull found the color red compelling, and it would charge the person wearing a garment of that hue. In the same way Will's shirt fairly seemed to cry out to her to touch it, to run her hand softly over the folds, to—

While she stared at the shirt Will leaned across quickly and kissed her very gently on the lips. She shut her eyes for a moment, letting his mouth linger, and then she drew quickly back in alarm.

Immediately Will sprang to his feet and walked a little away from her, his back turned, and his hands clenching and unclenching.

Even through her own confusion and the tremor shaking her entire body, she saw that he was trying desperately to control himself. She must do the same. She rose to her feet and went to pick up her stockings and shoes. They were still damp, as was the bottom of her dress, but those were only minor problems.

Holding her shoes and stockings in her hand she turned and began to pick her way carefully back to camp.

"Here, let me carry those. And watch where you step. There are sharp stones, and, and—" He stopped and stared at her.

She kept moving, not daring to look back at him. Her thoughts of him shamed and terrified her. If only she could get back to the clearing—

With a few bounds he jumped past her and now stood in her path, his dark eyes blazing and his fists clenched. "You are driving me beyond all human endurance, Lucinda, and you know it!"

She looked quickly at him and immediately turned her eyes downward once more. "I don't know what you mean," she whispered.

"Damn it, woman, I'm not made of wood! I have feelings just as you do, and a heart, and a pulse. Here, look at this!" He held out his arm, and to her surprise, Lucinda saw that it was shaking.

"You tease and you tantalize, and you drive me wild. Your eyes and your lips say yes, and when I touch you, you respond at first. Then you object, as if I'd wronged you. You have no right to torment me in this way."

"I—I haven't tormented you," she whispered, looking at him through her thick lashes, but it was without conviction. For even as she denied it she knew that he wasn't entirely mistaken.

"For pity's sake, Lucinda, stop pretending. I've kissed enough women to tell who is experienced—"

Lucinda clenched her own hand then, and her blue eyes sparked in anger. "I've no doubt you have made free with all sorts! Well, I'm not to be toyed with in the same fashion! Whenever you kiss me you take me by surprise. I am *not* pretending. I've never kissed a man before, nor do I intend to ever again except my husband-to-be!"

She squeezed past him on the path and hurried away, fearing—or was it hoping?—that he would come after her. He did not. He merely yelled at her retreating form, "I don't believe you for one moment! No inexperienced woman could respond to kisses as you have done. You're just playing games. Oh, I've no doubt you'll find some poor idiot who will let you trick him into marrying you so you can then make a fool out of him, but it sure as blazes isn't going to be me! And I don't envy this mythical husband of yours your quick temper. As my old nurse used to say, you can catch more flies with honey than with vinegar!"

Lucinda was running now, in spite of her throbbing ankle and her bare feet, the soles acutely sensitive to the pebbles and sharp pine needles.

He was so hateful she simply had to get as far from him as possible! Now she was overjoyed that she would be leaving the following day. She'd never have to expose herself to his fiendish tongue any more.

When she reached the cabin she shut the door and threw herself on her blanket in angry despair. He wouldn't have dared to talk to her that way if Tom or her father had been here to protect her. He only behaved this way because she was far from home with no grown man to defend her honor. She began to shed tears of rage and indignation, casting about for some way to show him, to make him pay for having so demeaned her, for having insinuated that she was a scheming, unprincipled vixen.

Lucinda kept to her cabin until mid-afternoon. When Davy had knocked at her door at noon she had told him to eat without her, pleading a headache and lack of appetite.

It was certainly true that the lump in her throat would have prevented her from swallowing a morsel, but it was her heart rather than her head that ached. She was thoroughly tired of the whole business. "Tomorrow, tomorrow," she kept whispering longingly. She would leave tomorrow regardless. If her mule was still not totally healed she would walk all the way beside him, sore ankle or no, rather than spend another day anywhere near Will Masterson.

When she finally emerged from her cabin she found Davy excitedly handing his gold dust to James to be weighed. Catching sight of his sister, Davy was dismayed. "Shucks, you weren't supposed to see me. I wanted to surprise you by buying all the stuff and paying for it myself," he pouted.

"Why, thank you, Davy, that's very thoughtful. I'm surprised now instead of later," Lucinda said, giving him a hug. "You certainly have been a great financial help."

Davy brightened under his sister's expression of pleasure, and James smiled also.

"Be sure you weigh it correctly, please," Lucinda cautioned James. She didn't wish him to humor them but to accept accurate payment for the provisions.

James suggested that they not purchase too much and slow themselves down on the trail. He calculated what they would need to take them the rest of the way, for they would have to call a halt when they reached the tall mountains. They could stop back at the camp and pick up enough food for their return journey to Sacramento.

The thought of returning without Tom made Lucinda sick at heart.

From the way James kept glancing in her direction, Lucinda felt that he had not been reconciled to letting her go on her way without him.

She found it somewhat ironic that she had to fend off both the Mastersons, one for being too presumptuous and the other too unselfishly kind.

Lucinda told Davy to pack the supplies directly onto their mules, since they would be leaving first thing in the morning.

When she came back to the clearing she found James hovering near her cabin. "We still haven't settled the matter of my coming along with you on this lap of your trip."

"I can't accept your offer, James, much as I appreciate your kindness in making it. Davy and I were fine on our own, and there's no reason we shouldn't be so again."

He granted that it might be true, but explained that the closer they got to the Sierra Nevada mountain range, the rougher the going would be. The mountains were impassable in spots, and that feature made the place attractive for outlaws, who would ride down at night and raid claims, plunder, and sometimes even murder.

Lucinda couldn't see that one lone man would be much help against that sort of band of robbers, but she didn't say so. Instead she steadfastly clung to her determination to go on alone with Davy and beseeched James not to frighten them further.

James finally gave in but she saw that she had hurt his feelings. She was sorry, for that was not her intention. However, she simply couldn't put herself any further in his debt.

It occurred to her more than once, after James' description of conditions near the mountains, that perhaps Tom had been captured by bandits and that was why he had never sent word. Could they have persuaded Tom to join them? Surely that was impossible.

While Lucinda was puttering in her cabin, smoothing out and packing her clothes, there was a knock at her door.

It was the cook, who poked his head inside and said that they were going to have a little farewell celebration for the Evans kids, as he called them. Over Lucinda's shy protests he then said that she might do one small thing to help and that was to show him how to fry doughnuts.

She immediately agreed if he would let her do them with step-by-step instructions, to which he nodded.

Lucinda put on her second-best frock, of palest pink. The delicate color brought out the vivid blue of her eyes and enhanced the pink blush in her cheeks and lips. Since it was to be her last night she decided to let her hair hang loose, and she brushed it for a full one hundred strokes so that it fell in silky, heavy waves over her shoulders.

She moved the small mirror off the wall, trying to see how her dress looked, but she couldn't do more than catch a glimpse of it here and there. She wasn't aware of the startlingly beautiful picture she made, for the garment hugged her bosom and waist as if it had been molded to her body, flaring out over her crinolines.

Just as she stepped outside she bumped into Davy, who looked at her in astonishment.

"What's the matter, Davy, isn't it all right?" Lucinda asked him anxiously.

"Uh, yeah, but maybe it's too all right. I mean you look like a princess or something. Are you going to fry doughnuts in that dress?"

Davy was right, Lucinda saw. She would have to make some adjustments. First she pinned up her hair and covered it with her bonnet, and then she put on an apron.

The meal was a success, and the men seemed to be in a fine mood. It wasn't long before Lucinda realized that one reason for their euphoria was a fresh supply of whisky, which the cook had brought back with him.

In fact, the glummest men at the party were the Masterson brothers. James kept looking at her sadly, while Will avoided looking at her at all. James had put on a white shirt, tie, and black coat in honor of the occasion. Will still wore his red shirt, as if to show his indifference to the proceedings.

After supper they all sat around the fire. Even the card players forgot their game this once. Song after song was sung as the harmonica wove its plaintive notes around the rhythmic plunking of the guitar strings.

Lucinda had removed her apron. Now the heat of the fire and the flush of excitement made her take her bonnet off as well. She unpinned her hair and let it fall to her waist, much as it accidentally had done when she had first arrived. It had almost the same effect on the men, for the singing petered out and a great collective sigh went up.

One of the men who was quick with verses took the guitar and on the spot altered the words of "Oh, Suzannah," substituting "Lucinda" and coming up with:

Oh, Lucinda, oh, don't you cry for me,
For I've gone to California with my washbowl
     on my knee.

His merriment was contagious, helped by the whisky that was flowing freely. Lucinda declined to touch it, and the Masterson brothers had only a drop themselves. Davy didn't need any spirits to raise his own to an extraordinary pitch of excitement.

Then the musicians struck up a lively tune. First on his feet with a request for a dance was the nimble little cook. Lucinda accepted, and as they danced, making a ludicrous couple, she was sure, the men cheered and clapped.

Every time her partner whirled her around, a flash of red caught Lucinda's eye. By the end of the dance, however, it was no longer visible.

Lucinda dropped to her knees near the fire, declining all further invitations to dance, giving as an excuse her still tricky ankle. The men shouted in disappointment, but James broke in to calm them and control the proceedings.

Will had vanished, and Lucinda was vexed with herself for looking around her and straining her eyes in the darkness, as if expecting him to return at any moment. She should have been pleased that she could relax away from his constant gaze. While he had been sitting at the fire he had never taken his eyes off her. He hadn't been smiling, either, but had looked as glowering and resentful as ever.

Why, then, did something seem to be lacking in the festivities now? Just a few moments ago Lucinda had felt gay and light-hearted, and appreciative of the efforts of the miners to make her last night a happy occasion. Now, as she looked at all of them, the celebration seemed excessive and rather silly. They were just a collection of gold hunters cavorting somewhat intemperately and making a great fuss over nothing. She hated herself for her uncharitable thoughts, but there they were.

When she decently could, Lucinda excused herself, saying that she was quite exhausted and wished to retire, as they planned to decamp very early in the morning.

The miners crowded around her and she shook each one's hand in turn. Davy was sulking, for he didn't want the evening to end. Finally Lucinda gave him permission to stay up a while longer.

James remained at her side and escorted her to her cabin. When they reached her door, Lucinda held out her hand.

Taking it in his own, James held it for a few moments. "I wonder if you would walk a little way with me, Lucinda," he requested solemnly.

She could hardly refuse, so, her hand still in his, they went slowly to the edge of the clearing and towards the woods.

When they were alone James stopped and turned to face her. He looked sheepish and embarrassed.

"I—I hardly know how to begin, Lucinda," he said, lingering over her name. "I shouldn't like you to laugh at me."

"Of course I won't," she replied, looking curiously at him. Lucinda was puzzled but could only stand patiently waiting for him to proceed.

"When Will and I left Virginia to come prospecting we put all thoughts of an ordinary life from our minds, Lucinda," he finally began. "We wanted excitement, riches, and most of all, perhaps, adventure. We neither of us thought we wished to follow in the footsteps of our parents and older brothers and sisters, who seemed very staid and dull to us then."

He paused and looked at her meaningfully. Lucinda returned his look with a clear, open gaze of her own, while she waited for him to continue.

He sighed. "The last couple of years have given us everything we dreamed of, and maybe even a little more. I don't mind telling you honestly, my dear Lucinda, that we have done extremely well in the matter of our gold strike. We can retire at a moment's notice when we so wish."

Lucinda wondered what he was getting at, and why he had to keep saying that disturbing "we," for each time it made her jump slightly as a picture of Will flashed before her eyes.

"I—I never thought I'd wish to settle down. Even a few months ago I would have laughed at the notion. But now—" He stopped, and again his eyes canvassed her features, but he found no particular encouragement there.

Sighing once more, he went on, as if each word lay heavy on his heart. "I think the time has come for me to leave off prospecting, Lucinda."

"Really? And go back to Virginia?" she asked with interest.

He shook his head slowly. "I'd like to remain in California. There is a great future here, I think, in all sorts of ways. I won't bore you with business details. The point is, when I settle down, it will have to be with a woman for whom I care more than for any other."

Lucinda suddenly felt an emptiness in the pit of her stomach. Did he—was he trying to tell her—

She looked at him warily, and found that he was

blinking his eyes rapidly as if warding off a blow. He was waiting for her to speak.

"I think—I'm afraid that if you're going to say—I mean—" Lucinda stopped then because it simply couldn't be true that he was going to say what she thought.

He said nothing at all. Instead, he tightened his hand holding hers and pulled her gently towards him. Then he put his arms around her and kissed her. He kept kissing her for some minutes.

Lucinda didn't struggle, but neither did she respond. She was in a turmoil, for this embrace came as an unexpected complication.

Finally James withdrew his lips from hers. "I love you, Lucinda. I'm asking you to be my wife. Otherwise I have no right to take such liberties."

She almost said, "Your brother has no such scruples," but she swallowed down such horrid words at a time like this. Her face flushed deeply, and she felt distressed. Good, sweet, kind James, honorable and forthright. If only she could have said, "I love you too," but she couldn't.

For she had felt nothing when he kissed her. Except, perhaps, great affection, such as she had towards her brothers.

That would not do. Besides, when she remembered the way Will had kissed her. . . .

"Lucinda?" James had his hands on her shoulders and was looking at her with such a sorrowful expression in his warm brown eyes that a tear came to Lucinda's own.

"Oh, James, you've been so kind to me! I owe you more than I can ever repay. I am exceedingly fond of you, of course, terribly fond, but—but—"

"But you don't return my feelings, is that it?"

She nodded and lowered her head.

"I see. I'm not sure it matters greatly. I believe I have enough love for both of us. After all, you're still very young and inexperienced. It may be that given time—"

She shook her head repeatedly. "I'm afraid not, because, you see, I—I guess I love another."

She was surprised to hear herself say that, for it was not what she had intended. Yet, the instant she said the words she knew they were true. She did love another. She loved Will Masterson. There was no denying it to herself any longer. She wasn't merely receptive to anybody's kisses. If she had been able to feel towards James as she did towards his brother she would have been overjoyed. For there would not have had to be a painful renunciation. James loved her and wished to marry her. How simple it would have been!

Nevertheless she didn't love James and couldn't marry him. That much was clear.

She stole a look at James' face then, and was relieved to see that though it was sad and chastened it wasn't totally shattered.

"I understand, my dear Lucinda. Do forgive me if I spoke out of turn. I had no idea or I wouldn't have put you in such an awkward position. When I think of it, I have no right to be surprised. Such a beautiful girl as you, with such a fine character, would attract suitors wherever you went. I have no reason to think I was the first. In spite of the gold fever, there are surely a few men left in Illinois." Having tried to save her from further embarrassment by attempting a joke, James now managed a friendly smile.

Lucinda was too despondent to contradict James' conjecture that she was in love with a man back home. What did it matter, since her love was hopeless.

"You have done me a great honor, James, by asking me to be your wife, and I shall always cherish you as a close and dear friend," Lucinda said gently.

"So be it, my dear. I shall never say a word more on the subject. All I can do now is wish you the very best of luck." With his hands still on her shoulders, James bent his head and kissed her gently on her brow.

"James!" a voice rang out angrily.

James and Lucinda jumped apart, only to see Will standing several yards away. He wasn't close enough to have overheard the conversation but undoubtedly he had misinterpreted that last chaste brotherly kiss.

"Is this going to be an all-night affair, James, or can you come with me for a few minutes? Certain things need attending to," Will snarled angrily.

With an apologetic look at Lucinda, James turned to follow Will's angry strides back to the clearing.

Lucinda had a momentary impulse to call out to Will, to tell him that things weren't at all what they had seemed to him. Of course she did no such thing. What would have been the use? What did it matter what Will thought?

James would no doubt tell Will the truth of the situation anyway. Lucinda was momentarily irked with James for having obediently turned and followed his brother, just leaving her standing there. It seemed strange that Will, who was the younger of the two, should have much the greater force of personality.

As she made her way slowly back to her cabin, Lucinda was filled with despair. If this was love, she wanted no part of it. She had been unprepared for such disappointment. Her father had courted her mother, who had been jubilant to accept his proposal. They had married and lived happily. Lucinda had always thought that was the way of romance. Why, then, not for her? Why should she be doomed to have an ache in her heart for a man who wanted the pleasures of love but none of the responsibilities?

The only thing that gave her some small comfort was the knowledge that it wasn't Lucinda, personally, who Will feared would tie him down. Even the beauteous Louise had not been able to captivate him sufficiently to change his mind. Where the belle of Virginia had failed, how could a simple farm girl like Lucinda hope to succeed?

Of course, she didn't have any hopes at all. It was just that James' unexpected declaration had made the situation even more fraught with disappointment. Lucinda had always found that when she couldn't have something that she wanted, the offer of something else only deepened her melancholy.

Will hadn't even bid her goodbye. Well, that was that. She had no intention of seeking him out. And it was not to be only goodbye but farewell. No matter what, Lucinda determined that she would not pass this way again to reopen her wounds. Away from Will, perhaps they would heal and she would be able to forget her hopeless longings.

Chapter 10

Lucinda and Davy hit the trail just before dawn, for she was determined not to have to face the Mastersons that last morning. The air was still wet with dew, and the dampness clung to their clothes as they brushed against the dripping leaves on the narrow path leading out of camp.

They were headed due east, so they could see the sky begin to lighten and a faint peach blush appear over the horizon. It was going to be a fine day, and Lucinda felt her troubles lifting as they departed from the source of most of them.

They rode for a couple of hours before stopping to have breakfast. Davy went into the river with his gold pan, only to emerge glumly half an hour later having found nothing.

For several hours they jogged slowly on without halting, slackening their pace as they passed men working their claims to inquire if a farmer from Illinois had passed this way. After repeated shrugs and shakes of the head, Lucinda and Davy ceased to ask. Instead Lucinda merely glanced at the prospectors surreptitiously from under her bonnet as they went slowly past on their mules.

As the trail climbed higher into the mountains the terrain became more difficult. They could already see the rugged snow-capped peaks in the distance.

It was still early when they made their camp and ate a light supper. By the time it grew dark they were rolled up in their blankets.

Sister and brother had said very little during the day. They both seemed to be suffering from loneliness. At the Masterson camp they had become accustomed to all the bustling commotion. Now, with little else to divert them, they thought of Tom all day long and of the bleak prospect of locating him in this vastness.

When Lucinda tried to turn her thoughts from Tom she succeeded only in thinking of Will and James Masterson. She was disquieted when she remembered the strangely unexpected proposal of marriage made to her by James. Although she felt honored, and certainly somewhat flattered, she recognized too that she was probably the only marriageable girl he had met since leaving Virginia. She doubted that James would have fancied himself in love with her if, say, a Southern beauty such as Louise had happened by the camp. No, Lucinda told herself firmly, she was not going to let circumstances bring out any latent vanity. She would long remember James' encomium on Louise's beauty and grace. Whenever she had a tendency to be pleased with herself Lucinda would be sure to recall that she couldn't be considered in the same category as Louise.

Even so, Lucinda couldn't get the Masterson brothers out of her mind. In the quiet of her bed, she sought to discover some sign of romantic feeling for James. She toted up his fine qualities and compared them with all the lesser ones of his brother, but it was no good. She loved James like a sister, but the very thought of Will, of his dark, glossy curls, his brooding eyes, his firm jaw and deeply clefted chin, his ravenous lips, all increased her breathing, quickened her pulse, and set her blood racing.

Time would help. Only a few weeks ago she'd never heart of Will, and yet she had survived very nicely for eighteen years. With each passing day thoughts of him would recede until he would be only a faint memory.

For the next several days Davy and Lucinda stuck to the same monotonous routine. They were drawing close to the end of the river. Once they reached the high mountains they would not be able to go farther. Moreover, they doubted that any prospectors who weren't skillful mountain climbers would be found beyond that point. Lucinda was sure that Tom wouldn't be among them.

To add to their growing despondency, the weather had turned. It rained steadily for two days, soaking them and their sacks of provisions and making them feel dreary, indeed. It was hard to get a fire going, and almost as difficult to keep it from fizzling.

As if to punctuate their failure, they came that afternoon to the beginning of the steep mountain trail. One look was enough to convince them both that they hadn't a hope of getting themselves or their heavily laden mules up there, even if they had had the heart to go on. So this was to be it. They had combed the river and found nothing.

Lucinda jumped off her mule in disgust, saying that they might as well make camp even though it was scarcely dusk. They would have to start back the following day.

They rigged up a makeshift lean-to against an overhanging rock by means of a couple of branches and their tarpaulin. Nevertheless it was a bedraggled pair that silently ate beans and a bit of rabbit, drank some hot coffee, and huddled near the remains of a fire attempting to escape into slumber.

Davy crept as close to Lucinda as he could, and she put her arm around him. He hadn't behaved this way since he was a small boy. Usually he became embarrassed at too much affection. Lucinda saw that he must be feeling very low indeed, and she hugged him in sympathy.

"Reckon we ought to start back?" Davy asked dejectedly.

"I guess so, Davy. We certainly can't go any farther in this direction."

"You know, Cindy, I really thought we'd find Tom," Davy said suddenly in a burst of disappointment.

Lucinda patted Davy's head. "I know. I did too."

That was all they said. In a few minutes Davy was breathing regularly. For Lucinda sleep took much longer. She hadn't felt so sad for a long time. Not having found Tom meant that they would have spent all that money in vain. Lucinda was steeling herself to have to insist that they return home, although she knew that her little brother was going to beg to be allowed to devote some time to gold prospecting.

It would be a terrible trip back to Sacramento. She would have to write to her mother and say that they had failed. And when she and Davy finally reached home they would be worse off than ever before, for the farm would have suffered without Davy's help, and her own teaching position would have been filled by somebody else.

Was there an alternative to returning home? Lucinda couldn't think of any. Of course, if they had found gold they could have sent for the rest of their family and started up a farm in California. Lucinda found it infinitely more interesting than Illinois. She loved the mountains and the fresh, coolly flowing rivers, the giant redwood forests, the gentle breezes blowing in from the coast. Why, she had not even seen the sea.

Lucinda told herself that her liking for California had nothing whatever to do with Will Masterson. Even if by some wonderful chance she would be able to remain in California he would play no further part in her life. She could never compare in his estimation to the lost Louise. In any event he was a wanderer, a restless prospector who didn't want to link his life with that of another. Besides no sane man would take a bride to live in a mining camp, and surely no sensible woman would agree.

If only she could forget him quickly, forget his wild kisses that had left her breathless with incomprehensible longing. How she wished she had never met him! If she ever did meet the sort of man who might be right for her, a sober, upright farmer from back home, she would not be able to give him her first kisses or feel for him what she had squandered recklessly on Will Masterson.

Her mother had always cautioned her against having ideas not in keeping with her social position. Perhaps quite disparate types of people all mingled together in a mining camp, but Lucinda well knew the unwritten rules about one's station in life. She, a humble farm girl, couldn't aspire to the society of gentlemen farmers from Virginia. What held true for Will did so equally for James. She could not have returned to Virginia as his bride, only to be scorned by his family and friends as an upstart. However, a nagging realization crept into her thoughts, and that was that things were bound to be different in California. People from all areas and walks of life were beginning to settle here and would make their own rules and develop their own hierarchy. If she and Will had had enough money to build a beautiful house. . . .

Scolding herself for her wildly fanciful images, Lucinda shut her eyes tightly and did her utmost to think of something unconnected with California or Tom or Will Masterson. She conjured up a picture of her pupils at the schoolhouse, forcing one image to follow another, until she finally fell into a restless sleep.

****

Everything looked brighter in the morning, for the sun was making a brilliant display of itself, as if to compensate for its recent absence. Even Davy bounded out of bed with a smile and ran for his map, which he pored over with great concentration while Lucinda prepared the breakfast.

"Look here, Cindy," Davy said, his voice shrill with excitement. He had been studying his map for some minutes. "We haven't been to all the branches of this river after all!" Lucinda glanced at his pointing finger.

"It's really not marked very clearly, Davy. Surely we would have noticed it on the way here. It may be another river and not a tributary of this one. However," she hastened to add, as she saw his face fall, "there's still no reason to retrace our steps when we can, with little time lost, return a different way."

"Then you're for it?" shouted Davy.

"Yes. Now calm down and let's pack up."

Somehow the thought of exploring new ground encouraged both of them and they went about their tasks more happily than they had for several days. At least the new route had prospectors dotted on both sides of the water, although as they progressed Lucinda saw that no claims had actually been staked. This meant that nobody had found a "glory hole" or anything like it.

When they stopped for lunch Davy tried his luck in the river while Lucinda, on impulse, picked a large bouquet of wildflowers and stuck them in the saddle of her mule, much to her brother's amusement.

When Davy scrambled out of the river, his eye again fell on the flowers and he called out to his sister, "The posies brought me luck, Cindy. Look!" Sure enough he had found some gold particles.

Lucinda knew that he would request that they make their camp on the spot so he could wash for more but she headed him off firmly. She pointed out that they simply couldn't dawdle, for their supplies were going fast and in spite of Davy's find they would run out of food and money if they didn't reach Sacramento within the following week.

"But if I strike it rich—"

"That's enough, Davy. I'm sorry but we can't afford the gamble."

And he had to be content with that. Lucinda had further objections but she didn't wish to frighten Davy with them. She had noticed, on this lap of their trip, that there was a much more furtive look to the men prospecting. Some of them seemed to be lurking idly near the river, as if looking for lucrative prospectors. Lucinda, remembering all the warnings she had had from James about bandits down from the high mountains, didn't wish to linger in the area any longer than necessary, for her conjectures frightened her. What if someone had seen Davy and heard him telling her of his find? They might be followed and set upon.

Lucinda was determined to be even more vigilant. In some ways she was sorry they hadn't retraced their steps, for this part of the river had more heavy brush on both banks and was far less easy to negotiate. Even worse, there were some excellent places for bandits to conceal themselves from view.

They rode on, Davy's little face puckered with disappointment at having to give in to his sister. They passed two men working a claim who looked up at them.

"Howdy, folks," one of them called out respectfully, tipping his hat. "You riding straight on following the river?"

"Yeah," shouted Davy. "What about it?"

"Just be careful, sonny, and keep that rifle right handy. There's a crazy man up yonder. Would just as soon shoot a hole in you as give you the time of day."

"Never mind, Davy, let's ride on and keep a sharp lookout," Lucinda told her brother.

On and on they went, until the light began to fail and a burnt orange globe shimmered before them in the western sky.

"Shucks, Cindy, if I don't get off this mule and move around I don't think I'll be able to walk ever again," Davy complained.

Lucinda sighed, for she, too, was numb and weary. "All right. We'll stop for a few minutes."

Davy reached for his pan and began to wade into the water, screwing up his face as the iciness penetrated through his boots.

"Oh, dear, do you have to do that now?" Lucinda called after him. "It's getting too dark to see."

Davy had moved quickly downriver and out of hearing.

Lucinda jumped off her mule and began to lead it on the narrow trail near the river while Davy's mule followed.

A few yards from Davy Lucinda saw a man in the river with his gold pan. From that distance he looked quite wild, with long shaggy hair and a beard down to his middle.

Lucinda's heart began to thump. Was this the man their informant had described as "crazy" a while back? She noticed that he had his rifle slung over his shoulder as he worked.

Just as she was about to warn Davy she saw the man straighten up and yell, "Hey you, there! Move on. This is my claim."

Something about his fierce appearance convinced Davy to obey. With a thumping heart Lucinda counted every step until Davy was back at her side.

"I wasn't anywhere near him," Davy grumbled. "Why does he have to be so mean?"

"Sh. Stay quiet a minute, Davy." Lucinda shaded her eyes with her hand, trying to get a good look at the stranger. It was difficult because the sun was just setting and the shadows cast by the tall trees flanking the river were deepening.

"You don't think that's Tom," Davy said, his voice incredulous. "He never had such long hair and a beard. Anyway, Tom wasn't so mean."

Lucinda stared and stared, her pulse quickening. What Davy said was true, of course, and yet there was something familiar about the man. Even his voice, when he had spoken to Davy, had sparked some memory in Lucinda.

"It could be Tom, Davy. Just look at the way he moves. Oh, Davy, quick. Let's go up closer and try to talk to him."

"I dunno," Davy said, looking at his sister dubiously.

"He could be that crazy man we were told to look out for."

"I know. We won't do anything foolish. Let's just try to be friendly and see what happens. And keep your rifle handy, but for goodness' sake don't point it at him or do anything to scare him."

"Yes'm," promised Davy.

Slowly they made their way towards the prospector, walking their mules. Davy was carrying his rifle tensely, ready at any minute to use it if he had to.

When they were only a few yards from the stranger he spotted them and immediately lowered his pan. "Don't come any closer," he warned, lifting his rifle off his shoulder.

"Tom, it is you! I know your voice! Tom, dear, it's Lucinda and Davy. Don't you know us?"

"Cindy, it isn't," insisted Davy, his eyes growing wide with apprehension.

"What's that you say?" the man asked guardedly.

"Tom Evans! It's your sister and brother. It's us, Lucinda and Davy," she called out again. "We've come all the way from Illinois to find you."

The man was silent now, but hesitant. He held his rifle in his hands as if he wasn't quite sure what to do with it.

Davy plucked up courage then and called out, "If you're not Tom Evans, then who are you?"

The man hesitated. "That's just it, sonny. I don't rightly know."

"But I know, Tom, truly I do," cried Lucinda. "I know your voice. I couldn't forget my own brother, could I? Anyway, why don't you come and talk to us. Even if I'm mistaken and you're not Tom Evans, we don't mean you any harm. Surely you can see that. Davy, put your rifle down."

Davy was skeptical and reluctant, but he obeyed his sister.

"I assure you, you have nothing to fear from us," Lucinda repeated.

The stranger, shouldering his own rifle, slowly sloshed through the water towards them. Then he climbed out of the river and stood a few feet directly in front of them.

"Shucks, I don't know, Cindy," Davy whispered to his sister.

"You have no idea at all of who you are?" Lucinda asked the man.

He shook his head with a forlorn gesture. "Nope. I don't know where I come from or how long I've been here, or how I came to be here at all."

"Oh, Tom, oh dear, if only you could remember!" She began to talk of their home, of their farm. She described their mother and their little sisters. She told the man everything she could remember about Tom, starting from her childhood. No longer afraid of him, she talked on and on.

He listened raptly but made no sign of recognition. Davy, his head turning first to look at Lucinda, then at the man, realized that Lucinda was convinced that this was indeed their brother, and so he became convinced too, in spite of the man's alarming appearance.

"You taught me how to shoot, Tom, remember? I was only nine when you left home but already I could knock an apple off a tree like you showed me."

The man shook his head sadly and held out both hands in an empty gesture.

"Listen, Tom, why don't we build a fire and have something to eat," suggested Lucinda. "You may not know us but we certainly know you. Davy, gather some firewood," she commanded.

Lucinda held out her hand. "Don't be afraid, Tom, please."

He shrank from her touch. Nevertheless, once Davy got the fire going he did sit at the far end, regarding Lucinda and Davy steadily, his perplexed blue eyes flicking over them.

Lucinda felt a lump rising in her throat. What could have happened to him to make him lose all memory of his family? And yet he seemed in his right mind, he didn't talk wildly or irrationally. The best thing was that he was alive, and he seemed to be in good physical health.

While she prepared the meal, Lucinda kept talking, glancing up at him now and again hoping for some sign of recognition in his eyes.

He didn't say much, and Lucinda didn't press him. She glared at Davy once or twice when he asked too many questions, which only seemed to bewilder the man.

"Don't you even recognize her cooking?" Davy asked, his mouth full of beans and pancakes.

"I'm afraid I don't, though it's mighty good. Listen, I —I'd sure like to find out who I am and that I have a sister and brother and folks back home. But I can't rightly pretend that it's so, can I?"

"But, but how could you forget?" Davy asked, puzzled. "You taught me how to plow the fields and how to ride a pony and how to fish and skim stones in the pond. 'Course you didn't have that old beard and all that hair then."

"But the color is the same," Lucinda hastened to add. There was no doubt at all in her mind now. Tom's voice was unmistakable.

"You used to carry Betsy and Annie on your shoulders. They're six and seven now, so they would have been four and five when you last saw them." Lucinda almost wept then, remembering how much Tom had adored his little sisters.

"Oh, yeah, Tom, and you got real angry with Annie when she used to pinch the scar on your shoulder. Don't you remember? You got it when you came after me 'cause I snitched your corncob and was trying to smoke it. And you caught your shoulder on that sharp branch and tore it? And you whipped me?" Davy said this shakily, for he had always felt terrible about the incident.

"Of course, Tom, the scar!" Lucinda shouted excitedly. "I forgot all about it. On your right shoulder."

Tom blinked his eyes then, and frowned, almost as if
he had remembered something. He undid his top buttons and pushed the shirt to one side, exposing a part of
his shoulder.

"You see anything?" he asked wistfully.

"Sure!" exclaimed Davy gleefully. "That's it, all
right!"

Lucinda leaned close and confirmed Davy's observation.

Tom tried to look pleased with his new-found identity
but he couldn't because no memory came to him. Lucinda could see that even in his forgetful state the same old
honesty prevailed. He could have pretended, but he
didn't. So it was not such a very different Tom after all.

"If you let me cut your hair and shave off your beard
you might recognize yourself in the reflection of the water, Tom," she suggested gently. "Have you—have you
had the beard long?"

He shook his head and sighed. "I don't know. I don't
know anything much. From the first day when I woke
up with a bump on my head and only the clothes on my
back, I've counted about four hundred days."

They tried to reconstruct where he had been exactly
but without success. It was obvious that Tom had been
attacked and robbed, for he had begun his new life with
nothing.

"First I worked for some fellows to get enough money
to buy me a mule and a pick and shovel and so forth and
set off on my own. I knew how to pan for gold, that was
clear, and that's all I remembered. I thought if I could
find enough gold I could make some sort of life for myself, even if I never learned who I really was."

"And did you find gold?" Davy asked breathlessly.

Lucinda gently nudged her little brother. "That's
enough questions, Davy."

"But, but anyway, Tom, you're going to come home with us, aren't you?"

Tom thought that over a bit, poking uncertainly at the fire. "I honestly don't know, Davy. You say 'home' and it doesn't mean anything to me. Just think how it would hurt your ma if I got there and couldn't remember a dang thing." He tossed the stick away in despair and rubbed his head, as if trying to force some memory into it.

"We're all tired," Lucinda said gently, "and it's been a long day. Why don't we get some sleep? We can talk it over tomorrow when we're feeling fresh. The main thing, Tom, is that we found you and you're all right."

He shook his shaggy head sadly. "I dunno. It almost makes it worse, trying to remember, trying to fit all those things you've been telling me into that blank head of mine. I know I should be feeling grateful to you for coming all the way here and looking for me. It must've been real hard, with all these roughnecks and all. A girl and a boy all by themselves. Anyway, I sure would like to have you for my folks." He said this shyly, and Lucinda's heart went out to him.

"Never mind, Tom," she said soothingly. "It will come back soon. It's bound to, the more you see of us."

She ached to throw her arms around him and hug him, but she saw that there was no point in doing so. He would only shy away from her, for to him she and Davy were strangers.

Davy was totally bewildered. As he and Lucinda lay side by side at one end of the fire, Tom having curled up a few feet away from them, Davy whispered to her, "How could he forget everything that way?"

"If he was hit on the head, it's possible. And there was nothing to remind him, you see, for such a long time. The robbers took everything. His papers, our letters, probably. And then he had to think how to survive." Her voice broke. She was near to tears, thinking of how close they had come to losing Tom altogether.

"Will he ever remember, Cindy?"

"I'm sure he will. Go to sleep now, Davy."

Long after Davy was sound asleep Lucinda remained awake, racking her brain to think of a way to jog Tom's memory. From the way she heard Tom toss in his blanket she knew that he too was being kept awake by his dilemma. How odd it was to be treated like a stranger by someone who had been around for as long as she could remember. Tom had always taken care of her after their father's death; he had in some ways become a substitute father.

If only she and Davy could get Tom to agree to come back home with them she was sure that his memory would return.

Tom seemed even more shy in the morning, and as he helped Lucinda and Davy to prepare breakfast, the lines of puzzlement creasing his forehead remained constant.

While they ate, a couple of flies buzzed annoyingly around their plates. Davy swiped at them with his hand, and then began to sing "The Blue Tail Fly."

Smiling at Davy, Lucinda joined in the chorus of "Jimmy crack corn, and I don't care, my master's gone away."

Suddenly, Tom, who had been drinking from his mug of coffee, began to cough and splutter.

The other two stopped and looked at him anxiously. "Are you all right?" asked Davy.

Tom waved his hands, to indicate that he was, although he had swallowed the wrong way. When he stopped gasping he jumped to his feet. Still having difficulty in breathing normally, he began to choke out the second verse of the song.

Thrilled, Lucinda and Davy let him sing it all by himself, and then joined in the chorus.

"Cindy? It is Cindy, isn't it?" Tom suddenly called out, a look of recognition coming into his eyes.

"Oh, Tom!" Lucinda flew up to him and hugged him,

while Davy crowded close to Tom just behind her.

Tom still looked somewhat bewildered, and he kept rubbing his head, as his memory returned in bits and pieces.

"Our old workhorse was named Graytop," he announced.

"Yes," shrieked Davy, "he was!"

Gradually, as Tom talked in an excited manner, he was able to recall the farm and their mother and sisters. He was even able to remember the death of their father, and the funeral. And deciding to go to California.

"But what happened to you?" cried Davy. "Why did you stop writing to us?"

Tom shook his head at the question. "I can't remember. I can't even remember leaving home. It's the old memories that have come back, not the recent ones."

"It's all right, it doesn't matter," Lucinda comforted him. She feared that Tom had been through a terrible experience. Perhaps it was just as well that it remain forgotten.

"Tom, why were you so mean to me yesterday? Telling me to get out of the river and all?"

"Well, Davy, whatever did happen to me left me very scared of strangers. I don't like folks coming too close, I'm not sure why. But there's a lot of bad men in these parts. They ride in groups. It's never just one on his own. So I got kind of used to talking to myself, acting crazy, so they'd leave me alone."

"Gee, if you'd started talking to yourself we'd probably have scooted out of here too," said Davy.

"Well," Tom smiled weakly, "I wasn't too afraid of a boy and his sister, even though I wasn't friendly." He ruffled Davy's hair. "One thing I do remember is how small you were and how big you've got."

Davy stuck out his chest proudly.

All morning they talked and talked, while Lucinda cut Tom's hair and shaved his beard.

"There!" Lucinda exclaimed. "Look into the water at your reflection. Don't you recognize yourself now?"

Tom rather thought he did, but it pained Lucinda greatly to see how pale his face was, and how much thinner than when he'd gone away. One thing that made her rejoice was that he was a full-fledged man now. He had grown to his full height, and his shoulders had broadened.

"Oh, Tom!" Impulsively Lucinda hugged him. "I think this must be the happiest day of my life! We had begun to give up hope."

"Yes, but it was my idea to come back this way, wasn't it, Cindy?" Davy cried. "I was the one who saw this branch of the river on the map."

Lucinda was more than glad to let Davy take all of the credit.

They all spoke at once, then, the words tumbling over each other. They would hasten to return to Sacramento as soon as possible to send word to their mother. She would be overjoyed, and they all agreed they would keep some of the more unpleasant details to themselves and not worry their mother unduly.

"Did you have any luck with the gold?" asked Davy. "Look, Tom, I have all this left over, after I paid for the provisions and things." Davy ran to get his pouch and show Tom.

His brother looked at it with bright eyes. "Why Davy, that sure is a fine stake. You've done real well for the short time you've been here."

"And I want to get some more and make us all rich," Davy went on, carried away by his excitement. He sped towards the mule again to find his pan.

Tom winked at Lucinda, and she was delighted to see how much more like his old self he became with every passing minute.

Davy waded into the stream and showed his brother how he washed the dirt. Tom duly registered his surprise and praise, and for a while he washed dirt in his own pan alongside of Davy.

Tears of joy sprang to Lucinda's eyes as she watched her brothers. For she had dreamed so many times that such a thing would come to pass. Just for once her imagination hadn't played her false.

Instead of just picking up gravel from the riverbed, Tom used his pick and shovel to get at the banks of the river, and they were rewarded with nuggets as well as gold dust. By the end of the day Davy had a pouch full of nuggets.

"Sh," cautioned Tom finally. "You don't want to call the bandits down from the hills with all that hollering."

Davy heeded his brother's words, but his eyes continued to shine with overflowing happiness. He did stop yelling and simply confined himself to running up and back to work off some of his excitement.

"I'm sorry to sort of act like a wet blanket but it's important, Cindy, at least until we get out of here. Matter of fact, we probably should have made a start this morning, but I knew there was some gold here and I wanted to give Davy a good day, because there's nothing much left where we're heading back."

"That was thoughtful, Tom. Isn't Davy splendid? Hasn't he grown into a fine boy?" she asked, smiling with fond delight as Davy now carefully replaced his gold pouch in the saddle bag.

"He sure has, and he's not the only one." Tom looked proudly at Lucinda. "You've grown into a fine young woman yourself," Tom said. "Very pretty, and with a rare kind of courage. When I think of you coming all the way out here in a wagon train, and then riding a mule up into these hills—well, I almost get sick realizing what could have happened to you."

When Davy went off looking for rabbits Lucinda gave her older brother the details of their trip.

"I don't remember writing you any letters, Cindy, but

I suppose it's a good thing I mentioned the name of this river. Of course, I never dreamed in a million years that you'd come looking for me. Although now I'm mighty glad you did." He gave his sister a hug.

Tom was quite interested in Lucinda's description of the Masterson brothers. She was careful to keep from Tom her feelings for Will or the proposal made to her by James. She wasn't sure if her story was totally plausible but Tom seemed to take for granted that she was telling him the truth, and that gentlemen farmers would have behaved in just the polite, gallant way she said they had.

Tom decided that they should remain where they were for one more night and move out early the next morning.

It was a joyful trio that sat around the fire that evening, talking earnestly, for they had two years of conversation to catch up with. In addition, the more they discussed the past the more Tom seemed to remember. They believed, finally, that everything had come back to him with the exception of his trip to California and his prospecting up until the time he was beaten and robbed.

That night they lay sleeping near the remains of the fire when Lucinda was suddenly awakened by a noise. She jumped up in fright and saw two figures moving in the shadows near the mules.

"Tom, Davy, is that you?" she called out. At her side Davy and Tom both started from their blankets, and all three realized at once that there were two strangers near the mules.

Tom grabbed his rifle and Davy did the same. Slowly they crept towards the mules. Then Tom rushed forward and tackled one of the intruders, while Davy shot into the air twice, yelling, "All right, come on, men!"

Lucinda, petrified, stayed where she was for she realized, even in her panic, that she couldn't be of any help without a weapon and might even impede her brothers from routing the intruders.

For a few moments she held her breath in the utmost

fear, and only when she saw Tom and Davy returning with the mules did she relax.

"We scared them off!" Davy proudly informed her. "Tom gave them a hiding while I made believe there were a lot of us."

"Our Davy's a clever lad," Tom added admiringly. "Get dressed, Cindy. I think they may have been scouting for a gang. We'd better get away from here just in case they come back in greater numbers."

Lucinda and Davy hastened to break camp, and in a little while they were riding as swiftly as they could in a westerly direction. They rode until dawn, and then Tom found a place for them to stop.

They were exhausted and quite cold, in the damp chill of the early morning, but at least they were safe. They had ridden far from the mountains, and Tom was sure they had left the bandits well behind.

Lucinda made some coffee and the three sat huddled close to the fire drinking it and warming their cold fingers.

"Cindy, you and Davy get some sleep now. I'll keep watch."

Lucinda tried to tell Tom that she would keep watch and he should try to rest but he wouldn't hear of it. She finally realized that he was back to his old self and that he was in command of the little group now.

Happy to relinquish the responsibility, for she felt, as she always had, that Tom knew best, Lucinda rolled up in her blankets and was fast asleep within moments. Unknown to her, Davy awakened after a couple of hours and took the watch while Tom slept.

When Lucinda finally awoke it was to a smell of bacon and coffee.

"Hey, lazybones," Davy yelled, as her blonde head emerged from the blankets. "Come and get it. You don't want your breakfast to get cold now, do you, Cindy Evans!" Davy mimicked just the tone his sister always used when he was reluctant to wake up.

Davy and Tom were smiling conspiratorially, and Lucinda joined in the joke. She knew it pleased them to be able to serve her breakfast for once, and she praised their efforts highly.

They talked soberly of the night's experience. Tom, puffing his pipe, glanced at his sister and brother with a grim expression on his face. "Chasing those bandits last night brought back the rest of what I'd forgotten."

Lucinda and Davy sat still, listening in rapt silence.

Tom related that he'd got to California safely, after a rather hazardous journey, and found, as so many others before him, that the hills were not exactly paved with gold as he had thought. So he had worked hard and learned the ropes. Slowly and steadily he had accumulated enough gold, he had thought, to enable him to start for home. They would have enough to keep the farm going, hire some help, and so forth, though it was hardly a fortune. Then, one night, he had been set upon. There must have been half a dozen robbers, and they had beaten him senseless and left him for dead. They had taken everything, even his boots.

"When I came to I couldn't remember a thing. It's the most awful feeling in the world, as if you've just sprung fully grown onto the earth. I didn't tell folks because I was too ashamed. I just started from scratch all over again. I never really had the gold fever, but I kept going because I didn't know what else to do. Now that I remember I'm a farmer I'm mighty glad, because I've had enough of this life."

"Then we're going back home already?" Davy asked, a disappointed note creeping into his voice. "And without much money?"

Tom looked at him then. He grinned. "Who said so? Shucks, I've been working for a year. You think I'm such an incompetent prospector that I've got nothing to show for it?"

Davy's eyes grew wide. "Then show us!"

Tom rose and went to his mules. Lucinda and Davy,

exchanging glances, followed him. He opened his saddle bags. Undoing the careful layers of blankets inside, he reached in both hands. "Here, and here, and here," he proclaimed, blinding them with the glittering sight that met their eyes. Tom poured a handful of nuggets into Davy's hands.

The boy's eyes nearly popped out of his head. He was too deeply stunned to utter a sound, and so was Lucinda, who was gawking with as much astonishment as her younger brother.

"There's enough here to make us all rich for the rest of our lives. Now that I know who we all are," laughed Tom happily.

Chapter 11

It was a happy trio that headed down the trail in the direction of Sacramento. No longer did Davy yearn to stop and look for gold en route. Now he simply wanted to make all haste to transport the gold they had to a bank in exchange for money. Then he longed to return home and spend it. In fact, every hour he changed his plans completely, from purchasing the best fishing rod money could buy to the most elaborate rifle, the finest horse, a boat, a herd of cattle. . . .

Tom and Lucinda allowed Davy to dream to his heart's content. By the time the money was ready for spending Davy would have exhausted his wilder fancies and could then be persuaded to do something sensible. Tom privately told Lucinda he would like to put the bulk of Davy's share into a trust for him to use as he wished when he came of age.

Meanwhile, Davy kept close to the gold carried by Tom's two mules, and Lucinda couldn't seem to take her eyes off Tom, almost as if she believed if she diverted her gaze he would vanish into the air.

"Cindy, you're going to wear out my face just by looking at it," protested Tom, laughing. He was now the old Tom in every respect, for he had lost his pallor after a couple of days in the sun. The worry frowns had gone, as well as the thin cheeks. Lucinda had seen to that in the portions she fed her older brother.

Her main apprehension at this time was passing through the Masterson camp once more. Davy had pointed out that it would be right on their way. And they could use some more supplies. Besides, shouldn't they pay a call on James and Will to let them know they had been successful in finding Tom? Tom wanted to meet the Mastersons and thank them for having befriended Lucinda and Davy.

Lucinda had many misgivings but was afraid to say too much lest Tom discover the reasons for her reluctance. In spite of her vow to forget Will and the hope that his image would fade quickly from her mind, he was as present in her thoughts as he had been a week previously. Regardless of the new plans she and Tom were making, of her joy in their reunion, when she lay down to sleep she found that she was haunted by Will's strong, darkly handsome face, by his piercing black eyes, and his demanding lips.

At first she tried to console herself for the continuance of her obsession by saying that enough time hadn't passed. The memory of her encounters with Will was still too fresh. The surrounding countryside was too reminiscent of him, and the gold prospectors they saw in the course of their travels. Every time she glimpsed a red flannel shirt her heart missed a beat. If, however, she left California, things would be different. Nevertheless every time she thought of leaving, her eyes unaccountably filled with tears. She would shake them from her golden lashes impatiently. What was the matter with her, anyway? Was she never to be satisfied? All that she had wished for months was to find Tom alive and well. That wish had more than come true, for he was also rich.

All her dreams couldn't be realized, however, and she must resign herself to the disappointment of her romantic notions about Will Masterson. For they would stop only briefly at the Masterson camp. And everything would have changed. Will would not dare to importune her with Tom protecting her. By now James would most likely have become reconciled to her loss. Could she at least behave as if she were reconciled to the loss of Will?

She longed to be able to treat Will with as much scorn

as he had treated her. True, she was still a farm girl but she was poor no more. They would be able to have the best farm that money could buy, and hired men to work it and make it prosper. She should have pretty clothes after all, and a fine carriage. Her mother could surround herself with servants and never have to lift her finger for the rest of her life. Her little sisters could grow up to be ladies, educated to do fine embroidery and play the piano. They could acquire all the skills that Lucinda had always envied.

The last night before reaching the Masterson camp Lucinda slept hardly at all. Her imagination quite outdid itself. First, she pictured herself riding into camp triumphantly with Tom at her side. They would have a celebration, and Lucinda would be wearing her prettiest frock and looking radiant. She would wring new respect from James, much as she imagined Louise would have done. At this point Lucinda considered whether or not she could be correct, cool, and disdainful to them all, as befitted her new status in life. Or should she behave in a gay and flirtatious manner, like a Southern belle, fluttering her eyelashes and emitting provocative smiles, now that she had Tom to protect her? Whichever role she elected, she would behave coolly to Will. She would hardly notice him at all. And her heart would not turn over at the sight of him, she promised herself sternly, nor would her eyes glow with pleasure and excitement at seeing him again.

Will Masterson would understand, finally, that she was more to be reckoned with than he had thought, that she wasn't merely a lowly country girl who would suffer his arrogant, cavalier treatment of her.

Lucinda rose at dawn before her brothers so that she could spend some time in beautifying herself without eliciting their teasing comments.

So by the time Tom and Davy were stirring she had bathed and washed and dried her hair, cleansing herself of all the ravages of the trail. She would wear a simple dress for traveling. If her calculations were correct, they would reach the Masterson camp close to sundown. Then she would change her clothes and appear to her best advantage.

The following morning she would depart knowing that she had gotten the best of Will Masterson after all. He would know that her future held a life of ease and luxury. He would be sorry he hadn't valued her more highly. He would think of her long after she had gone; long after she had fallen in love with somebody else.

Before she was completely carried away by her foolishness, Lucinda gave herself a hard pinch in her arm. "Stop that nonsense instantly," she told herself firmly. "It is Louise he regrets, not you. Perhaps if you had met him for the first time some months from now. . . . But it's too late. He's seen you bedraggled and in a temper, and at your absolute worst."

No matter how she lectured herself, however, she couldn't help hoping that somehow she would contrive to make a sensational impression at camp.

Lucinda went through the day in a daze, as if she were two people. One part of her responded to the conversations with her brothers and was aware of her immediate surroundings. The other part was already at the Masterson camp conquering all the miners with her beauty and delicate manners, her imperious smiles and tinkling laughter.

Davy was too busy weaving dreams of his own to notice Lucinda's half-attentive behavior but Tom perceived her strange divided self quite early in the day.

"Where are you, Cindy, dancing at a masked ball in the White House or what?" he gently teased her, drawing blushes and denials from his embarrassed sister. He looked at her shrewdly, causing her to redden guiltily.

When they actually rode into the Masterson camp nothing happened as Lucinda had imagined it would. First, as soon as he sighted the clearing Davy began shouting that they had located their brother, and the miners stopped their work and approached the three with congratulations. Second, all eyes were on Tom and not on Lucinda. And third, Will Masterson was not in camp.

Lucinda found herself unable to control her wildly beating heart and her trembling. Apparently the thought of seeing Will still affected her greatly. Now, in fact, she began to have a sinking feeling that he had gone from here and she would never see him again. But that was what she wanted, wasn't it?

She felt too lacking in control even to inquire but Davy had no hesitancy. "Where's Will?" he asked James as they sat around having a welcoming coffee.

"I believe he's having a swim in the pond farther up-river," James explained. "That's always been his habit. Helps him to relax after a day of work."

Lucinda felt the color rise to her cheeks. The pond was where he had surprised her in her shift. She had accused him of deliberately spying on her and making her uncomfortable. Now she learned that he had been accustomed to swim there himself!

The very thought of their encounter in the pond caused her to grow agitated. Her trembling hand, holding her cup, sloshed some of the liquid onto her skirts. She jumped to her feet, as Tom inquired with concern if she had scalded herself.

She shook her head, wiping the garment furiously. She felt very foolish. Nothing was going quite as she had planned. Even James was not noticing her as of old. His attention was completely taken by Tom. To complete her distress, she looked up and saw Will approaching the group.

His dark curls were wet and he was bare-chested, his trousers rolled to his knees. Carrying his shirt and boots, he drew nearer.

Lucinda began to quiver all over. She quickly sat down, lest she fall into a swoon and make things even worse.

Before he had reached them, Will suddenly caught sight of Lucinda and stopped in his tracks. After a pause he continued to tread warily in their direction.

Lucinda grew hot all over, and then immediately cold, as if she had a fever. Far from having lessened with time, her feelings for Will were more intense than ever.

"Will, over here," James called out. "We have visitors."

As Will came nearer Lucinda forgot herself momentarily in shock at his haggard appearance. He had great circles under his eyes as if he hadn't slept in days, and his face was drawn and thinner. His eyes looked larger by comparison and shone with a great brilliance as if he were possessed.

He cast a glowering look at her, and then his brooding glance fell upon Tom. Lucinda saw Will bite his lips in distress.

"Howdy, Will," cried Davy, jumping up and rushing to his side. "We're back! And we found Tom! We found our brother after all. Aren't you glad?" Davy demanded, tugging at Will's arm.

Will's pale face suddenly reddened as the blood returned with a rush. He sighed profoundly. Then he ruffled Davy's hair, subsequently coming right up to Tom and holding out his hand in a friendly welcome.

Tom shook hands warmly, but the look on his face was one of curiosity. Will had a foreign appearance that made him look most dissimilar to his brother, for his dark curls were still damp from his swim and his bare bronzed chest and arms seemed powerful and exotic, like something out of a story book.

Nevertheless, Tom greeted Will in his open, frank way. "I'm pleased to meet you, Will," he said, "and I want to thank you and James for taking such good care of my family for me."

"No need, no need," Will assured Tom. "It's a wonderful surprise to learn that you've been located after all. It's surely something of a miracle." Will actually did sound glad, and he kept grinning at Tom.

While Will exchanged some words with her older brother, Lucinda feasted her eyes surreptitiously from under her bonnet. She couldn't help herself. She had to admit grudgingly that she was overcome at seeing Will again, although she remained uneasy at his haggard appearance. What had happened to make him look so changed?

Now was the time for her to pretend to be a grand lady, as in her dream, but she found she could do nothing of the kind. Pretending in front of others was just not in her nature. She would have to remain satisfied with what she was.

"Aren't you going to have some coffee, Will?" James asked.

Will shook his head. "As a matter of fact I came back for my rifle. That mountain lion that's been pestering the mules and horses is lurking near the pond. I think if I stalk him I'll put an end to his nightly marauding."

"Here, let me go with you," Tom said, jumping up. "I've been prospecting as far as the Sierra, and I've shot several of those beasts. Mighty nasty they are if they manage to spring on a man. I saw a fellow get awfully mauled once."

"Me too. I want to go too!" shouted Davy. "I can shoot, Tom, you know I can."

"No, Davy, you stay here and protect your sister," Tom said firmly. "Why, if we should miss it and it came into camp you'd be needed to keep it at bay."

"James could stay here," Davy said, pouting.

"Sorry, Davy," said James. "I'm going with your brother and Will. I believe you are more needed here in camp."

"Shucks, you're just trying to make me feel good," Davy grumbled, "but you don't fool me. You think I'm too young!" He spoke with utter disgust, while the three men tried to stifle their smiles.

"Be careful," Lucinda called shakily after them. She

felt afraid, and it gave her a most peculiar sensation to watch the three men who were most important to her preparing to put themselves in danger.

Davy petulantly kicked the dusty ground with the toe of his boot. Lucinda sought to take his mind off his disappointment by encouraging him to talk about his plans for his newly found riches.

More than an hour passed. The sun went down, and still there was no sign of the three hunters. Lucinda began to be concerned. Surely once the sun set they wouldn't be able to see the mountain lion in the thick foliage. At that point she heard several muffled shots from the woods.

Her heart pounding, Lucinda fervently hoped that the reports meant they had been successful in shooting their prey. She kept looking in their direction, expecting at any moment to see the three emerging from the wooded trail into the meadow but nobody came.

Davy, growing bored, joined the miners at the sluice. Lucinda had washed and dried the coffee pot and cups. Now she paced restlessly up and back, not knowing what to do.

The darkness fell quickly. The cook appeared with twigs to start the fire. Lucinda knew she ought to offer to help him prepare the meal but she was too uneasy to concentrate on anything. Surely they should have returned by now, when it was too dark to hunt any further.

The more she thought of it, the more fearful she became. What if one of the men had been hurt by the beast, or even shot by mistake? What if one of them was lying on the ground, bleeding? Up and back she walked, trying to assuage her fears, berating herself for her foolishness. They were three strong, able men, experienced with their rifles. Surely nothing could have gone wrong, could it?

Finally she simply couldn't bear the suspense any longer. Without telling a soul, she decided to walk a little way into the woods and see if she could find the others. She wouldn't go close enough for them to spot her, for she was quite embarrassed at her foolish fears. It was simply that she couldn't rest until she had ascertained that Tom and the Mastersons were all right.

Lucinda set off through the meadow and then continued along the narrow trail, stepping carefully and mindful of all the warnings about snakes and bears as well as traps the men periodically set to snare rabbits.

It was quite dark now, and she found it difficult to see very clearly, for the moon had not yet risen. On and on she went, a fluttering in her stomach. She was afraid to continue deep into the woods and yet she couldn't return to camp without knowing what had happened.

There was an open space up ahead. Lucinda strained to see more clearly as her eyes became accustomed to the dark, and the stars shone down unhindered by the trees. Surely the men couldn't have advanced much farther, for she had passed the pond minutes ago.

Lucinda crossed the clearing. As she headed towards the narrow path that continued into the woods, she saw a pair of glittering eyes in the brush staring straight at her.

"Tom?" she called uncertainly.

There was a growling noise.

"Cindy! Look out!" Tom's warning came from another direction.

As she turned her head a shadow sprang out of the brush at her. She screamed and tripped as she tried to run. At the same moment something hurled itself at her and knocked her to the ground.

She felt all the blood leaving her body. Just before she swooned she faintly heard several shots ring out.

When Lucinda regained consciousness she was lying on the ground. Her eyelashes fluttered open and she saw Tom bending over her, James kneeling at her side.

"How do you feel?" Tom asked her.

"All right, I think. I—I'd like to sit up, please."

Tom helped her to a sitting position and put his hand on her forehead.

"What—what happened?" she asked, still dazed.

There was a momentary silence, broken by Tom. "Cindy, what ever made you come out after us? Surely you must have known it was a foolhardy thing to do. We were stalking a dangerous animal. We would have shot at anything that moved. If you hadn't screamed—"

Lucinda tried to struggle to her feet.

"No, not yet," James advised gently. "Rest for a moment more. You've suffered a shock."

She felt frantic because although James and Tom were hovering over her she couldn't catch sight of Will. Had something happened to him? Those shots she had heard. . . .

"Cindy, for heaven's sake!" Tom said to her, exasperated. "Don't you understand? You walked into this clearing totally unprotected, and the mountain lion sprang at you. If Will hadn't made a lunge for you, knocking you out of its path so that James and I could shoot at it, you'd be a goner. Will saved your life."

"But—but is he all right?" she asked, her voice quavering dangerously at the edge of hysteria.

"Perfectly all right," came Will's voice, and then he moved closer. His face looked white and tense, and it smote her heart.

"I'm—I'm sorry," she cried out brokenly. "I thought something must have happened because you all were gone so long. And—and it was dark. I didn't understand how you could hope to see anything in such blackness—"

"Do you not realize, Lucinda," came Will's ironic voice, "that the creature is a cat and as such its eyes glitter in the dark?"

"Oh. Oh, goodness, then—then—when I saw those eyes and I thought it was one of you—"

"Exactly. Cindy, you have behaved mighty foolishly," Tom added sternly. "You have been on your own for too long. I hate to think of what could have happened to you all this time without a man to protect you."

Lucinda, sitting leaning against his arm, hung her head shamefacedly. "I'm truly sorry," she whispered. "Did—did you get the mountain lion?"

"Oh, yes," affirmed Tom. "And now we'll have to bury it. But we'd better get you back to camp first. Will, do you want to take her, please. You seem to have twisted your shoulder, and I suppose it would be better to let us do the digging."

"Very well," Will agreed in a low voice. "Can you walk, Lucinda, or shall I carry you?"

"I can walk very well, thank you," Lucinda assured him, trying to regain some of her dignity.

James and Tom helped her to her feet, and she smoothed her skirts dejectedly. "I'll—I'll see you back at camp then," she murmured to them. Then she turned to follow Will, who had begun to make his way through the brush.

Lucinda was glad that Will walked ahead of her without speaking. Glad, too, that it was too dark for him to see her face, for she felt absolutely mortified. So much for the elegant impression she had wished to make in camp! Not only hadn't she been cool, sophisticated, and coquettish, she had blundered into a hunting party and nearly gotten herself and the others killed. And worst of all, the man she had wanted to inspire with awe by her dazzling appearance had saved her life!

No wonder he walked ahead of her, letting her fend for herself. No wonder he had not a word to say to her. Would the ladylike Louise ever have behaved in such a fashion? No, indeed. It was unthinkable. If Will had thought badly of Lucinda before this, he would hold her even lower in his estimation now.

Trying to keep pace with him, Lucinda stumbled and nearly fell. "Can you—please wait a moment," she pleaded, her voice faltering as she struggled to regain her footing.

He stopped then and turned to look at her. "You said you were all right. You said you didn't need any help," he reminded her, his tone unaccountably bitter.

"I—I am all right. If you don't go too quickly." As she said these words she stumbled once more, and this time she fell.

She heard Will swearing under his breath. He came back to where she foundered. Then she felt his strong arms lifting her. She wanted to protest that she was able to walk by herself, that he needn't carry her, but she was afraid to unleash more anger. Hadn't she tripped twice already?

Silently she let him bear her in his arms. As her head bumped against his bare chest she could feel the warmth of his body and the smell of the sun and the clear water of the pond on his skin. Her nearness to Will frightened her more than the thought of the mountain lion. She ached with an attempt to shrink into herself and not be so acutely aware of every inch of his bare skin, of every muscle and sinew.

Lucinda finally broke the silence, to take her mind off the way he held her close to his chest. "I—I do apologize for causing you all this trouble. And—and thank you for saving my life."

Will grunted noncommittally.

"I'm truly grateful for everything you and James have done for us," she continued in a whisper. At the mention of James he stiffened.

"Your reckless behavior is beyond belief. Not content with the miracle that you and your young brother escaped harm on your unlikely journey, with the second miracle that you succeeded in locating Tom, you further tempt fate by walking into the woods in the darkness as blithely as if you were going to market in the middle of the afternoon."

"It was foolish, I know. But I was so afraid that something had happened—"

"And if it had, then what? What conceivable help could you have been? If there had been an accident your tears would have hardly helped by salting the wounds."

Lucinda chafed under his brutal words, but she remained silent. He was right, of course. Oh, she had turned out to be a fine lady, indeed! The best thing for her would be to return to Illinois. There in familiar surroundings she would recover from her madness. She tried to console herself with the thought of the wonderful mansion they would build, of the rich furnishings it would contain, of the beautiful frocks she would have made especially to suit her, of the balls she would attend, the eligible young men she would meet. But it was small consolation, for Will would not be there, and her triumph would be a hollow one.

On and on Will walked with his burden, and Lucinda realized for the first time how very far from the camp she had ventured. "If—if you're getting tired of carrying me I can surely walk now," she murmured.

He didn't bother to answer her but kept up his steady pace. In a few moments they had reached the edge of the woods and were in the meadow that led directly to camp. Already in the distance Lucinda could see the red glow of the camp fire.

In the meadow, the tall grass gently brushed against their legs as Will waded through it. The air was fragrant with the odor of wildflowers, and Lucinda inhaled deeply. Overhead the stars shone brilliantly to complement the rising of the moon, full and majestic, casting its eerie glow on everything below it.

Lucinda glanced at Will's face, the skin drawn taut across his features. Her hands, resting as lightly upon his bare shoulders as they could, felt cold and stiff.

He began to breathe heavily, and she was sure her weight, slight though she was, had finally begun to tire him.

"Please put me down now. You're exhausted. I can walk here perfectly well and it's light enough to see."

He stopped then and set her on her feet, his chest still heaving. For a moment they stood so close to one another that she could feel his hot breath on her forehead.

She quickly turned and half ran towards the clearing, her heart thumping against her ribs as if in warning. For she had been on the point of flinging herself into Will's arms. She had yearned to bury her face in his chest, to kiss his smooth, fragrant skin. Her thoughts made her flush and grow weak with shame. She now saw, to her horror, that she no longer had any control whatsoever over her feeling. She could only just manage to keep a rein over her actions.

"Damn!" Will stopped suddenly and raised one foot, bending down to touch it, his face contorted with pain.

"What's wrong?" she asked, hurrying back towards him. "Have you stepped on something?"

"Of course I've stepped on something! What kind of idiotic question is that," he spat at her, exploding in fury.

Wincing, he hopped to a rock and carefully lowered himself on it, removing his rifle from his shoulder.

Forgetting everything except that he was hurt, Lucinda ran up to him and knelt in front of his foot, peering at it. "Why, it's bleeding!" she exclaimed. Without hesitation she ripped a long piece from the bottom of her petticoat and bound it around his foot. She had to push her bonnet to the back of her head so that she could see what she was doing.

Intent on her task, for his foot was bleeding freely, she worked as quickly as possible. When she was satisfied with her makeshift bandage, she lifted her eyes to his. To her consternation she saw that he was looking at her with a glittering, reproachful expression.

Flustered, she rose to her feet. "That should do until we get back to camp. Please lean on me now. I'm quite all right, and if you put too much weight on that foot it will make the bleeding worse."

She had to bite her tongue to keep from reprimanding him for going off on a hunt in his bare feet. If the situation had been reversed, how scathing he would have been towards her. Lucinda really didn't see why he could say anything he pleased just because he was a man, and she had to behave like a simpering fool just because she was a woman. Sighing heavily, she remembered that Louise had captivated him with that sort of behavior.

Grimacing with pain, Will put his arm around her shoulder. Then, using his rifle as a crutch, he let her lead him.

"Do you know what it was you stepped on?" she questioned. "I couldn't see anything when I examined your foot."

"Pine needle, I think," he muttered. She saw that he had to save his breath for his effort. "Why don't I rest here, and you get some of the men to help me," he requested.

She didn't want to leave him but decided to do his bidding. Quickly she sped into the clearing, and in a few minutes was doubling back followed by two of the miners. They lifted Will easily and carried him back to the fire.

There, Lucinda insisted on taking charge. Davy helped by bringing hot water, proclaiming that his sister was expert at finding splinters that were too small for any other ordinary person to spot.

By the light of the lamp Lucinda undid the bandage and went to work on Will's foot. Very soon she discerned the cause of the pain. It was, indeed, a long sharp pine needle, which she gently drew out. Then she washed the foot with hot water and bound it up in a fresh cloth.

While she attended to her task the men joked good-naturedly about her nursing skills. After all her unfortunate adventures, Lucinda felt that perhaps she had redeemed herself in a small way.

As soon as his foot was bound Will put on his boots, claiming that his foot was fine. Nodding at Lucinda, he made his way to his cabin.

When Tom and James returned they all ate, surrounded by the men who acted as an eager audience to hear the saga of the mountain lion.

Of course Lucinda's part in it came out, and Davy protested that he was the only one to have missed out on the fun.

Will returned to the fire to inform Lucinda that he had moved once more into his brother's cabin so that she could spend the night in his.

"Now, no protests, Lucinda," James broke in. "I'm sure your brother will agree that you will be more comfortable," he finished, appealing to Tom.

Tom and James had obviously become friends already. Tom did agree, and he thanked Will for his consideration.

James was being careful to treat Lucinda with a fond, if rather distant, politeness. Lucinda noticed that Tom carefully observed his attitude towards her. She knew Tom was very perceptive and she feared he would guess her feelings about Will if she didn't do her utmost to conceal them.

After the meal, Lucinda went to her cabin and changed to her best dress. She wasn't even sure why she bothered, for her entire plan of conquest had gone awry. What she wore could hardly matter at this point. And yet she put on her dress of pale blue which heightened the startling blue of her eyes. The fitted bodice and sleeves of the dress brought out the exquisite contours of her shoulders, firm breasts, tiny waist, and gently curving hips. She brushed her yellow hair until it shone. Then she took two locks from the sides and tied them behind her head with a blue ribbon.

Putting on her treasured matching slippers, she was pleased at the dainty appearance of her feet. The last touch to her costume was a little delicate blue fan.

Perhaps her ladylike appearance now would cause the others to forget that she had gone tripping through the brush like a pagan. When she stepped from the cabin the fire light flickered over her and set her off to good advantage. All conversation stopped. Her appearance certainly created the sensational effect she desired, except that Jake broke the spell by emitting a low whistle, for which he then apologized to a momentarily scowling Tom.

Lucinda blushed deeply as she took a seat next to her older brother, smoothing down her petticoats. She was vexed with herself for looking swiftly around the faces for a particular one. She didn't find it. Will had disappeared while she dressed.

Drinking some more coffee, Lucinda tried her best to put all thoughts of Will from her mind. Indeed, she became distracted by what Tom was saying to James. He spoke of returning to California with the family and buying a farm in one of the lush valleys.

"I like this place," Tom declared. "I think there's a great future in California. What do you think, Cindy? Could you get used to living here?"

"I suppose so," she whispered, wondering why her heart was beating a tattoo against her rib cage. "I mean, it would be better farming, wouldn't it, without such severe winters." She stopped then, for she hadn't thought the matter through and her feelings were confused.

Davy had no such conflicts, proclaiming loudly that he wanted to remain in California and learn how to climb mountains and how to sail in clipper ships going in and out of San Francisco Bay.

It was when Lucinda felt a tremor working itself up her back that she knew Will was watching her. She lifted her head and saw him standing a few feet from the fire in the shadows. She shivered suddenly, as if she had caught a chill.

"Come and join us, Will," Tom called out to him.

"We've been discussing the pros and cons of farming here and back home."

Will crouched down next to Tom. "So you're planning to return to farming? Tired of being an Argonaut?"

"Maybe. At least I'd be able to say for sure if I knew what an Argonaut was," Tom replied, smiling.

"I know, I know," Davy cut in enthusiastically. "Cindy read it to me out of a book. They were heroes of long ago who went with Jason to look for the Golden Fleece, and the name of their boat was the Argos. They found the fleece, too."

"Good for you, Davy," commended Tom, grinning at the boy. "I see you have a good memory for your lessons."

"Shucks, that's not a lesson. That's a story!"

Everyone laughed at that. Lucinda tried to join in but her pulse was racing and she remained overly conscious of Will's presence. Her hands grew clammy and she fanned herself quickly, to cover the way she was trembling.

"If you're looking for farming land," James was telling Tom, "I'd recommend the San Joaquin Valley. . . ."

Lucinda stole a glance at Will and surprised him in the act of regarding her as well with that brooding expression in his eyes. She lowered her gaze immediately, wondering what he was thinking. Did he admire her dress? Was he sorry he would have no opportunity to try to kiss her again, now that she was under Tom's protection? It was clear that Will, like James, had taken to Tom. Most people couldn't fail to respond to her brother's warmth and vitality.

She turned her eyes to Tom now, determined to concentrate on the conversation and forget that Will was among those seated in the circle around the fire, his dark curls and red shirt evoking disturbing memories which she earnestly wished to banish forever.

They were discussing farming in the valley, and Lucinda learned that it wasn't very far from Sacramento. She had mixed feelings as she listened. In one respect she would have been delighted to live in California. She had already a great affection for the place. However, if she would always feel as wretched as this when having even the most minor contact with Will Masterson, might it not be better to put half a continent between them?

Chapter 12

Will had stopped looking at Lucinda and entered into the conversation. As he talked, Lucinda realized that he had a wealth of knowledge about farming. In spite of having had no such experience in California, he was knowledgeable about soils and the best crops to grow, as well as how to go about obtaining the land.

This was the sort of talk that bored the prospectors, so they began to drift away to their card game.

Noticing the general exodus, James suddenly called out, "Come on, men, that's hardly the way to entertain our visitors. How about some music?" He sent the cook for the whisky jug.

Like the Mastersons, Tom wasn't a drinking man. He took only a small amount to be sociable and allowed his sister to have exactly one drop, mixed with water. After a look at his brother's pouting face, Tom granted Davy the same privilege.

The men grew voluble and began to clamor for songs. Tom had a clear, fine tenor, and he used it to harmonious advantage.

Lucinda, sitting by the fire and watching Tom with pleasure, found her fingers itching for something more to do than flutter a fan in front of her. She returned briefly to her cabin to leave the fan and take up her sewing basket. Idle hands had never been encouraged at home. Lucinda doubted that her changed circumstances would endear her to idleness after all.

She took her place at the fire once more and threaded her needle, No, she wasn't quite destined to be a belle

and devote herself to attending balls. In spite of any new
luxuries she would have to put her time to better use.
She would travel, perhaps sail on a clipper ship across
the sea. And it would be magnificent to visit cities such
as New York, Boston, San Francisco. And when she
tired of travel she would, perhaps, open a school.

Absorbed in her sewing, and her thoughts, Lucinda
wasn't aware that James had shifted his position so as to
sit beside her.

He smiled warily at her. "I haven't had a moment
alone to tell you how extremely happy I am that you
have found Tom after all. And he is every bit as fine a
man as you said. It is, as my brother remarked, a miracle
that you have been reunited. I didn't want to tell you
before this, Lucinda, but I had heard many heart-
breaking stories that began like yours but ended much
less satisfactorily."

"I understand," Lucinda responded softly. "I know
that we have been uncommonly fortunate, and I'm deeply grateful."

"I suppose now you'll be able to—to—well, settle
matters with—with the object of your affections," James
said quietly.

Lucinda felt a bright flush come to her cheeks and she
wielded her needle rapidly without answering. She
didn't quite know what to say.

"Will you be remaining in Illinois or returning to California?" he further pressed her.

"I don't really know, James. I'm quite confused. Everything is so changed suddenly. I'm not sure of my
plans, but—but my feelings remain the same," she finished quickly.

She threw James a look of compassion and then lowered her eyes to her mending. It was an awkward moment, for she didn't wish to encourage James to renew
his suit, nor did she care to cause him pain.

He was sensitive to her mood, however, and changed
the subject of his own accord.

Every so often Lucinda looked up and saw Tom, Davy, and Will at the other side of the fire. It was such a strange grouping, and yet it seemed right somehow. If only—if only. . . .

She must stop thinking about it. She and her brothers would be gone tomorrow, Of course, if they ever returned to California. . . .

Tom had begun requesting different songs. He seemed to delight in the memory of first this one and then the next. When someone sang a ballad of unrequited love, Will moved back into the shadows, took his rifle on his knee, and began to clean it thoroughly. It was as if he wished to have no further part in the proceedings.

No doubt he was thinking once more of Louise. A lump came into Lucinda's throat, and she was angry with herself for caring what Will thought, and about whom.

If there hadn't been this terrible tension and hostility between her and Will they could have had much to say to one another, Lucinda thought sadly. They were interested in many of the same things; for example, the kinds of books they read. Whenever Lucinda had overheard Will talking to his brother, or this evening to Tom, she had found his opinions and observations most agreeable. It was only with her that he acted antagonistic and contrary. But then, he had never hidden from her his feelings that she was unsatisfactory, schoolmarmish and outspoken. In fact, her only asset, from his point of view, had been her availability and foolish willingness to accept his kisses. How she regretted having permitted them! For if she had kept herself aloof, perhaps the story could have had a different ending.

She was deeply involved in her own thoughts, so started sharply when she found the object of them crouching beside her and reaching for the coffee pot which was warming in the fire. Her fingers began to tremble uncontrollably, and she bowed her head low to keep the flush that covered her face from being observed.

Will stood next to her and sipped from his cup, while she kept her eyes on her mending.

"You ought to be looking happier than you do after having been reconciled with Tom," he said softly but with an edge to his voice.

"I'm perfectly happy, thank you," Lucinda retorted harshly, perhaps because it was a lie, and she bit off the thread sharply.

"You don't look it. Oh, yes, you're dressed in your Sunday best but the glow is lacking. I wonder why. From what Davy tells me, you'll never have to hoe potatoes again. No, ma'am, you're going to be a fine lady from now on." His tone held the old mockery, as he eased himself down next to her and added some more coffee to his cup.

Lucinda simmered with annoyance. Davy should have said nothing, not even to Will. Tom had cautioned the boy and he should have obeyed. She rankled, too, under Will's uncharitable words.

"I suppose it would displease you to know that I might be able to have an easier time, wouldn't it?" She glanced at him with sparks of anger in her eyes. "Not for me a life a luxury, you imply. I suppose you don't think I'd be able to appreciate the finer things. Only the ladies of Virginia are fit to sit idle all day, twirling their parasols and making polite conversation."

"Are those your aspirations?" he asked her drily.

She looked down disconsolately. After all her daydreaming and her steadfast resolutions, she talked to him the same way as always. And he mocked her as always. It was no use trying to pretend with Will, for she was just not the kind of woman who could please him.

Tying a knot in the thread she began to sew once more. "My aspirations, no. I like the idea of riches and luxury as much as anyone, but not a life of idleness. I suppose you can't understand that I wouldn't care to giggle foolishly behind my fan and talk of nothing but frocks and balls. I'm afraid I'm made differently. Such a useless life of endless gossip would bore me to tears," she finished.

She glanced up at him, a challenge in her angry blue eyes. Let him laugh at her if he wished.

He did not laugh, however. He returned her dark look with one of his own, but was silent for a few moments.

Dimly Lucinda heard the singing of the others but she had no idea what song was being sung, for with all her faculties she was concentrating on every word and movement of Will Masterson.

He pulled out his pipe and tobacco. "What do you intend to do?" he murmured in a low, sad voice.

"I'll help my mother run the house, I suppose, and see to the servants. I'll take up embroidery and have piano lessons. I'll supervise the education of my sisters, and perhaps even start a school."

He looked at her strangely. "All work and—and no—play?" His voice was almost inaudible.

She considered the question for a moment. "I'd like to travel. I've never even seen the ocean. I might like to go across it to a foreign land, to see some of the place I've read about." She flushed deeply under his constant gaze. "Anyway," she continued, to cover her embarrassment, "I doubt when we're through putting by money for the important things that there will be terribly much left over."

"What would you say are the important things?"

"A well-deserved rest for my mother, and security in her later years. A good education for Davy, and money for a fair start when he comes of age. And Tom will want his own farm one day, when he—when he marries."

Lucinda grew melancholy at the mere mention of marriage, and a quick glance at Will showed that he did the same. They sat silently for some moments, each sad for a different reason, she supposed. He was undoubtedly pining for Louise and his missed opportunity.

"Say them aloud, Lucinda. Your thoughts. I'm interested."

She couldn't imagine why, but she granted his wish nonetheless. "I was thinking about the pleasure of teaching children. I don't know that anything has ever given me more satisfaction than watching a child look at a meaningless jumble of letters of the alphabet and suddenly understand that the letters make up words. That first look of comprehension fills me with the utmost wonder and joy. And pride that I have helped to achieve such understanding. I love to read myself, and teaching others is surely one reason I have been put on earth." She stopped then, overcome by her easy loquaciousness. And the absense of any cutting remark on Will's part.

"I—I never thanked you for leaving behind several volumes in your cabin when I was using it." She wanted to say his name, and didn't dare. Her heart began to fail her. She had been talking to Will as if he were a friend. But he could never be that to her, as James perhaps could, because she loved him to distraction. She doubted she could spend more than five minutes in Will's company without wishing to feel his arms crushing her to him, and his hard mouth compelling her to surrender her own.

Now her thoughts made her hot with shame, and she desperately sought for an end to their conversation. It came from Tom, unexpectedly.

"Cindy, I'd sure like a cup of coffee. All this singing has made me feel awfully dry."

Lucinda hastily scrambled to her feet. She took Tom's cup and filled it. When she brought it to him he smiled at her. "Why don't you sit by me for a while and sing 'Black is the color of my true love's hair.' I remember how sweetly you sing it. Please, even if you're shy. For me, Cindy."

Lucinda couldn't resist such a plea from Tom. As the guitarist played a soft accompaniment, Lucinda folded her hands and began to sing. It had been such a long time. Now as she sang the words, she was struck with dismay that every sentiment in the song applied to her feeling about Will. She sang of the purest eyes, the bravest hands. She sang that she loved the ground whereon he stands. When she came to the words, "And if my love no more I see, my life will surely fade away," her light, sweet voice faltered and grew husky. She had begun by looking at Tom, for she hadn't dared to glance at Will once. Now she was staring moodily into the fire, the song over, her emotions devastated.

The sound of applause from the miners drew her from her reverie.

"Why that was beautiful, Lucinda," James exclaimed in wonderment.

"He's right, Cindy," echoed Tom. "You never sang it better." Tom turned to the others. "When I left home Cindy was only a kid. I guess I can't get used to her being all grown up now."

Lucinda felt as if she would sink through the ground. Surely everyone in the camp had known that she had been singing the song to Will Masterson.

But if anyone was aware of it, nobody made any sign. Instead the miners clamored for another song. She declined gently, pleading a strained voice and tiredness, although what she really meant was a broken heart.

Flushing under the praise and the disappointed groans of the men that she would not sing any more, Lucinda picked up her mending, which gave her an excuse to look down. If it was torture to be away from Will, it was worse to be with him. Her emotions were as ungovernable as the wind and the rain. They welled up inside her and spilled forth, giving her no peace.

Then she heard Will's voice, leading the others in a merry song. She could hear, however, that his heart wasn't in it. He was feeling anything but merry himself. He had his own broken heart to bear.

A terrible sadness stole over Lucinda. Her love for

Will was not just some childish fancy. It wasn't a whim, either, she feared, or lack of experience. She had probably already met as many men as most women. Will was simply her choice. It was he whom she loved, with every breath in her body. He might mock her, he might make her furious and bring out the worst of her temper. She loved him all the same, with a steady, undying flame, and it would be ever thus, even if she never set eyes upon him after today. There was not going to be a lessening of love with the passing of time. Lucinda knew now that however long she lived, however far she went from here, she would compare every other man to Will Masterson, and find any other man wanting.

"Sing 'Clementine,' James, do!" Davy begged him.

James readily agreed, and an air of jollity pervaded the others, singers and clappers alike. Only Lucinda felt left out of the proceedings. Try as she might she couldn't force a smile to her lips or a glow to her sad eyes. She made the greatest effort to join in the chorus of 'Clementine' but her lips stubbornly refused to move. In fact they trembled so that she feared she would burst into sobs.

"How about 'On Top of Old Smoky'?" James suggested to his brother, who was still holding the guitar.

Will played some chords without answering. Davy had picked up the plea and began chanting 'Old Smoky' over and over, jumping up and down in his seat impatiently.

Finally Will began to sing it. As the first words issued from his lips Lucinda was shaken by a tremor of misery. For Will sang as if every word cut him to the heart. "I lost my true lover, from a-courting too slow," he sang, and the bitter disappointment in his voice was all too evident to Lucinda.

Will looked straight at her then, a dark look of anguish. What was he trying to tell her? She believed it was that she mustn't hope for anything, for his heart had been stolen by another girl long ago. No doubt Will felt about Louise as Lucinda would feel in future years about him.

Lucinda gasped as her fingers fumbling with the needle caused her to stick herself painfully. Turning her palm upwards, she gazed in fascination as a tiny dot of blood appeared on her finger.

"For a-courting's a pleasure. and parting's a grief," Will sang mournfully, bringing tears to her eyes. "But a false-hearted lover is worse than a thief."

The truth of those words devastated Lucinda, for Will had stolen her heart and she never would be able to reclaim it.

> For a thief he will rob you, and take what you
> have,
> But a false-hearted lover will send you to your
> grave.

Yes, he surely would, Lucinda believed, as she lowered her head and moved even farther from the light of the fire so that nobody would see the tears flowing down her cheeks.

She was overcome by the sorrow of the words, the haunting beauty of the melody, and the unbearable magnetism of Will's voice, husky and vibrant, the deep timbre reflecting the depth of the passion with which he sang.

> The grave will decay you, and turn you to
> dust,
> Not one girl in a hundred a poor boy can
> trust.

That sentiment, bitterly rendered, was no doubt the result of Will's jilting by Louise.

> They'll hug you and kiss you,
> And tell you more lies
> Than the cross ties on the railroad
> Or stars in the skies.

Lucinda couldn't bear it any longer, and as he started on the final chorus she rose shakily to her feet and tiptoed into the shadows. Her soft slippers made no sound.

At first she thought she'd go directly to her cabin but she felt much too distressed to retire to her bed. Instead she walked blindly away from camp. She wanted to get beyond the sound of Will's mournful song.

Lucinda kept going until all she could hear was the soft chirping of the crickets and the rustling of the wind through the trees. She looked up at the full moon, shining with a more golden light, in this land of gold, than anywhere else. She regarded it sadly, for she knew that the next time she saw it she would undoubtedly be many miles from here.

There was an aching in her chest that she feared would never go away. Oh, if only she'd never set eyes on Will Masterson! How happy she'd be now to have found Tom, instead of having to divide that happiness with the pain of leaving Will.

A noise directly behind her caused her to spin around in fright. There stood Will himself.

"I—I thought it might be a grizzly bear," Lucinda choked out hastily, to explain why she was suddenly trembling.

"I'm sorry if you're disappointed," he muttered in a low, ironic voice.

Lucinda was silent, for the sight of him had set her pulse racing wildly. She curled her fingers into her palms in an effort to control herself. She wanted not to look at him, yet couldn't keep her eyes from his face. This would be the last time she would look upon the dark curls, the determined jaw, the dark, penetrating eyes, the reckless lips.

The bright moon cast its glow on his features and the signs of strain they showed. His eyes narrowed, as he looked in turn at her, and he began to chew his lower lip as if something was upsetting him. Still, his strong tall figure stood proud and erect.

"I'm sorry my singing drove you from the fire," he said at length, the hard irony still in his tone. "I consider that I had more reason to depart during your song."

She flushed deeply. "I—I didn't realize when I began to sing it that it was so—so obvious. I hadn't sung it since Tom left so long ago."

"Indeed. But you were not singing of Tom," Will retorted bitterly.

She lowered her eyes. "Do you have to say so? Is nothing inviolate?"

"Many things, to me. I could more accurately make that observation of you. You've made fools of us all."

She looked up at him, astonished. "*I* have? What in the world have I done?"

"You damn well know what you've done! Flirted with James, giving him to believe that you cared for him, when all the time—all the time—" He couldn't continue but his eyes flashed angrily at her.

"I did no such thing," she whispered, appalled by his accusation. "I treated James like a friend. I never felt anything—anything more than friendship and a sort of sisterly affection for him. And I did *not* indicate otherwise. Did he tell you I did?" she blazed at him.

"He was too crestfallen to tell me much of anything!" Will swallowed then, as if a thought was painful to him. "Are you—are you going back with Tom, and then returning to California?" His voice had dropped so low that she could hardly hear him.

"I—I suppose so," she murmured. Her agitation was increasing, and her breath began to come in short gasps through her parted lips.

"I suppose you'll be married by then," he whispered bitterly.

Married? Surely he was mocking her once more, and it was too cruel to bear. She could only bow her head so that he wouldn't see her eyes fill with tears.

"You *will* be married by then, will you not?" he persisted, raising his voice.

She couldn't bring herself to speak, but merely shook her head in anguish.

"No? But you told James you loved somebody else.

What about black, black, black, the color of your true
love's hair?" he mocked.

"He—he's not—in Illinois," she whispered. Was it
possible that Will didn't realize that she had been singing of him?

"He—he isn't? Where, then?"

"You know very well where," she whispered, her head
still bowed.

There was a short, tense silence.

"Tell me!" Will commanded hoarsely. He took a step
towards her.

"Stop torturing me," she whispered, lifting her wet
face. "It doesn't matter anyway, because he'd rather be
free."

Sobbing, she whirled and fled.

"Lucinda!" Will called after her. "Lucinda!" He
caught up to her and grabbed her shoulders, turning her
brutally towards him. His eyes burned. In a moment he
was kissing her wildly, desperately, crushing her to him
with savage intensity, his fingers digging into her back.

This was the culmination of all her fears, for she knew
as soon as he touched her that all her strength would fail
her, that all her resolve would melt into acceptance. She
abandoned herself totally to his embraces then, knowing
that she would rather be lost herself than ever lose him.

When he finally raised his lips from hers to draw a
breath he looked at her fiercely. "Is it me you love?"

"You know it is! Oh, please, stop tormenting me! Let
me go, please!" She tried to wrench herself away.

"Go where? Where will you go?" He was breathing
shallowly, and his hands holding her arms exerted a
fierce pressure.

"I'll go with Tom, back to Illinois. And if we return to
California I'll stay on the farm in the valley and try to
forget I ever met you!"

"And if I don't let you go?" He took one hand from
her arm and gently ran his finger down her wet cheek. A
muscle in his temple was flickering slightly.

His unexpectedly tender gesture completely over-whelmed her. "If you don't let me go," she burst out, "I'll remain here with you, in your cabin, and wash your clothes and cook your meals and follow you around like the most faithful dog. In spite of shame, in spite of ev-erything. So unhand me, if you wish to remain free!" She tried again to shake herself loose.

He held tightly to her. "Stop struggling, if you don't want me to hurt you. I don't want to let you go."

"Why not?" she cried. "You told me you wanted to be free!"

"No, Lucinda," he whispered. "I don't."

"You—you don't?" She looked at him mistrustfully. "I—I don't believe you."

"Why not?" he hissed, gripping both her arms again. "I like the little picture you paint of our future together. I, prospecting for gold, you, scrubbing my clothes clean on a rock, following in my wake, impervious to the scorn heaped upon you by friends and family. You did say you would do all that, didn't you?"

"Yes," she whispered. "I said so and I'd behave so. You can save your sarcasm. I know you're only mock-ing me."

"If you think I'm mocking you, why don't you go? Here," he added, releasing her arms. "Why should you stay? You're a wealthy young lady now. You will have dozens of honorable suitors—"

"I see!" she broke in. "You think it is only my money that recommends me."

"Not only. There's also your beauty, for example. And your spirit, your courage, your passion, not to omit your intelligence, your kindness, your sweetness. You don't believe me, I see. You think I mock you still. It strikes me that yours is a strange sort of love. How can you feel love for a man whom you consider so patently dishonorable?" He looked at her with a hurt expression in his glittering eyes.

"I—I don't know what you mean," she whispered.

rubbing her bruised arms where his fingers had dug into
them. She had lost all reserve now that he knew of her
feelings for him. "I'm not blaming you for anything,
Will. You kissed me but you never encouraged me to
lose my heart. On the contrary, you made your position
quite clear from the beginning. That I fell in love with
you is my misfortune."

"Why didn't you heed my warning?"

She looked sadly at him, her blue eyes shining with
tears. "I didn't realize what was happening to me. I've
never loved before, nor shall again. I don't want any
part of love. It's too painful," she finished, her voice
breaking. Turning away, she shook with sobs.

"Lucinda, come here!" Will commanded.

She wanted to refuse, but something in his tone
caused her to obey.

He put his hand on her chin and tilted up her face.
"Why are you crying, you foolish girl? Don't you know
that I love *you?* Do you think I could have kissed you as
I did if I weren't hopelessly smitten with you? From the
moment your golden hair tumbled out of your bonnet I
knew I was lost. Now, dry those silly tears, my darling."

With that he enfolded her tenderly in his arms and
kissed her eyes, the tears on her cheeks, her forehead.
Then he gently kissed her lips.

Her arms stole around his neck without her aware-
ness. She couldn't quite grasp what was happening to
her. Had he really said that he loved her?

The kisses he gave her subsequently were very real,
indeed, for his gentleness gave way once again to
savagery. His mouth grew hard and possessive, while
her soft lips surrendered gladly.

The pair was too much enraptured to notice that
somebody had approached.

"What the devil is going on here?" Tom's clear voice
rang out irately. "What is all this?"

Will and Lucinda broke apart, but Will kept his arm
firmly around her waist.

"I'm sorry, Tom. I suppose I should have asked you formally if I could court your sister. It's just that I thought—well, there's been a misunderstanding—"

"I'll say there is," Tom broke in angrily. "Are you telling me you're expecting my sister to be a prospector's wife and live in a cabin with a dirt floor and—"

"No, of course not!" Will interrupted impatiently. "I've had enough of prospecting. I've found my golden girl, and I want to keep her all to myself. I was thinking of doing so on a farm next to yours, Tom, in the San Joaquin valley."

Tom took a step forward, his face lighting up with pleasure. "Do you mean that, Will?"

Will held out his hand, and they shook on it.

Tom glanced at his sister. "I don't have to ask how you feel about all this. I must admit I'm not entirely taken by surprise. The way you've been mooning around, I kind of thought you'd fallen for somebody. When I heard the way you sang that song—well, the man with the blackest hair was the one you didn't dare look at, so I knew it had to be Will."

Tom backed away suddenly, showing signs of embarrassment. "I'm only in the way here. I'm sure you've got lots of things to talk about."

"Tom, let me tell my brother myself, please," Will requested.

As Tom nodded and faded from view, Lucinda turned to look at Will, her face radiant with happiness. "Do you really mean it, Will? Oh, if you retract now you'll have Tom to deal with."

"Of course I mean it, my precious darling," he murmured, looking at her with eyes that were ready to devour her.

"But, but what about Louise? When you sang that song I was sure you were regretting her—"

"How the devil do you know about Louise?" he asked.

"When I first came here, and you were so opposed to

my remaining, James told me that you had become bitter about women because Louise married someone else after you'd left Virginia."

Will shook his head impatiently. "He's my brother and we're very close in many ways. In others, we don't understand each other at all."

"Then James was mistaken in thinking—in thinking —"

"That I was pining for Louise? Yes! I never loved her. It's true that in the beginning I was somewhat infatuated. I'd had little experience of women then. But I soon realized that she treated every man to her favors. She was an accomplished flirt, addicted to accumulating beaux. She was more interested in conquering all of Virginia than in being true to one man."

"But when I first heard you sing 'Old Smoky' so sadly, as if you regretted—"

"I regretted my disillusionment with love, not Louise. I had thought I'd never trust a woman again." He looked at Lucinda intently. "Tonight I was singing it to you but you were so uninterested you left in the middle of my song."

"Only because I didn't realize, and I couldn't bear to think—to think of Louise."

He smiled wickedly at her for a moment. "Were you jealous?"

"Horribly," she admitted, daring to smile back at him.

"Well, I'm glad," he said cruelly. "It serves you right for all the jealousy I've felt."

"But why? I gave you no cause." Trying to think back, Lucinda remained perplexed. "Surely when I responded to your kisses that first time—"

"Ah, but how was I to know? I hardly was acquainted with you. I understood very well that I was smitten, but I had no assurance that you weren't simply another coquette, flirting because it pleased you to exercise your power over men."

"I told you, did I not, that I'd never kissed another."

"So you did, my darling, but I doubted your words. For I thought a beauty like you could never have come this far, with only a boy to protect her, and remained so innocent. I was so much in love with you by then that I was afraid to let you know it and give you the power to wound me. And then, it seemed to me that you switched your attentions to James. I could hardly blame you. He has a more gentle nature. I am perfectly aware that my own is quite ungovernable." As he said this the muscle in his temple twitched once more.

He swallowed in agitation. "I can never do anything by halves. I was mad with wanting you. I felt if I showed it and you—you laughed at me I'd have to do something desperate."

He held her close to him for a moment, and she could feel how rapidly his heart beat against her ear.

She lifted her face and looked at him, her heart so full of love for him that she thought it might burst.

"I had no idea you cared for me," she murmured against his chest. "I thought you thoroughly despised me and were comparing me unfavorably with Louise."

He snorted. "Compare you unfavorably! Why she behaved in a vain and frivolous way, exactly as you described so devastatingly a while ago by the fire. Gossiping and twirling her parasol. I didn't know such a one as you existed, who would risk danger and even death, not only to cross the country but to dare to come into these hills—"

"Shh." She put her fingers against his lips. "After all your previous criticism I may swoon from too much praise."

"If you do, I'll catch you in my arms, so," he murmured, picking her up suddenly and clasping her to him. "When I realized your devotion to Davy, your determination to locate Tom, the way you mended our clothes and cooked our meals, I thought I'd go mad, for I was convinced that I'd already lost you to James."

"But if you had said only one word to me—"

"I couldn't. My pride wouldn't let me." He swung her to the ground and stepped back from her a little way.

She saw in his face then what he had kept hidden—his sensitivity and his vulnerability.

"The day I saw you in the woods with my brother, Lucinda, when I saw him kiss you, I was sick with jealousy. He voluntarily told me that he had proposed to you and you had refused because you loved another. I— I never dreamed it could be me. I fear I jumped to the conclusion that you were a flirt after all, and that you had a beau back home and were simply toying with James and with me."

"Did you tell James how you felt? Or didn't your pride let you?"

"No, it wouldn't and I didn't. I was eaten with anguish and have hardly slept a night since you left." His face took on a pained look, in remembrance.

Gently Lucinda stroked his cheek, but when he attempted to embrace her she kept him at arm's distance. "Yet, you let me go. Straight out of camp and out of your life."

Lucinda stepped away and turned her back, considering that if he could have done that he surely couldn't love her very much.

Will grabbed her roughly and turned her to face him. "If you knew how miserable I felt! I could say nothing to anyone, not even James. I cursed myself over and over for having let you go. I was going to come after you. And then, when I saw that you had returned, and I noticed Tom, the jealousy nearly drove me mad in that first moment. I thought that he was your love. When Davy said it was Tom I nearly fainted with relief."

Lucinda remembered then how peculiarly he had behaved when meeting her brother.

"It got worse and worse," Will murmured, with his lips against her forehead, holding her gently close to him. "When I saw that mountain lion spring I acted from pure instinct and without thought at all. When I carried you back, feeling you against my chest, and later when you knelt and doctored my foot, oh, my darling what control it took to keep from carrying you off into the woods regardless of the consequences. Look, look at my hands." He held them out, and she could see deep nail marks in the palms where he had dug in his fingers.

"I thought," she whispered, "that everyone in camp knew I was singing that song to you."

"And I thought the same when I sang 'Old Smoky.' But you vanished. It was then I knew I had to come after you. I meant to hear from your own lips that I had a rival. Even when you said I was the one I could hardly believe it."

"No, you were so convinced that I was a 'false-hearted lover.' Oh, I could never be that! The only thing that saddens me, Will, is James. Do you think he will ever forgive us?"

"Of course he will. His is a forgiving nature. He's wanted to quit prospecting for the last year. I believe he will be only too happy to go down into the valley and find himself some lovely lass to comfort him."

"As you would have done if I hadn't returned your love?" Lucinda asked him, gently teasing.

He suddenly gripped her with such force that she jumped in fear. "Never! I told you that I'm nothing like James!" he said savagely. "James never needed you as I do, nor wanted you as I do!" He strained her to him and kissed her again and again, while she drank in his embrace and the passionate words of love murmured between kisses as hungrily as sand absorbs rain.

As they broke apart for a moment, Will said, "You're not returning to Illinois with Tom. Oh no, my darling, I'm going to make up for my slow courting by insisting on a very quick wedding."

She blushed. "Are—are you sure you want to settle down on a farm? Won't you miss the excitement of searching for gold?" she asked, her eyes shining.

"All the excitement I need is in your lips," he whispered. Then, moving both hands to her hair he entwined his fingers tightly in the silken strands. "And all the gold I'll ever want is right here.

"Do you love me, Lucinda? I need to hear you say it because I've doubted it for so long."

"I love you, I love you," she said, between kisses.

As his arms closed around her and his lips sought hers she had the most wonderful sensation that reality, for once, was surpassing her wildest dreams.

Don't Miss these Ace Romance Bestsellers!

_____#75157 **SAVAGE SURRENDER** $1.95
The million-copy bestseller by Natasha Peters,
author of Dangerous Obsession.

_____#29802 **GOLD MOUNTAIN** $1.95

_____#88965 **WILD VALLEY** $1.95
Two vivid and exciting novels by
Phoenix Island author, Charlotte Paul.

_____#80040 **TENDER TORMENT** $1.95
A sweeping romantic saga in the
Dangerous Obsession tradition.

Available wherever paperbacks are sold or use this coupon.

DAOMA WINSTON

09245	The Carnaby Curse And Castle of Closing Doors	$1.50
14175	Death Watch	$1.50
16690	The Dream Killers	$1.95
*49680	The Love of Lucifer	$1.50
86512	A Visit After Dark	$1.25
87070	Walk Around the Square	$1.25

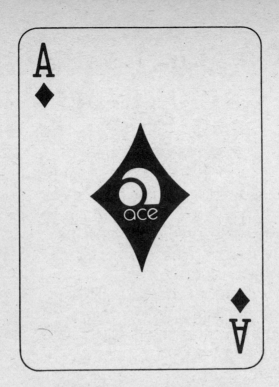

There are a lot more
where this one came from!

ORDER your FREE catalog of ACE paperbacks here. We have hundreds of inexpensive
books where this one came from priced from
75¢ to $2.50. Now you can read all the books
you have always wanted to at tremendous
savings. Order your *free* catalog of ACE
paperbacks now.

ACE BOOKS ● Box 576, Times Square Station ● New York, N.Y. 10036